MOLLY KEANE

was born in Co. Kildare, Ireland, in 1904 into "a rather serious Hunting and Fishing Church-going family" who gave her little education at the hands of governesses. Her father originally came from a Somerset family and her mother, a poetess, was the author of "The Songs of the Glens of Antrim". Molly Keane's interests when young were "hunting and horses and having a good time"; she began writing only as a means of supplementing her dress allowance, and chose the pseudonym M. J. Farrell "to hide my literary side from my sporting friends". She wrote her first novel, *The Knight of the Cheerful Countenance*, at the age of seventeen.

As M. J. Farrell, Molly Keane published ten novels between 1928 and 1952: *Young Entry* (1928), *Taking Chances* (1929), *Mad Puppetstown* (1931), *Conversation Piece* (1932), *Devoted Ladies* (1934), *Full House* (1935), *The Rising Tide* (1937), *Two Days in Aragon* (1941), *Loving Without Tears* (1951) and *Treasure Hunt* (1952). All of these are now published by Virago. She was also a successful playwright, of whom James Agate said "I would back this impish writer to hold her own against Noel Coward himself." Her plays with John Perry, always directed by John Gielgud include *Spring Meeting* (1938), *Ducks and Drakes* (1942), *Treasure Hunt* (1949) and *Dazzling Prospect* (1961).

The tragic death of her husband at the age of thirty-six stopped her writing for many years. It was not until 1981 that another novel – *Good Behaviour* – was published, this time under her real name. Molly Keane has two daughters and lives in Co. Waterford. *Time after Time* appeared in 1983, *Loving and Giving* was published in 1988. Her cookery book, *Nursery Cooking*, was published in 1985.

VIRAGO
MODERN
CLASSIC

NUMBER
368

Molly Keane
(M. J. Farrell)

CONVERSATION PIECE

Published by VIRAGO PRESS Limited 1991
20–23 Mandela Street, Camden Town, London NW1 0HQ

First published in Great Britain by Collins in 1932

Virago edition offset from Collins first edition

Printed in Great Britain
by Cox & Wyman Ltd., Reading, Berks.

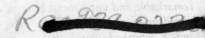

Molly Keane: An Interview with Polly Devlin

Molly Keane, as M. J. Farrell, wrote, on the whole, of the lives, preoccupations and pastimes of that moneyed, hunting, curiously dislocated class of people in Ireland, the Anglo-Irish, skating over the political angry geographical reality that was Ireland in the first quarter of this century. In some books, notably Two Days in Aragon, she tackles the enormous, vexed problem of the turbulent relationships existing in Ireland between the Anglo-Irish and the various factions of the 'native' Irish; in others she goes back to the golden days of the Edwardian swansong of the Anglo-Irish. But in all her books she presents – and thus preserves – a detailed and exquisite picture of the last days of the Irish raj; she celebrates, by affectionately chronicling, the beauty and atavistic qualities of the Irish great houses, marooned dreams of tranquillity and decaying splendour standing in their depleted demesnes, lived in by people who refuse to see – or believe in – the fires and diaspora before them. Both Ballyrankin, her parents' house, and Woodrooff, the Perry house, where she spent long formative periods before her marriage, were burned in the Troubles.

Her books are witty, sardonic, human comedies, edged by black humour, and like all good comedies sadness and pathos lie close to the glittering surface. But they are now more than novels: they deliver a remarkable and vivid social history, an impeccably observed, occasionally delinquent record, full of relevance and revelation of a way of life and a vanished world that has not otherwise been given its due recognition in the country where it once existed.

P.D. Molly, when did you first start writing?

M.K. When I'd been to school for a short time I got some sort of bug – I don't know what it was – some sort of virus I suppose. But everyone thought (and my mother was determined) that I was getting tuberculosis, so as a cure for that I was put to bed. Now, the only thing I could ever do at school was what they called English Composition. So for an escape and through sheer boredom I began to write a book. I wrote away under the bedclothes, and honestly I must have written about fifty or sixty thousand words or more, and I thought it was pure Shakespeare. Well, not Shakespeare exactly – more Dornford Yates.

P.D. And this was *The Knight of the Cheerful Countenance*?

M.K. Yes. Looking back, perhaps it wasn't as bad as I think. It was probably tremendously pictorial because the only thing I thought about was hunting, and the only thing I wanted was glamour and lovely men.

P.D. A lot of young girls think of glamour and lovely men but they don't sit down and write a novel.

M.K. Yes, but I was on my own, without the lovely men. Well, there was one I fancied, but he wasn't any good for me.

P.D. Do you think it was the influence of your mother that made you write?

M.K. No, not at all, she would have been horrified at the idea of my writing a sort of Romance.

P.D. But she was a writer?

M.K. But she wasn't a serious writer. When she was young she'd been quite a good minor poetess – Moira O'Neill, the Poetess of the Glens – and I don't want to despise her poems because I think some of them are rather magical. She was terribly idle. But we thought they were lovely when we were small.

P.D. So do you think at some level –

M.K. – we were influenced by her? I'm sure I was, but it's so curious because by the time I got to writing I was terribly at odds with her. – I'd sort of grown up and I was having great fun with my grown-up cousins and she disapproved of it all. She was frightened for me, just as I would have been frightened if my daughter was, say, in the drugs scene. I think, probably, having led a tremendously secluded life, she was terribly frightened of my knowing people whom she considered fast, which was anyone who had any fun at all.

P.D. Did you ever become friends with her?

M.K. No, alas, no. I mean when I was a child I had no one else to love. I was a terrible lover, and I *adored* her, though I hardly ever saw her; but she did have a sort of rapport with children.

P.D. Did she come round to loving your books?

M.K. No.

P.D. Had she read them?

M.K. I don't know. I never discussed them. Ever.

P.D. But wasn't not knowing unsatisfactory?

M.K. We were at different ends of a civilization. I mean I was frightfully jolly and funny and off to all the doings I could and she thought this was dreadful and she didn't know what was going to happen – I don't know *what* she thought.

P.D. And the relationship between you and your father was a significant one?

M.K. No. None at all. There wasn't any. No, he was completely of a life apart. The only time I think I was ever near to him was when he was dying and my mother had this phobia about doing nothing and not having proper nurses and I looked after him, and I insisted I go and get the old nurse from the village so that she would sit with him all night, and that really turned my mother against me.

P.D. Was he an uncomplaining man?

M.K. Very.

P.D. Was he like the father in *Good Behaviour*?

M.K. No, he wasn't as jolly. He was very well behaved.

P.D. Did you love him?

M.K. No. I admired him because he was such a good horseman. I admired that about him.

P.D. Are you nervous by temperament?

M.K. Yes.

P.D. And shy?

M.K. I think so. Yes, I think I am. I think I'm nervous. I was always disliked as a child. My mother didn't really like me and the aunts were ghastly to me and my father had absolutely nothing to do with me.

P.D. Did you feel isolated . . . unloved?

M.K. Yes, I think I did. As a very young child I sort of depended on my mother and thought she was everything – but I don't think I got much out of her.

P.D. That's a dreadful legacy, isn't it?

M.K. No. I don't know. It's what made me fight myself free. Now Susan, my sister, had always been much more popular. She'd always been gentler and quieter and jolly good at various things and she got on so awfully well.

P.D. Fight yourself free of what?

M.K. Fight myself free of that secluded life – that nunnery of a life, which it really was. Because anything like young men were frightfully disapproved of, and as for anything being done to help us – nothing was done, except the horses of course.

P.D. I remember that story about your mother seeing you lying on the grass showing your knickers.

M.K. Yes, and I must have been only eight or nine.

P.D. And she was genuinely shocked?

M.K. Yes, she was. I remember discussing this with Susan, who really had a much more liberal point of view about it all. And she said, 'You see our mother's generation felt that modesty was a thing that almost had to be beaten into people – that it wasn't naturally born in them. They must be shown and made to be aware that that was a necessary element in life.'

P.D. And in *Two Days in Aragon* there's a moment when Nan and Mrs Fox are discussing sex and they talk about it with a real prurient interest. You make it clear that they didn't perceive anything loving or life-enhancing about sex.

M.K. A disgusting business, yes. And there was so little discussion about it. I remember there was a frightful scandal because we had a sweet old groom who was an ex-steeplechase jockey and he jumped down a stile coming out of the laurels back into the stable yard and he broke his neck and was found dead at the bottom of the stile. And the insurance looked into the whole thing and said he had been in the laurels having a go with the cook and there was a desperate hush about that. And there was another awful scandal, how they couldn't have known all about it I cannot imagine, when a little housemaid had a baby in her bedroom, having done all her work and everything and gone into her bedroom and had the baby and there was an old cook who thought something must be wrong.

P.D. And this was Ballyrankin?

M.K. Yes, and the girl had gone out, how she could have done it, having just had a baby, and she found the baby in a large cardboard box, a dress box addressed to me from some big shop – well strung up and the address in large letters and labels, you know how things were in those days – addressed to me and she was just about to float it down the river. Can you imagine the scandal? How my mother can never have noticed that this girl was just about to give birth.

P.D. I can never understand these stories. At the end of pregnancy it's so *obvious*.

M.K. There's absolutely no mistake, is there? And Cook knew she was, but the cook didn't say to my mother, 'Look, this girl ought to be brought home.' So there's the baby floating down like the Lady of Shallot in a box tied up with string and brown paper and well labelled as Miss Skrine. The poor girl must have been desperate. Oh, those days. To think of them is so extraordinary.

P.D. And were you quite different from your brothers and sister?

M.K. Yes, very different.

P.D. And had they led the same secluded lives?

M.K. Well, no . . . They didn't actually because my brothers were in the Army and Navy and that sort of thing that the boys all went into then, and had been to school in England. They all liked my mother, as boys always do, and got on with her.

P.D. You had one sister?

M.K. One sister, Susan, much older. She was four years older, but it made a big difference then; and she'd gone to school in England. And then she'd got tuberculosis.

P.D. Did your sister like your books?

M.K. I think she did. She disapproved and admired both. She thought they were terribly disloyal to the Anglos – the Anglo-Irish.

P.D. Because she was very loyal?

M.K. Oh, tremendously so. Dangerously so. And my mother couldn't think of anything beyond it.

P.D. And was Ireland a foreign country to her, or her country?

M.K. It was my mother's country. It was Anglo-Irish country, except for the poems of the Glens of Antrim. She was a great one for the dialect and I think that she used the dialect to keep her distance.

P.D. Was she an unhappy woman?

M.K. No, she adored my father. She was frightfully happily married to him, and she adored her sons.

P.D. But a show of emotion was not a clever thing to show?

M.K. When we were little she could be affectionate, but when one was older it somehow went altogether because of this tremendous disapproval. I understand now that I was everything that she thought was all wrong.

P.D. But then what happened when *The Knight of the Cheerful Countenance* came out? Did she just ignore it – pretend it hadn't happened?

M.K. I think she shuddered and read it – or read some of it.

P.D. And you continued to stay at home?

M.K. I stayed at home on and off. In those days the funny thing was that if you were asked to stay somewhere you stayed for weeks.

P.D. Had you thought about a career?

M.K. No, it didn't exist. Absolutely not. And the only thing I thought about writing was that it would give me some money so that I could go on having lots of fun and going to horse shows and hunting and enjoying myself with my friends – and actually, what did I get for my first book? About £70, I think.

P.D. But what did you envisage your life to be if you didn't think of a career?

M.K. I just enjoyed life like it was . . . I adored parties. If I thought of anything I should have thought of some sort of dream-happy marriage.

P.D. That's what people did think of?

M.K. Yes, I'm sure they did. And yet they kept awfully quiet about it. One thing I do remember very plainly that children now, girls now, discuss every iota of sex, or lack of sex, with their gentlemen. I do know that I never opened my mouth to my greatest, closest friends about my adventures. I just didn't, and they didn't to me.

P.D. It was taboo?

M.K. No, it was more . . . I don't know how to describe what we were. I think for one thing the language about sex hadn't been invented. I don't remember the word sex occurring . . . ever . . . It just wasn't there. There was a tremendously romantic outlook. I do remember, when I was awfully young, on my very first walk-out I thought I'd practically reached heaven, and where had I got to? Practically nowhere!

P.D. But leading this ambivalent and lonely life in a large house . . .

M.K. But then I had friends outside it . . . I mean I had my hunting and my hunting friends and I had a great friend who lived about four miles away. We were so childish compared to the people of our age today. We were like children of twelve, the sorts of things that amused us. Or just a bit more sophisticated. I mean there was a bottle of sherry and there were the gramophone records, and the hunting was tremendous. When I was young it was the central thing in my life, and any sort of social success depended on being good at it, and success meant a lot to me, really a lot, because it spelt people. It spelt people spoiling me, it spelt people being good to me. Because I had nothing to give back. I was just a lone girl who was fairly amusing and not even frightfully good-looking and I did have a *lovely* time.

P.D. And did the native life affect you?

M.K. Well, we loved all the people.

P.D. And listened to them?

M.K. Yes. Always. It was a kind of fashion then to see who could imitate the Irish peasant, or who could tell a good story about them. That was very popular. I think that was what gave me an enormous memory about dialogue. I can't do dialogue well today, but then it was no trouble to me. I simply could remember what had been said to me, especially anything that hit me as funny. I think everyone longed to be a good entertainer; and I was very good at it, which sounds a vain thing to say, but I know I was. And I got myself into what I thought was exciting society by just being jolly funny – and knowing how to be sharp and funny about people. It must just have been born in me because I didn't learn it from anybody.

P.D. Was your father like that?

M.K. No. He couldn't have been more English and I don't think he was a very clever man. But he was an awfully nice man, and a marvellous horseman, and totally conventional.

P.D. So, you're nineteen, you've written one book, it's been published. Do people know you've written it?

M.K. No!

P.D. Was it hard not to be boastful?

M.K. Oh, no. I was rather secretive about it. I think I told my great chum Daphne. But in the end it leaked out.

P.D. And the name M. J. Farrell? You'd chosen it at random?

M.K. Yes, because it was awfully different from my own name and all that.

P.D. And it is true that you chose it –

M.K. – from a pub, as I rode home . . . Very boring, but yes, I think I did. I wish I was as good as the other Farrell, who was drowned.

P.D. Did you decide then you were going to be a writer?

M.K. My feet nearly left the ground when I heard it was going to be published and I decided that that was the way to get another £70, so I wrote another novel, *Young Entry*, and then Billy [William] Collins, the publisher, stole me away. I thought he was awfully attractive.

P.D. And were you a celebrity?

M.K. No. I was little Miss Nobody. I don't know why Billy Collins went on, but he did go on publishing my books and telling me to write more. No, I was absolutely nothing.

P.D. And when did you use the word 'writer' to describe yourself?

M.K. I never did.

P.D. Have you ever done?

M.K. No . . . sometimes when I had to sign passports or forms I'd put playwright and author, but that was years later. You see I didn't have to sign forms about income tax or anything else then. I remember I did have a terrible income tax argument, which I managed to win, and so didn't have to pay tax on the £70.

P.D. And did you think, 'I'm going to write a book every two years'?

M.K. Yes.

P.D. No trouble thinking up plots? Getting time?

M.K. Funnily enough I never had much trouble then. I do now of course. I think how hopeless I was – I don't know. It was always tough work for me to write anything except that first book which I thought was so marvellous. I just took time off to write and otherwise enjoyed myself. It wasn't my occupation or my job. I used to come home from having jolly times in Tipperary or wherever and sit down and write a bit for *Blackwood's Magazine* and thought I was getting enormous money – say £30 – for a lot of words. I thought it was marvellous.

P.D. For reviews?

M.K. No, for short stories. Very respectable short stories, sort of hunting and everything. They were done in the book then called *Conversation Pieces*.

P.D. Was writing hard work?

M.K. Always terribly hard work. The grims, absolutely the grims.

P.D. And how did you start your Woodrooff life with the Perrys?

M.K. Oh, that was a big secret. I'd met John's father, William Perry, out hunting and he said, 'You must come and stay at Woodrooff.' And I pretended I was going to stay with a respectable friend and instead took the train to Clonmel, and when I got there it was just seething with young people, like that marvellous daughter of his, Sylvia Masters, and darling Dolly Perry whom I loved.

P.D. So this was an enchantment?

M.K. Oh, *marvellous*. I was never so happy in my life as in those first years at Woodrooff, it was carefree and lovely and the most exciting kind of racing people and everything, and I loved it, had a marvellous time. And I suppose it was there I met Bobby.

P.D. Had your husband read your books before you married?

M.K. Oh yes, very much. But he was never in the least involved in the writing. He used to say, 'I simply won't even look at your books until they're in hardback, because I might be an influence and I might be hopeless.'

P.D. So now you're married, you've come through the war, you're continuing to write and quite suddenly, out of the blue, Bobby died.

M.K. What killed him was a clot after an operation. He was perfectly all right, he was leaving the nursing home the next day. I was having lunch with Gilbert Miller about a play and I thought I'd just go in before I went to lunch. A nurse met me and said, 'Matron wants a word with you, could you wait in the hall.' And Matron came in and said, 'You must be brave, dear, your husband's dead.' It really was unbelievable – I hate to think about it.

P.D. And you'd got two small children? Sally and Virginia?

M.K. Mm. It was a bit much.

P.D. Was your husband's death the cause of the creative block in your writing? Is this a romantic idea or a real one?

M.K. I think it's a combination. I did write a bit after Bobby died. I was in the middle of a play, but I couldn't go on. Then four years later John Gielgud and Binkie Beaumont said, 'Moll, come on, write another play.' Money, you see, got so scarce after Bobby died. So I wrote *Treasure Hunt*. Sybil Thorndike was in it and John Gielgud directed it: it was a great success. I was pretty desolate when I wrote it.

P.D. And had you written during the war years?

M.K. Yes, I'd written *Two Days in Aragon*. I was awfully tormented by the theatre. Binkie Beaumont was always pestering me to do a play for him, and then not doing it.

P.D. What started you writing plays?

M.K. Well, *Spring Meeting*.

P.D. Yes, but how?

M.K. Oh, John Perry saying to me, 'Oh, Molly, you must write a play and I'll get John Gielgud to read it.' And I said I couldn't possibly write a play, and he said, 'Oh, that's all right, just write a play about your own life,' and I suppose *Spring Meeting* is more like my life than anything. Roger Livesey – a very good actor – played the old man, who was very much a portrait of John Perry's father – old Willy. So it *was* my life, I think, very much.

P.D. Well, then, all possibility of anonymity had gone.

M.K. Oh, absolutely, totally gone, everyone from Ireland came to London for the first night.

P.D. Did you enjoy it – or were you rather shivering?

M.K. I was frightened, but it was wonderful.

P.D. What a glamorous thing – to have a first night in the West End.

M.K. It was for a girl from the bogs – it really was. And all the old people I really loved, like old Mrs Hall, famous old Master of Hounds, I remember she came wearing a marvellous red dress with a pigskin handbag.

P.D. But you must have been a terrific star.

M.K. In a funny way, you see, I was, because they all adored it, and everybody in the hunting world in England loved it. It was extraordinary. It ran and ran and was sold out night after night, week after week. Of course it was a tiny little theatre, which was perfect – the Ambassadors – sweet little theatre. But it was just absolutely extraordinary.

P.D. And what about the well-known pitfalls of novelists becoming playwrights?

M.K. It was just a fluke, I suppose.

P.D. No, because you did it so many times. Did you read up about plots – points and all that?

M.K. No, honestly. If you told me tomorrow to sit down and said, 'Here's a million pounds to produce a play,' you wouldn't get one that would work. I've written two that were big successes, three that weren't done, and one that was a staggering failure – *Dazzling Prospect*, which came out just at the time of *Look Back in Anger*, though I don't think that was the entire reason for its failure.

P.D. Were you devastated by its failure? By the criticism?

M.K. Yes I was, absolutely. I felt very wounded. I thought, well, I've come to the end of all I can do. I'm obviously no good. Then I really shut up.

P.D. When did you start writing *Good Behaviour*?

M.K. Late in the Seventies. The children were grown up and I was doing nothing and I started writing. It was such a secret. Like my first book written under the bedclothes. I thought, 'Absolutely ridiculous, I know it will be a total failure, but I will have a go.'

P.D. And was it a joy to find yourself writing again?

M.K. No, no.

P.D. Just as painful as ever? And yet you did it. That's called artistic imperative.

M.K. No, no, it's just obstinacy, literary obstinacy. No, it's true if someone had said 'this is hopeless' I'd have dropped it at that moment – and when Billy Collins turned it flat down I was really shocked. I had sort of discussed it with him and said wouldn't it be funny to have a fool who doesn't see what was happening. And he said, 'Moll, what a wonderful, marvellous idea, get on with that.' And then flat turn-down. 'It's far too black a comedy, my best readers have said that and I've read it carefully, but if you will make some, or all, of the characters slightly more attractive we'll do it.' And I really had the guts to say, though I terribly wanted the money, to say no. So then I put it away and thought, well, that's finished.

P.D. And the legend of Peggy Ashcroft –

M.K. Not a legend, it's true. It's exactly what happened. She came to stay and got 'flu and was in bed and was frightfully bored and said, 'Molly, haven't you got anything you've written that I could read?' So I said, 'No, there isn't.' And then I said, 'Well, there is this book and I know it's absolutely ghastly and it's been turned down flat.' And, you know, she was absolutely crazy about it, thought it was wonderful.

P.D. And was it a terrific surprise, its great success?

M.K. Yes. I was simply ecstatic over the Booker . . . too extraordinary.

P.D. And you were well and truly re-launched. And you're starting another book?

M.K. Faintly. I must do it. I will do it. I don't know what it will amount to.

P.D. Do you know when you start a book how it's going to end?

M.K. No, I really don't know. If I had a proper education I probably would, but I'm not able to make a scenario. If I do make a scenario it just makes me sick. *Time after Time* was much better constructed than anything I'd done.

P.D. So your plot happens as the book moves along?

M.K. I think so. I mean the characters make the plot to me.

P.D. And are the characters fully fledged before you start or do they develop as you write?

M.K. They're not fully fledged, but they're in my head.

P.D. Are they based on people you know?

M.K. Absolutely, I don't think there is a truly original ghost of an idea in my head. I couldn't use specific characters.

P.D. But Aroon in *Good Behaviour* was a remarkable, original character and a very powerful woman.

M.K. Well, I'm so old . . . I've seen those women of my generation, the ones who didn't have success, leading barren lives and growing into *directrices*, as it were, as they grew older. I often think that snobbery is as strong as sex for a great many people. They cannot and will not give up or accept.

P.D. Was it bad manners to be imaginative or emotional then?

M.K. Oh yes, absolutely.

P.D. And was this reticence more agreeable, do you think?

M.K. No. I think it was very harmful. I know when Bobby died in 1938 I couldn't think of anything except shutting up my grief and not being a bore about it, even to my best friends.

P.D. And that was harmful?

M.K. Very, I'm sure of it, and very harmful to Sally, because she was only six when Bobby died and I thought she'd die when I told her. She absolutely adored him. I can't describe it. I wouldn't describe it. But I was so terrified that if I talked about him I'd howl and cry and that would be bad for her. So I did everything I could for her, ponies, brought her to Switzerland to ski, everything you could think of to entertain her and take her mind off it. She never mentioned it, she never spoke of it. Talk about good manners. Immediately after I went back to Ireland I went to collect her. She'd been staying with her cousins at Cappoquin House. It was a frightfully frosty garden in October, we had to go back in to lunch and she was only six and she said, 'Mummy, mummy, we must stop crying, we mustn't let' – I've forgotten the butler's name – 'we mustn't let him see us crying.' That sort of awful good behaviour must be impregnated into people somehow. Why should she have thought that? And yet it would have been part of my life. I would have been mopping my tears before I went back into the house. And another thing she said was, 'Mummy, mummy, what will you do, you'll never live without a man.'

P.D. Do you think that's the genesis of *Good Behaviour*?

M.K. No. I thought it was such a funny story, *Good Behaviour*. I thought it was funny – a black comedy.

P.D. But had you thought long about the results of –

M.K. – behaving like that? No, I hadn't.

P.D. It just sprang?

M.K. I don't know about that. It was just generated from knowing so many people like Aroon, not *so* many, but quite a few, and thinking why they were as they were – having the long back-spring knowledge of them growing up with me . . . and what their own lives had been like.

P.D. Do you type?

M.K. I can't type. Pen and paper.

P.D. And do you re-write and re-write?

M.K. I don't terribly because I write so slowly. I do a bit, of course, but I write on one page of an exercise book and then I leave a blank page so that I can correct opposite.

P.D. Do you often have to go back and change motivation?

M.K. No, I don't, because I am so ignorant, you see. I don't know how books are made. I mean give me a book and I'll read it like a story, but I wouldn't ever take it to pieces and say how it is done. I just wouldn't.

P.D. The insights, the descriptions, when you're re-reading them, they're how you think?

M.K. I hardly ever re-read them. I mean it's all a great surprise to me – if you were to give me some old book of mine I'd read it with great surprise as though I had no connection with it at all. I promise you.

P.D. Have you had a happy life?

M.K. Happy and unhappy both. Terribly happy in patches, not happy in patches. I suppose most people's lives are.

P.D. But compared to many Irish women of your class and generation?

M.K. Yes, compared to so many I have had a very amusing and marvellous life – God, yes, I know I have. I wish I could enjoy this kind of success more, but I'm too old for it I think.

P.D. Are you surprised by the shifts and turns in your writing?

M.K. I don't understand anything about my writing. I really don't understand why it's successful and I don't understand why it should fail either. It's all on a level to me.

CONTENTS

PULLINSTOWN

It was Sir Richard who asked me to stay at Pullins-town for the Springwell Harriers' point-to-point meeting. That his children had nothing to do with the invitation was evident from the very politeness of their greetings—greetings which they concluded as swiftly as the conventions permitted, leaving me to the conversational mercies of their father. But he, after a question as to how my journey had prospered with me, and a comment on the rival un-punctuality of trains and boats, sank his haggard (and once splendid) shoulders into the back of his chair, and, setting his old-fashioned steel pince-nez all askew on his nose, devoted himself to the day's paper in a manner that brooked of no inter-ruptions on less trivial matters. Since my cousins (in a second and third degree) made no demands on my attention, I looked about me and maintained what I hoped was a becoming silence.

The hall where we were sitting was lovely. Whoever designed this old Irish house had cer-tainly a peculiar sense of the satisfying fitness of curving walls, of ceiling mouldings continuously beautiful, while the graceful proportioning of a distant stairway drew the eyes down the length of the oval room and upwards to the light coming in kindly dusty radiance through a great window on the stairs. Sheraton had made the hooped table on which lay a medley of hunting-whips, ash-plant switches, gloves, two silver hunting-horns, and a vast number of dusty letters and unopened papers. Through the doors of a glass-fronted cupboard (his work too), I could see reels and lines, glimpses of wool and bright feathers for fly-tying, with bottles of pink prawns, silver eels' tails and golden sprats, all lures for the kingly salmon. There were pictures on the walls, not many, but Raeburn must have painted that lady in the dress like a luminous white cloud. She looked out of her picture with foxy eyes very like those of the silent little cousin who was now reading a discarded sheet of her father's newspaper with inherited concentration. The gentleman in the bright blue coat might have been Sir Richard in fancy dress, but he was a Sir Richard who had died fighting for King James at the battle of the Boyne. This they told me afterwards.

Still my cousins, Willow and Dick, sat saying never a word. Sir Richard sniffed a little, depre-catingly, as he read the paper, and Willow, the light slanting over her, appeared absorbed in her sheet. She was like her own name to look at, Willow, pale as a peeled sally wand, hair and all, and green flickering eyes. Her brother Dick was an arrogant and beautiful sixteen. I disliked the pair of them heartily.

A door opened, breaking the spell of quiet, and

a wheezing and decrepit old butler came in to arrange a tea-table in the window.

"Is that the evening paper you have, Miss Willow? Excuse me, Did Silver-Tip win in Mallow?"

"He did not. The weight beat him." Miss Willow did not lift her eyes during her brief reply, nor when she added, "Run up to the Post Office, James, after your tea, and buy me fifty Gold Flake. Only I have a little job to do for the Sir, I'd go myself."

"And what about James?" inquired the old butler with restrained acerbity. "Haven't he one hundred and one little jobs to do for the Sir? God is my witness, Miss Willow, the feet is bet up under me this living minyute, and how I'll last out the length o' dinner in the boots is unknown to me, leave alone to travel the roads after thim nasty trash o' cigarettes. Thim's only poison to you, child, believe you me."

"It's a pity about poor James." Willow addressed her brother. "I suppose the boots wouldn't carry him as far as the river to catch a salmon in the Tinker's stream to-night. Who stole my claret hackles, I wonder?" This last with sudden vicious intensity.

"An' who whipped six pullets' eggs out o' me pantry to go feed her ould racehorse," James countered nimbly, "that poor Molly Byrne had gothered for the Sir——"

" If Molly Byrne had as much as six eggs in the day from those hens, she'd run mad from this to Ballybui telling it out the two sides of the road.

" Are you ready for your tea, Sir Richard ? " She whirled round suddenly on her father, " James, show Mr. Oliver his room."

So I was sufficiently one of the family, I reflected, as I followed James's shuffling footsteps up the stairs, to be Mr. Oliver—it was rather pleasing. James peered at me, blinking in the afternoon sun that flooded the bedroom to which he led me.

" The maker's name is on the blade," he announced with dramatic suddenness. " Ye'r the dead spit and image of the father. God, why wouldn't I know ye out of him ? Wasn't he rared on the place along with the Sir ? He was, 'faith. Sure meself was hall-boy under ould Dinny Mahon those times. Your poor Da could remember me well—many a good fish I stuck the gaff in for him the days I'd cod ould Dinny and slip away down to him on the river. Didn't he send me a silk out of India and red feathers ye couldn't beat to tie in a fiery fly—may Almighty God grant him to see the light o' the glory of heaven—he was a good sort."

I was glad some one remembered my father. He had told me so much and so often of his early days there with those Irish cousins that I had come to Pullinstown with a feeling of intimacy for the place and for my cousins which the very politeness of their first greeting to me had dispelled as strangely as the silence that followed it. James left me with a restored right to my pleasant intimacies.

My room was a large one. A vast bed with twisted fluted bedposts, ruthlessly cut down, took up most of one wall—the furnishing otherwise was sparse. A cupboard was full of my cousin Willow's summer clothes, while a large, coffin-like receptacle contained what looked like her mother's or grandmother's. There remained a yellow-painted chest of drawers. I opened the top drawer, which was empty, but as it obstinately refused to close again, I could only hope that the other three were empty too.

The view from the two tall windows held me longer even than my struggle with the chest of drawers. I looked down across garden beds, their disorder saved from depression by the army of daffodils that flung gold regiments alike over the beds and through the grass that divided them, out across a park-like field where five young horses and a donkey moved soberly, and a grey shield of water held the quiet evening light, over the best of a fair hunting country to the far secrecy of the mountains. And looking, I envied my father those wild young days of his fox-hunting and fishing, shooting snipe, and skylarking with those Irish cousins here in Westcommon.

They had waited tea for me, I found to my embarrassment, and with an incoherent apology for my delay, I sat down beside Willow. She bestirred herself to be polite.

" The Sir—er—father was telling us you are an artist," she said, with less interest if with more dislike than she might have displayed had father told her I was a Mormon. " Well, I would like to be able to paint pictures," she continued, studiously avoiding the eye of her brother directed meaningly at her from across the table, a jeer in his silence.

" You would, I'm sure," said he suddenly.

" I would," his sister flashed round on him. " I'd paint a picture of you falling off Good-Day over the last fence in Cooladine last week."

" I did not fall off her—the mare stood on her head and well you know it."

" And small wonder for her—the way you had the head pulled off her going into every fence. Dick's an awful coward—isn't that right, Sir Richard ? "

" I wouldn't mind him being a coward if he wasn't a fool as well." Sir Richard eyed his heir sternly. " When did I give you permission to enter the mare in the open race to-morrow ? " he demanded.

Dick blushed. " I was waiting to ask you. May I ? "

" You may not. The mare will go in the Ladies' Race, and Willow can ride her."

" Oh, father——" Young Dick's blush sank

deeper in his skin. " I did *not* fall off her." On the point of tears he was.

" I'll ride my own horse in the Ladies' Race or I'll not ride at all." Willow's small silvery face expressed more acute determination than I have often seen. " If I can't beat those Leinster girls on Romance, I'll not beat them on that rotten brute Good-Day. You know right well she'll run out with me. Dick's the only one can get any good of her, and well you know it, Sir Richard."

" I'd sooner put an old woman up to ride the mare than that nasty little officer." Sir Richard tapped the table forbiddingly with a lump of sugar before dropping it into his teacup.

" Well, *I'll* not ride her," said Willow. She pushed back her chair, lit a cigarette, and walked out into the bright tangled garden. After a minute Dick followed her, and two sour-looking little terriers of indeterminate breed followed him without fuss. He would show them sport, I thought, watching the light swing of his shoulders in the seedy old tweed coat. It was as stern a business to him as to them.

Sir Richard looked out after his retreating family. " That's a right good boy," he said, with sudden almost impersonal approval, " and b'Gad—a terror to ride. Why wouldn't he? He's bred the right way, though I say it myself. But he'll never be as good as Willow. She's a divil."

Compared to the terror and the devil of his be-

getting, I felt that I must appear but a poor specimen
to my cousin. However, he suffered my interest
in an incomplete series of old coaching prints with
kindly tolerance, and showed me a Queen Anne
chair, a Sèvres cup, and some blue glass bottles
with quickening interest. " I forget about these
things," he complained ; " the children don't care
for them, you see ; it's all the horses with them.
Come out and have a look at the skins—would you
care to ? "

We followed a greened path round one of the
long, grey wings that flanked on each side the
square block of the house, and turning the corner
came to the high stone archway leading into the
stable-yard. In the dusk of the archway young Dick
and Willow stood, fair, like two slight swords in
that dark place.

" Father," said they, " Tom Kenny is here with
a horse."

" Well, I have no time to waste looking at the
horses Tom Kenny peddles around the country.
What sort is it ? "

" Oh, a common brute," said Willow, with
indifferent decision. " The man only came over
to see you about the fox covert in Lyran."

" Well, if you say it's a common brute, there's
some hope of seeing a bit of bone and substance
about the horse. If *you* don't like him, he may be
worth looking at." Sir Richard advanced into the
yard, and I, following him, caught just the edge of

the perfectly colourless wink that passed between his son and daughter. The match of their guile being now well and truly laid to the desired train, they proceeded carelessly on their way. A minute later the two terriers, a guilty pig-bucket look about them, hurried out of the yard in pursuit.

Inside the archway I paused. I love stables and horses and grooms, the cheerful sound of buckets, the heady smell of straw, the orderly fussiness of a saddle-room ; always the same and ever different. The mind halts, feeling its way into gear with a new brave set of values at the moment when one sets foot within a stable-yard.

The stables at Pullinstown had been built for a larger stud than lodged there now. More than a few doors were fastened up, but there was still a stir and movement about some of the boxes. A lean old hunter's head looked quietly out across the half-door of his box, hollows of age above his eyes, the stamp of quality and bravery on him unmistakably. Next door the shrill voice of the very young complained against this new unknown discipline—the sweat of the breaking tackle still black on an untrimmed neck. A bright bay three-year-old this was, full of quality, and would be up to fourteen stone before he was done with. Such a set of limbs on him too. Bone there you'd be hard to span. "That's the sort," said Sir Richard, nodding at him. "Ah, if I was twenty years younger I'd give myself a present of that horse. Go back to

your stable, I'd say ; I'll never sell you. Good-Day
and Romance are over there. I sold a couple of
horses last week. Now listen—I *hate* to sell a horse
that suits the children ; but they must go—make
room for more—this place is rotten with horses.
Well, Tom "—he craned round to a small dark man
who appeared quietly from the black mouth of
the saddle-room door—" did you get that furze
stubbed out of the hill yet ? "

" B'God I did, sir. Now look-at, the torment I
got on the hill of Lyran there's no man will believe.
I'm destroyed workin' in it. A pairson wouldn't
get their health with them old furzy pricks in their
body as thick as pins in a bottle. And then to say
five pounds is all the hunt should give me for me
trouble ! I'm a poor man, Sir Richard, and a long
backwards family to rare, and a delicate dying
brother on the place."

" Did Doctor Murphy give you a bottle for
him ? " Sir Richard interrupted the recital. " I
told him he should go see poor Dan last
week."

" Ah, he did, he did, sir. Sure, then the bottle the
doctor left played puck with him altogether, though
indeed the doctor is a nice quiet man, and he had to
busht out crying when he clapped an eye on poor
Dan. He was near an hour there with him, going
hither and over on his body with a yoke he had stuck
in his two ears. Indeed he was very nice, and Dan
was greatly improved in himself after he going.

Faith, he slapped into the bottle o' medicine, and he'd take a sup now and a sup again till—be the holy, I'll not lie to ye, sir—whatever was in the bottle was going through him in standing leps. I thought he'd die," Tom Kenny concluded with a pleasant laugh.

"Did he take the dose the doctor ordered?" Sir Richard's long knotted fingers were crossed before him on the handle of his walking stick. His head was bent in grave attention to the tale. What, I wondered, of Tom Kenny's horse? And what, again, of his brother?

"Is it what poor Doctor Murphy told him?" A pitying smile appeared for a moment on Tom Kenny's face. "Well, I'll always give it in to the doctor, he's dam nice, but sure a child itself'd nearly know what good would one two teaspoons do wandering the inside through of a great big wilderness of a man the like o' poor Danny. Sure he drank down what was in the bottle, o' course, and that was little enough for the money, God knows."

"Ah, psha!" Impossible to describe the mixture of anger and hopeless tolerence in Sir Richard's exclamation. "Well"—he lifted his head, stabbing at the ground with the point of his walking-stick—"I suppose it's to pay funeral expenses you're trying to sell the horse."

"Now God is my witness, Sir Richard, if I was to get the half o' what this young horse is worth, it'd be more money than poor Danny'll ever see at his funeral or any other time in his life."

" Ah, have done chatting and pull out the horse till I see what sort he is." Sir Richard bent to the match in his cupped hands.

Following on this, Tom Kenny retired into a distant loose-box, from which there issued presently sounds of an encouraging nature, in voices so varied as to suggest that a large proportion of the male staff of Pullinstown had assembled in the box.

" Stand over, Willy. Mind out would he split ye ! "

" Go on out you, Tom, before him."

" Sure every horse ye'll see rared a pet is wayward always."

" Well, now isn't he the make and shape of a horse should have a dash o' speed ? "

" Is it them Grefelda horses ? Did ye ever see one yet wasn't as slow as a man ? "

" Well, he's very pettish, Tom. What way will we entice him ? "

" *Hit him a belt o' the stick !* " came with sudden thunder from across the yard where Sir Richard still stood. Whether or not his advice was acted upon, a moment later the Grefelda horse shot like a rocket out of the stable door, his owner hazardously attached to his head by a single rein of a snaffle bridle.

" Woa—boy—woa the little horse." Tom Kenny

led him forward, nagging him to a becoming stance with every circumstance of pompous ownership.

I am a poor enough judge of a horse in the rough, but this one seemed to me to have the right outline. There was here a valuable alliance of quality and substance, and as he was walked away and back to us, a length of stride promising that he should gallop.

" That'll do," said Sir Richard, after a prolonged, sphinx-like inspection. " I'm sorry to see he plucks that hock, Tom ; only for that he's not a bad sort at all. Turn him around again. Ah, a pity ! "

" May God forgive yer honour," was Tom Kenny's pious retort ; " ye might make a peg-top o' this horse before ye'd see the sign of a string-halt on him. Isn't that right, Pheelan ? " He appealed to a small man with a wry neck and a surprising jackdaw blue eye, who had stood by throughout the affair in a deprecating silence, unshaken even by this appeal.

" What height is he ? Sixteen hands ? " Sir Richard stood in to the horse.

" Sixteen one, as God is my judge," corrected the owner. " Well, now," he compromised, as Sir Richard remained unshaken, " look—he's within the black o' yer nail of it."

Even this distance I judged, after a glance at Tom Kenny's outstretched thumb, would leave him no more than a strong sixteen. However that might be, I more than liked the horse, and so I rather suspected did Sir Richard, the more when I saw him shake his head and turn a regretful back to the affair.

"Sir Richard"—Tom Kenny's head shot forward tortoise-like from his coat collar—"look-at—eighty pounds is my price—eighty pounds in two nut-shells."

"Well, Tom," Sir Richard smiled benignantly, "I'm always ready to help a friend, as you know." He paused, his head bent again in thought. "Now if I was to ride the horse, and that is to say if I *like* the horse, I wouldn't say I mightn't give you sixty-five pounds for him," came with sudden generous resolve.

"May God forgive you, sir." Tom Kenny turned from the impious suggestion with scarcely concealed horror. Tears loomed in his voice as he continued in rapt encomium, "Don't ye know yerself ye might do the rounds o' the world before ye'd meet a horse the like o' that ! This horse'll sow and he'll plough and he'll sweep the harvest in off o' the fields for ye. Look at ! " (with sudden drama). "If ye were to bring this horse home with ye to-day, ye mightn't have a stick o' harvest left standing to-morra night. And he'll be a divil below a binder."

"Faith, true for you, Tom Kenny. That one's very lonely for the plough," Pheelan of the jackdaw eyes struck in with irresistible sarcasm. "Sure, it's for Master Dick to hunt him the Sir'll buy him."

Without a change of expression, Tom Kenny tacked into the wind again. " Well, ye'd tire three men galloping this horse, and there's not a ditch in the globe of Ireland where ye'd fall him," said he with entire and beautiful conviction.

" Ah, have done. Get up on him, you, Pheelan, and see would you like him." Sir Richard spoke with brief decision.

Following on this the prospective purchase was ridden and galloped into a white lather by Pheelan, whose hissed " Buy him, sir ; he's a *topper !* " I overheard as Sir Richard prepared to mount, and having done so, whacked the now most meek and biddable horse solemnly round the yard with his walking-stick, before he changed hands for the sum of sixty-eight pounds, a yearling heifer, and thirty shillings back for " luck."

" And damned expensive, too," said my cousin as, the deal concluded, we pursued our way onwards to look at the young horses ; " only I *hate* bargaining and talking I'd have bought him twice as cheap. . . . Isn't that a great view ? You should paint that. I would if I was an artist."

We had walked up a hilly lane-way, splitting a flock of sheep driven by a young lad as we went. The river lay low on our right hand now. Everywhere the gorse shone like sweet gold money, and primroses spread pale lavish flames. The whole air was full of a smoky gold light. It lay low against the rose of the ploughed fields. It was weighted

with the scent of the gorse. The young horses were
splendidly bathed in light. They grouped themselves nobly against the hillside before they swung
away from us, with streaming manes and tails,
to crest the hill like a wave, and thunder away into
the evening. Nor, though we stayed there an
hour, could we get near them again. My cousin,
as last exasperated, led me back to the house and
dinner.

" Don't change," he said as we parted ; so only
his own round skull-cap of bruised purple velvet
lent ceremony to the occasion of my first dinner at
Pullinstown. Willow had not changed, and Dick
came up from the river just as we sat down. Willow's
hair was as pale as wood ashes in the candle-light,
and her infrequent, shadowy voice oddly pleasing.
Still she did not talk to me, but held stubborn
argument with James as to the date on which the
salmon we were eating had last swum in the river.
Dick talked to her. He had risen a fish twice on a
strange local fly called a " goat's claret." They both
addressed their father as " Sir Richard " in cere-
monious voices, and he talked to me about my
father and the fun they had together, James, as he
ministered punctiliously to our needs, occasionally
supplying the vital point of a half-remembered
anecdote or forgotten name.

After dinner we played bridge, the army of
cards falling and whispering quietly between us
of our black and red skirmishes, adventures

and defeats. Sir Richard and I were three shillings down on the rubber when Willow put the old painted packs of cards back in their pale ivory fort and went out with Dick to plait her mare's mane for the race to-morrow.

" Why in God's name did you not do it by daylight, child ? " her father complained.

" Because Pheelan locked the stable door on me. He thinks no one but himself can plait up a mane."

"And he's right too, I dare say." Sir Richard contemplated his daughter with serene approval.

" I was ashamed of my life the way he had her mane in Cooladine." Willow was sorting reels of thick, linen thread. " Will you come, Dick ? " she said.

"And the reason why I play cards so well "— Dick rose to his feet, sliding my three shillings up and down his trouser pocket—" is because I can use my brains to think out problems." He was not boasting, merely voicing his private ruminations.

" Good-night, Sir Richard," they both said. " *Good*-night," they said to me with extreme politeness, and went out together.

Soon after this we went up to bed, Sir Richard and I, armed each with a shining silver candlestick like an evening star, and I sat for a while smoking a cigarette, leaning out of my window to the hushed bosom of the night. I saw a star caught in the flat water more silver than the moon. A white owl slanted by and was gone, low among the trees, and the sound of a fiddle jigging out some hesitant tune picked sweetly at the stillness.

"Play 'The wind that shakes the barley,'" a voice prompted the fiddler. "That's not it—it's the 'Snowy-breasted Pearl' yer in on now."

"Jig it for me, you."

"God, I wouldn't be able to jig it. There's the one turn on the whole o' them tunes—'twouldn't be easy to know them——"

I was sorry when the fiddling ceased, but when there drifted on the air a tale astir with every principle of drama, I forgot even that I was eavesdropping, and strained against the night to hear. . . . "Well, it was a long, lonely lane and two gates on it; that'll give ye an idea how long it was——" Followed a period of sibilant murmuring, and then a sudden protest: "Ah, go on! It's all very well to be talkin' how ye's box this one and box that one—if a fella lepped out on ye, what'd ye do?"

It was at this interesting moment that a window above my own shot open, and the irate voice of James ordered Lizzie Doyle and Mary Josey to their respective beds.

"Begone now!" he commanded, and with Biblical directions told the garden what he thought of a domestic staff that sat all day with their elbows up on the kitchen table drinking tea, and spent the nights trapseing the countryside.

"Oh, Jesus, Mary and Joseph! Isn't that frightful?" I heard amid the scuffle of retreat, and then, as though in submission to the moods of fate : "Well, the ways o' God are something fierce." In the succeeding silence I too betook myself to bed.

The morning was unbelievably young when I woke to the faint squawk and flapping of birds on the water below. A heron in a Scotch fir-tree was pencil-etched against the grey sky. In the very early mornings churches and bridges too have the air of nearly forgotten stories ; but never did romance so hinge itself to possibility for me as now when, like two sentinels of the morning's quietness, I saw Willow and Dick ride out of the stable arch and walk their horses away from sight into the slowly silvering morning. The breathless picture they made is with me still—both sitting a little carefully, perhaps, with saddles still cold on their horses' backs. And you could hardly have told, but for the square-cut pale hair of one, which of them was Willow and which was Dick. Bright and unkind the two blood-horses looked in the grey light, and their riders forlorn in the gallantry of the very young passed on to face who knows what horrors of schooling in cold blood at that deathly hour.

At breakfast they were touched with the unimpeachable importance of those who rise up early to accomplish dangerous matters while others are still in bed. I found them less romantic. Willow ate some strange cereal with lavish cream. " Good for the body," she said in reply to her father's comment. " Have some yourself. Will you have some ? " she added to me.

There was a patch of mud on the shoulder of Dick's tweed coat, and Sir Richard scolded and grumbled all through the meal at the rottenness of those who face young horses into impossible fences. Dick made neither defence nor answer. Occasionally he stuck a finger between his neck and the spotted handkerchief he wore round it, loosening its folds abstractedly. He ate an apple and one piece of dry toast very slowly, and just before he lit a cigarette he said, " There's no one can ride that mare, only myself. She's a queer-tempered divil, but when Cherry'd be good "—there was almost a croon in his voice—" *then* I'd give her an apple." Whereupon he went out of the room, shutting the door behind him, and Willow, who was feeding the dogs, said :

" That was an awful toss he took. I thought he was quinched. Ah—he was only winded. What time do you want to start for the races, father ? You should bring the lunch in your car. Dick and I have to go on early to walk the course."

Clearly I perceived that I was included under the heading lunch as their father's passenger. I saw them leave the house at about eleven, James

following them to pack a suitcase, a medley of
saddles, a weight cloth, a handful of boot
pulleys and jockeys, a mackintosh coat, a cutting-
whip and a spare horse-sheet into the crazy brass-
bound Ford car which waited pompously beneath
the great, granite-pillared porch.

"Good-bye, now." He fastened the last button
of the side curtains as the Ford started on its way
with that unearthly hiccup common to its species.

"Mind ! "—Willow put her head out of the car—
"see and squeeze the cherry brandy out of the
Sir for lunch."

James returned to the hall at a busy if rather
dickey trot. "Merciful God ! "—he halted in
horror—"if they didn't leave the little safety-
hat after them." He surveyed a black silk-
covered crash-helmet with dismay. "Ah, well,
it'll only have to follow on with ourselves and
the lunch."

This was my first intimation that James was to be
of the party. Had I known the ways of Pullinstown
more intimately it would never have occurred to
me that any expedition could be undertaken without
his presence. But never can I forget my first sight
of him an hour later in his race-going attire. He
wore a rather steeple-crowned bowler hat, green
with age, and a very long box-cloth overcoat with
strongly stitched shoulder patches and smartly cut
pocket flaps. It was a coat, indeed, that could only
have been worn with complete success by the most

famous of England's sporting peers. From his breast pocket peeped a pair of minute mother-of-pearl opera glasses (no doubt removed from one of the glass-topped tables in the drawing-room), and round his neck, tied with perfect symmetry, was a white flannel stock, polka dotted with red.

" James has to sit in front with me." Sir Richard, more then usually haggard and untidy, slid himself crabbedly behind the wheel of the big Bentley, cursing his sciatica in a brief aside. " He always remembers where the self-starter is. I never can find it. It's a cursed nuisance to me in race traffic. What's that, James ? " He pointed to a small fish-basket which James was stowing away in the back.

" There's a change o' feet for Miss Willow, Sir Richard. There's no way ye'll soak the cold only out o' wet boots, and ye couldn't tell but they'd slip the child into a river or a wet ditch, or maybe she'd be lying quinched under the mare in a boggy place. Sure——"

" Ah, get into the car, ye old fool, and stop talking. Maybe it's a coffin you should have brought with you, let alone the boots. Have we all now ? "

" We have, Sir Richard." James laid the crash-helmet on top of the lunch basket and stepped in beside his master.

By what seemed only a series of surprising accidents, Sir Richard fought his noisy way into

top gear, and, determined to stay in at all costs,
took risks with ass carts and other hazards of the
twisty roads which appalled me. What, I wondered,
would be our progress through the race traffic, if
indeed we ever came so near the course ? We had
left the wide demesne fields of Pullinstown behind
us now, and the country on either hand was more
enclosed. Banks I saw, tall single ones, and wondered if they raced over these in Ireland ; big stone
facers too, solid and kind, plenty of room on them ;
and an occasional loose-built stone wall—no two
consecutive fences quite alike and not a strand of
wire to be seen. The going was mostly grass, though
here and there a field of plough showed up rawly,
white gulls stooping and wheeling above it, dim
like sawn-out pearl in the grey soft air ; and always
the mountains, ringing the country like a precious
cup.

"That's a great bog for snipe," Sir Richard
would say. "That's a right snug bit of covert,"
or "That's the best pool on the river," pointing to
a secret turn of water low under distant woods.
" I killed a thirty-pound salmon there—on a
' Mystery,' it was. Two hours I had him on before
James got a chance to gaff him. Ah, he was a
tiger ! God ! I took a right fall over that fence one
time. No, but the high devil with the stones in it.
Wasn't his father out that day, James ? He was, of
course. Tell him I showed you the place King
Spider nearly killed me. He'll remember—dear

me, I'm forgetting he's dead—poor Harry ! Is this
the turn now, James ? To the right ? "

" Wheel left, Sir Richard, wheel left," James
corrected easily ; and wheel left we did, but with
such surprising velocity that the heavy car skidded
and spun about in the road, pointing at last in
the direction from which he had come.

" Oh, fie, Sir Richard ! " James, quite unmoved,
reached out a respectable black-trousered leg
towards the self-starter. " Do you not know the
smallest puck in the world is able to do the hell of
a job on that steering ? If the like o' that should
happen us in strong race traffic, we were three dead
men."

The race traffic, of which I had heard a good deal,
did not become apparent till we were within the
last couple of miles from our destination, when indeed
the narrow lane that led up to the car park was
congested enough. Old and young, the countryside
attended the races. Mothers of infants who could
not by any stretching of possibilities be left a day
long without sustenance, avoided the difficulty by
taking their progeny along with them ; and the
same held good, I imagined, in the case of those old
men who, had they remained at home, would
certainly have fallen into the fire or otherwise
injured themselves during the absence of the race-
goers. Ford cars conveyed parties of eight or more.
Pony carts, ass carts, and bicycles did their share,
while a fair sprinkling of expensive cars had to

regulate their pace by that of the slowest ass cart that preceded them in the queue. A shawled and handsome fury, selling race-cards, jumped on the step of our car during a momentary stoppage of the traffic; her tawny head blazed raggedly in the sunlight.

"Race-card—a shillin' the race-card," she bawled hideously. She carried a baby on her arm. I saw the outline of its round head beneath the heavy shawl, but, quite unimpeded by its burden, she leaped like a young goat from the step of our car to attack the next in the line.

"Easy, Sir Richard! Mind the cycle now! Stop, sir! They want the five bob for the car now. Wheel west for the gate. Cross out over the furzy bushes. Slip in there now; that's Miss Willow's car." So piloted by James we came at last to a standstill.

From the top of the little hill where the cars were parked, we could see below us the weighing tent and paddock (a few horses already stood there in their sheets), the bookies establishing themselves in their stand (we were in good time; they had not begun to bet on the first race yet), and at the foot of the hill the railing run in to the finish; while out in the country here and there the eye picked up the lonely flutter of a little white flag.

"Leave Red Flags on the Right and White Flags on the Left," I read on my race-card below "Conditions of the Meeting." And then :

" First Race, 1.30.

Hunt Race : A sweepstake for horses, the pro-
perty of members of the Springwell Hunt."

Then the Sporting Farmers' Open Race, and

" Third Race : Open Race—of £30, of which
the second receives £5.
1. Major O'Donnel's Wayward Gipsy (black,
yellow cap).
2. Mr. Devereux's ch. geld, Bright Love.
3. Sir Richard Pulleyn's br. mare Good-Day,
aged (blue, black cap)."

Six more runners were down to go for that race,
but I turned the card over and read : " Ladies'
Race. Open. For a cup." And Miss Pulleyn's
Romance heading the list.

" Romance'll win it," Sir Richard prophesied
bleakly, " but there's a lot of good horses against
the boy. Have you me glasses, James ? Have you
me stick ? Right. Come on now till we see the
horses saddled for this first race. We'll have lunch
then, James."

Down the hill towards the saddling enclosure
we went, almost fighting our way between groups
of gossiping country women, stalls of oranges and
bananas, roulette boards, and exponents of the
three-card trick.

" Clancy's horse'll win it, you'll see," I heard.

" See now—he's like nothin' only a horse ye'd see on paper ; he's like a horse was painted."

" What about Amber Girl ? " interpolated a rival's supporter.

" Well, what about her ? Now look-at, I seen this horse win a race in Ballyowen. Well, he was four length from the post and four horses in front of him, and the minute Clancy stirred on him he come through the lot to win be two lengths. Clancy made a matter o' ninety pound about it. Ah ! he never let him run idle."

" Well, what about Amber Girl ? " reiterated Amber Girl's supporter.

What indeed, I wondered ; how would she run against a horse that could accomplish so spectacular a finish after three miles over a country ? But I was never to hear. A section of the crowd melting at that moment, we pushed on towards the paddock, and here, lost in joint disapproving contemplation of the six starters waiting to be saddled for their race, we found Willow and Dick. They were as quiet as two fish in a pool, but I felt all the same that very little in that busy ring escaped their devastating attention.

" Is Pheelan here with the horses yet ? " Sir Richard asked them.

" He wasn't here five minutes ago. Did you not pass him on the road ? " Willow looked worried. " I hope he didn't go round by Mary Pheelan's pub," she said to Dick, as they went out of the

ring to look for him. And really, for Pheelan's sake,
I found myself hoping that he had not. Nor had
he. But his subsequent discovery, blamelessly
sheltering with the horses behind a gorse-crowned
bank of primroses, wrung from Willow a sufficiently
stinging reprimand.

Because of the search for Pheelan we missed most
of the first race, and I failed to accomplish my
nearest ambition, which was to see a bank jumped
at really close quarters. Through my glasses I could
see the distant horses flip on and off their fences with
the deceptive ease that distance lends to the most
strenuous effort, and the last fences before the finish
were two that did not take a lot of doing. A disappointing race from the spectator's point of view :
won in a distance. Three finished.

We ate our lunch after this. That is, Sir Richard
and I ate sandwiches, and Willow and Dick watched
us with the avid importance of jockeys.

Dick studied the field for his race : " The only
horse I'm afraid of is that Bright Love—that's a
Punchestown horse."

" Ah, it'll fall," from Willow, easily.

She read bits from the race-card. " Patrick
Byrne's Sissy—that's a great pattern of a cob.
Purplish waistcoat and white shirt sleeves. Could
he not say he was wearing the top half of his Sunday
suit ? "

" Doris is going to ride her own mare in the
Ladies' Race. You'll have to mind yourself, Willow."

" I rode against Doris in Duffcarry, father. I had right sport with her. Sure she was nearly crying with fright down at the start. ' Go slow into the last fence, girls,' I said, ' *whatever* you do—that's a murderous brute of a place.' I was only teasing them about it, but didn't Doris and Susan pull into a trot very nearly. Ah, that was where I slipped on a bit and they never caught me. A bad fence ?— not it—the sort you'd get up in the night to jump."

" You know, Dick," she said, " I hate the way they jump that narrow one—right on the turn."

" Oh, there's nothing in it."

We were watching the second race. They did not eat, but sat on their shooting-sticks and drank a thimbleful of black coffee each.

" I'll have a good drink with you after my race, Dick," Willow said. They dived into their Ford car, throwing out a suitcase and a weight cloth. James followed them down the hillside.

In the ring Willow held Good-Day, while Pheelan fussed and chided about her saddling. She was a little bit of a mare, Good-Day—a bright blood bay, all quality. The single rein of her plain snaffle was turned over her head. She looked to be fairly fit, and I guessed would take some beating. I said so to Sir Richard.

" Ah, a right mare if she was half ridden." Dick just caught the answer. I saw the tips of his ears go scarlet against the black cap that Willow was tying on his head. The wind blew cold through his jersey. It looked as though it must whistle through his body too, so fine drawn he was and so desperately keen. Pheelan gave him a leg up. As he sat, feeling the length of his stirrups, Good-Day turned her head round, nipping the air funnily.

" She'll be good to-day," Dick said, " you'll see," picking up his rubber-laced rein.

James came sidling up to say behind his hand, " Master Dick, keep east the fence before the wood —there's a paling gone out of it. Ye may gallop through. Mickey Doyle bid me tell you."

Dick smiled a little wintry smile and nodded.

They were out of the ring now, Pheelan leading the mare down through the crowd.

" Stop on the hill, father," said Willow ; " James and I are going down out into the country."

" Go down, you," Sir Richard said to me ; " you'd be more use than old James." I thought he looked distinctly shaky and just a thought grim as he walked slowly back to the car.

James and Willow and I took a short-cut down to the start. We jumped three formidable banks, pulling James after us, before we reached the place of vantage Willow had in her mind's eye.

Now we could see the field lined up for a start below us—eight horses in it—Dick and the little mare seemed so far away from any hope but each other. Willow was straining her eyes on them. A false start, and all to do over again. They were off. Hardly room to steady a horse before the first

fence, and Dick did not even try to do so. They were
up—they were over. Certainly Good-day wasted
no time over her fences. A rough piece of moorland
and every one taking a pull. The horses turned
away from us to drop into a laneway. Then we saw
them over two more fences. Good-Day leading
still—a raking chestnut striding along second ; then
the bay mare Wayward Gipsy and six more all in a
bunch. Two horses fell at the fourth fence, a little
puff of dust rising from the bank as they hit it. One
jockey remounted, and the other lay where he had
fallen, his horse galloping on. Willow did not even
put her glasses on him. She was aware of nothing
but Dick and Good-Day.

"The mare beat Bright Love over her fences," she
said, " but he'll gallop away from her, James, if
he stands up. He jumped that badly. Steady now,
Dick, take a pull on her, this is a divil. He's over.
Now we lose them. Come on, boys ; we'll slip
across to this big fence and see them come home."

Over a field we ran, Willow just beating me,
James a very bad third, to take up our stand beside
a high, narrow bank with a ditch on the landing
side. Not a choice obstacle for a tired horse. And
three fences from home they'd be racing too.
"Oh, a filthy spot," said Willow.

A little knot of country boys gathered round her.
"Eh, Miss Pulleyns, can ye see the horses ? Eh,
Miss Pulleyns, did they cross out the big ditch yet ?
Look-at, look-at ! Mr. Pulleyns is down."

"Almighty Lord God! Should the horse have fallen with him?" queried an emotional lady friend.

"No, but he fell from the horse beyond the wood."

"Oh! Oh! Is he hurted?"

"Hurt! He's killed surely. Isn't the head burst!"

Knowing that my glasses could not hope to equal the hawk-like vision of my informants, I said nothing, but focused them on a point beyond the plantation and waited for the horses to appear. When they did, Dick and Good-day were, as I had indeed supposed, still among them—lying third now, with the big chestnut Bright Love in the lead and Wayward Gipsy second, but I thought she was pretty well done with.

"He'll not catch the chestnut now," Willow said. "He's let him get too far in front of him. Wait now—this fence takes some doing. THEY'RE DOWN!" she said. "Ah, Dick wins now. Wayward Gipsy's beat."

"Come on, Master Dick," James piped, hopping from foot to foot in his excitement, his opera glasses clapped on the horses. "More power, Master Dick—he have the mare cot! 'Tis only a ride home now."

Two more fences and Good-Day was galloping down to the bank where we stood, Wayward Gipsy half a field behind her; Bright Love, remounted, a bad third; and the rest nowhere.

"Steady, Dick, now." The boy was burning

with the effort of his race. The sour little mare had jumped everything right ; nothing could go wrong with them now. He may have let her go on at it a bit faster than he need have done (I am no judge of pace in riding over banks). I only know she failed to get right on top, and came off that tall fence end over end in as unpleasant a looking crash as I hope I may never see again. It shakes one.

Young Dick lay hunched quietly where he had fallen, but the mare was up in a flash. It was I who caught her, and James who threw me into the saddle just as Wayward Gipsy jumped the fence beside us.

Never shall I forget the horror of that ride in. How I sat in Dick's five-pound saddle, the flaps wrinkling back from under my knees and the off stirrup gone in the fall, I shall never know—for one who fancies himself not a little over fences I must, across the two first very moderate banks I jumped in Ireland, have presented a sorry enough spectacle. Had there been an inch more left in Wayward Gipsy we were beaten. As it was, the judge just gave it to Good-Day—a short head on the post.

I weighed in all right. I knew I must ride nearly a stone above Dick's weight (a bit of a penalty for the little mare to carry home after such a shattering fall), and as I walked out of the tent I met Willow coming in to weigh out for her race.

"That was pretty quick of you," she said to me.

"I'd never have got the weight. Oh, Dick's all right—only shaken and badly winded. The Sir's running mad round the place looking for you."

Dick was saddling Willow's horse when I next saw him, and too busy to spare any time for me. She was late : three other horses had gone down to the start.

"Now, Doris," Willow called to a pretty girl who looked excited and nervous as a cat as she was put up by a firmly adoring young man, "all fences on this course to be jumped at a slow pace. I'm very shook indeed, with my only brother nearly quinched before my eyes."

The girl laughed ; she was all nerves, though I dare say a tigress when she got going. "Stay with me down to the post, Willow. I'll be kicked off for certain."

"Very dangerous work this, girls ! " Willow laughed, pulling up her leathers. "Now, Dick, I'm right." She caught my eye as she rode out of the ring and gave me a small friendly nod as I wished her good luck.

"Go down to the old spot," she said, "and I *hope* I won't need you as much as Dick did."

Nor did she. From the same view-point as before, Dick and James and myself watched the flash of Willow's blue shirt as she led round that course at a wicked pace. . . .

"Wait till Sir Richard sees her," Dick murmured ; "he'll not leave a feather on her body, and the reason is she's making every post a winning post."

A hot class of horses and the fastest run race of the day. Romance jumped the fence where we stood in perfect style—on and off—clever as a dog, never dwelling an instant, and galloped home to win in a distance.

Dick saw the last lady over without mishap before we turned to follow James back to the hill.

"Look!" said he suddenly, stooping to the ditch to pick up a half-buried stirrup-iron and leather. He turned it over. "It's me own." He looked at me, an expression almost of friendliness dawning in his face. "And you in trousers," he murmured.

We found Willow at the car, where her father was measuring her out a niggardly drink and expressing his unstinted disapproval of her method of winning a race, while James alternately begged her to put on her coat and eat a sandwich. Failing in both objects, he presented her with a small comb and glass, and bade her tease out her hair, for it was greatly tossed with the race.

"Ah, don't annoy me, James," Willow finished her drink, stuck her arms into the leather coat he held out for her, clapped a beret on her surprising hair, and said to her father, "I'll drive Dick and Oliver home. Major Barry wants you to take him. Come on, boys, till we gather up our winnings."

Later, as the Ford rocked and bumped its way out of the field, and I sat, shaken to the core, in the back seat with a horse-sheet over my knees and one of Willow's gold-flake cigarettes in my mouth, Dick turned round to say—

" And the reason why I think you should stop on for Punchestown is because that's a meeting you should really enjoy."

" That's right," Willow agreed.

And, strange as it may seem, I gloried to know the accolade of their acceptance mine.

THE VILLAINY OF MR. FOX

A WIRE from Willow brought me back to Pullinstown. The wire said : " Nice young horse. Five years old. Star turn. Come for hunt, Thursday. Willow."

It was quite two months since I had written to my cousin : " Let me know if you see anything extra brilliant out hunting. Must be up to thirteen stone, all quality, and must fairly gallop and be willing to have a go. They soon get into these fences if they are a bit keen."

The Wednesday morning, a gleaming and gentle November morning, found me battling with the unaccountable vagaries of the Irish Southern Railway. Horse or no horse, hunt or not, Pullinstown had laid its charming spell upon me. To return there was absurdly exciting. The gleam in the day stirred adventure and romance within me. I was impatient to arrive.

Slowly the little train chugged its way up the shining blue curves of the river, tidal here. Seven wild swans, as remote unto themselves as the seven brothers of Finola, waited out on the breast of the water ; theirs a breathless ecstasy of beauty that should never know the placid assurance of those sleek birds who glorify the Thames. I thought of the wild-fowling on this coastland, of the snipe by day, and duck flighting on a steely evening, and I knew again the stir of excitement that thrills to tears, or nearly.

The cold little station of Ennistiogue was tenanted by one pessimistic porter. When he had taken charge of my ticket and of His Majesty's mails, he informed me that every car in the town was gone to the races, and in regard to the train, " 'Twas as wayward and backward you couldn't say whether or no 'twould be in it at all." So he passed unhappily into the fastnesses of the booking office, in some dim way contriving to connect his inability to attend the races with my unwelcome arrival.

I did not for a moment expect that my cousins would remember the date and hour of my arrival, and it was with relief that I heard from without the station walls sounds only to be associated with a Ford car *in extremis*. It was not Willow's car, this scarred and mutilated specimen, but the charming youth who drove it welcomed my fare.

" Take ye out to Pullinstown ? " he said in response to my inquiries. " I will, of course ; why not ? I'm partly the train meself."

The explanation of this slightly cryptic remark I read in the freshly painted lettering on the back of the car—the proclamation I.S.R. quite shouted down the modest plate on which I could still just read, " Hackney 5 seater." It was a good twenty minutes before the engine woke again to horrid life. "She's near the one age with meself," said her driver with apologetic indulgence, "and, indeed, she's as cross an old yoke there's not another one could lay a hand on her, only I do be in on her tricks." He got into top gear with a roar and a jerk, and dodged nimbly round an ass cart, whose driver, an old woman of vast proportions, clung tenaciously to the middle of the road.

The great lodge gates of Pullinstown (Adams had proportioned their curves) were fast closed. I got out to open and shut them again, in the shy, thrusting faces of six young horses.

"Miss Willow and Master Dick have them ones rared great pets," said my driver, as we proceeded up the long straight avenue beneath a rigid rank of dripping lime-trees, their golden leaves pasted like flat paper money to the mud of the roadway. "Indeed, Mary-Josey Whelan (that's a housemaid is in it) was telling me Miss Willow have a little young donkey to folly her, and sleeps in a box in her bedroom. But, indeed, 'twas only for the cod o' the thing Mary-Josey tould me. I wouldn't mind that one. She's as wild as the deer."

The sad grey elegance of the house, the perfect outward balance of its sweeping wings, smote my mind like well-remembered music when I saw it again. The light of the quiet day shone back from the narrow dark slates that roofed it, and the high windows held a blank and unassailable stare of dignity. Beneath the heavy granite-pillared porch my driver disembarked myself and my baggage, and, frustrating with some difficulty the determination of two cats and a nearly grown hound puppy to squeeze past the wire-netting frame that protected alike the door paint and the house from their depredations, I walked into the hall.

No one was there save a small string-bodied terrier engaged in the absorbing work of scratching her ear (recently, I perceived, dressed with olive oil) and subsequently licking her toe. She abandoned this attractive pastime to give me a doubtful greeting. Decidedly she did not altogether remember.

The November light was kind to the great hall with its medley of lovely furnishings and crowded rubbish. A flavour of prawn bottles, opened long months ago, came faintly from the fishing-tackle cupboard, floating out against the memory of Willow's and Dick's Gold Flake and Sir Richard's cigars. A fire of hard Kilkenny coal burnt unwillingly in the flat wide hearth.

" Willow ! " I called.

" Dick ! "

Neither of my young cousins answered.

"James ! " I called, putting my head round the baize-covered door that divided the hall from the kitchen regions, but no answering pipe came from the butler's pantry.

Sir Richard's stick was gone from its accustomed corner in the hall, and I resigned myself to waiting till they returned to luncheon, or it might be tea, or indeed, more than likely, the following day.

"Oliver!" said a voice from the gallery above me. "We forgot you were coming," and my young cousin, Dick Pulleyns, came down the wide stairs. There's a gravity about Dick's good looks— I found myself thinking of those seven wild swans out on the morning river. Dick's hard, thin hand was as cool as a bone in my own. He looked at me with the solemnity of the very young, but this time his shyness was not unfriendly.

"And the reason why we forgot about you is that James is sick, and Willow and I are all day nursing him. As for the maids," said Dick, " now James's eye is off them, they're out ditching around the hay-lofts with the grooms every minute of the day. Really disgusting. Father is out," he said ; " he went down the Long Pasture to see one of the young horses that was kicked out at grass, and has a knee on it now as big as your head. Will you come up to James's room ? That's where we will most likely find Willow."

"How do you do, Oliver ? We're delighted you came. The Sir will be in to lunch." Willow shook my hand and returned to the fireplace, where she was balancing a large black kettle on the high and narrow grate of an Adams fireplace, its elegancies of beading, its cups and faint traceries thickened with the grime of years.

"Poor James is rather bad ; but it's entirely

his own fault, with a temperature of 101," said Willow, with grim professionality. "Didn't he drink off a whole Baby Power whisky that that damned Pheelan brought him, and then got out of his bed at ten o'clock at night to hunt the maids in from their lovers in the hayloft. But it is Pheelan," said Willow, "that I really blame. Sir Richard didn't leave one feather on him when he heard."

"Ah, poor Pheelan; don't be too hard on him, Miss Willow." James's voice came dimly from his bed. I went over to speak to him. Sewn into red flannel by Willow, he looked like the smallest, oldest woman ever seen. It was an old French bed in which he lay—a bed of painted wood and strong, fine basket-work, its faint apple-green and china-blue, grey-white and thin gold-leaf still bright. A sea-coloured piece of brocade dreamed across the grey homespun blankets and coarse sheets. Choked with cobwebs, and grimy with the hand-marks of many years, the same material curtained and canopied the high windows.

"How are you, James?" I asked.

"Indeed, I'm only very poorly, Mr. Oliver. There's like an impression on me schest. There's prods in me digesture rises like flames halfway in me t'roath. Me heart bates ex-tra. Only with the help o' God and Miss Willow to poultice me, I might pull out of it yet."

"You will, maybe," said Willow, "but certainly not with the help of Pheelan."

She looked more than ever like her name, Willow. A green high-collared jumper and an ancient pair of jhodpores did not appear inconvenient for her nursing ministrations. She poulticed James in linseed with efficient exactness, and clapping a heavy silver salver on his chest to top the lot, shook her head at him gravely. "James," she said, "I wouldn't wonder if you did no good."

Dick advanced solemnly to the other side of the pillow.

"What age are you, James? You're a lot older than the Sir in any case."

From beneath the massive salver James groaned faintly.

"Willow," I said, thinking it time to create a diversion, "your baby donkey is eating James's last poultice. Will that do it any harm?"

An engaging person, Willow's baby donkey, with its clicking black boots, spindling legs, and wrinkling black crepe nose. It had lain near the fire until Willow turned her back to administer James's poultice, when it promptly seized on the golden moment for depredation. I was glad that the donkey was no myth; the lively clatter of its black hoofs followed us out of James's bedroom and downstairs to lunch.

"Well, Oliver, me boy!" Sir Richard struggled out of his chair by the hall fire to greet me. "How's James, Willow?" he asked over my shoulder as we shook hands. "Better? Well, b'God, I'm

glad to hear it. The house is all to blazes without
him. Come in to lunch, Oliver ; that is if Willow
remembered to order any lunch for us."

Willow had remembered to the extent of a cold
goose, a vast ham, and a plum pudding as black
and rich as nearly a year's keeping, and at least
half a bottle of brandy, could make it. As was
their custom, Sir Richard's children ate in somewhat dignified silence, while their father cheerfully
supported the brunt of the conversation. He was a
good talker, cousin Richard, and, as his discourse
was always on his own nearest interests, never a
bore.

He ate practically nothing, but sat with his round
armchair pushed back a little way from the head
of the table. His preposterously thin shoulders
and elbows were searching angles under his loose
tweed coat. On the sideboard behind him stood a
regiment of silver candlesticks, some squat, some
curling upwards with the sinister grace of serpents ;
and on the wall behind the sideboard hung an ancestress painted in a green stomacher, with such
pearls as Raleigh might have given to an Irish
love. Her definite, small square hands were Willow's, and from the shivering fairness of her skin
I guessed that the coiffed-away hair might be as
pale a silver as Willow's is.

" So you're going to buy a horse from Fox ? "
Sir Richard tipped his glass of port to the light.
" Well, I hope you're proof against a good stick,

for that's about all you'll get out of him. Listen !
I suppose it's *those* two "—he nodded at his son and
daughter—" have you filled up with nonsense
about that horse. Now, mind you, I wouldn't
trust their judgment—not for a moment.

"And be careful what you ride belonging to the
Reverend Mr. Fox. With all respect to his cloth,
that's the biggest blackguard of a little jockey-
parson I ever came across. Wait till I tell you. I
went down there one time—it must be five years
ago now—to buy a horse. Well, the last horse he
pulled out was a real blood-like bay, now a horse
you'd *love* to look at.

"'Saddle him up, quick,' I said. So they put a
saddle on him, and Fox praising him up as the best
horse he ever had. (Great talker he always is.)
I got up on him anyhow, and rode him down a
lane-way from the yard (remember I was an old
man that time, and pretty bet up with this sciatica,
too), and I turned off into a field. Well, when he
felt the grass under him, he gathered himself up
into a little lump below me. He looked round at
the stirrup, and he made one bound to get away.
I gave him one job in the mouth, and turned his
head for a thick thorn hedge and got him back on
to the lane again, and when I rode him out on the
road he did the very same thing. *I* knew the sort
of him—if he'd got off, nothing in this world or the
next would stop him. I rode him back into the
yard and I got off him. I never said a word, good

or bad, about buying him to the fella. I wouldn't go into the house and I wouldn't have tea, and if I live to be a hundred I'll not go near that man's place again."

"And what about that mare you sold *him*, Sir Richard? The brown Stylograph mare, with such a bad heart you wouldn't care to ride her out of a jog," Willow put in.

"Ah, only for her constitution that was nearly the nicest mare I ever owned," said Sir Richard with indulgent reminiscence. "Now, I re-member——"

"Father," said Willow, "if we're to get to the Reverend Mr. Fox before night, we'll have to take your car. And keep an eye on James, won't you?"

"What's James doing with the best salver clapped on his chest?" inquired Sir Richard sharply.

"That's to keep some heat in the poultices." Willow pushed back her chair. "And mind my ass doesn't eat the linseed, Sir Richard; it's a dreadful purge."

"I'll *not* have that nasty ass following me about the house." Sir Richard spoke with immense decision. "No, b'gad, and I'll not have the dirty little thing in the house at all."

"Oh, *father*, such a clean little ass, and no bother to anyone. Wait till the spring months come, and I'll put it out then; I will really."

Dick looked up from the finicking labour of preparing really artistic dinners for his two little dogs. "The cook says you're to give her a tin of baking powder and some matches from the store-room before you go out, Willow."

"*Matches!*" Willow flamed. "*What* did she do with the box I gave her on Monday?"

Of such was the housekeeping at Pullinstown. Coal, flour, wine, and oil were there in untram-melled confusion, while such small fry in the shape of groceries as matches and baking-powder were kept sacredly behind lock and key. Moreover, I observed that the only times when the storeroom key was not lost were those at which it had been forgotten in the storeroom door.

Sue and Flicker, those two famous huntresses, ate their dinners with the squeamish delicacy of well-beloved dogs. When that was over they came to Dick as we sat in the hall. Their eyes dreamed on him ; for each other they cherished a frenzy of jealousy but just contained ; and for him, who never failed to show them sport, idolatry. Sue was a little white pig of a thing—more like a fierce white mouse, with her pink nose and extra long dock, than like a dog. She would hunt a rabbit if it was gone half an hour in front of her, and had drawn a badger by herself. The scars of many fox-bites honourably adorned her muzzle.

Flicker was sour and old-maidish, very much waisted, rather morose, steady and true to a fox scent. She bit visitors (sinking her teeth, too), and there was nothing Dick secretly enjoyed so much as this vice of hers. I told him now that I considered it a cheap form of amusement.

" *Cheap !* " said Dick. " Not when she bites the tinkers, it's not cheap. My Sue wouldn't do that. My Susie-Wusie, my bitchie-witchie——"

I left him, still maudlin, to put on a pair of riding-breeches.

Willow drove us in Sir Richard's big car. Dick and I sat in front with her. Sue and Flicker marking game in the shape of cats as we drove along. Willow drove fast over the execrable roads, but she knew their turnings to a hair's-breadth. We came to a country of little surprising hills, with the sea on our left-hand ruling a faint horizon across the sky.

" This is the Spree Harriers country," Willow said. There were many low stone walls, but built solid enough to put a horse down should he hit them.

" You wouldn't knock them down with a sledge," Willow said. There were banks, blind and narrow, by way of variety, and the country, they told me, rode very light.

" Do you hunt down here ? " I asked.

" With the Spree Harriers ? No, my God ! and the reason is that they're the rottenest lot of poaching blackguards in Ireland." Dick spoke with a complete finality that made me blush for my ignorance.

" *We* hunt with the West-common hounds," Willow said, " and there's nothing we hate like those Spree dogs. They poach our coverts the day before we go to draw them—they join the best end of our country, too. And they're always so short of blood they'll dig a vixen in March, or surround a fox in covert any day in the year. Oh, they're outlaws! A sort of farmer fellow hunts them—keeps the hounds on about a fiver a year."

" Does the parson we're going down to see hunt with him ? "

" Well "—Willow hesitated—" he's always *by way* of being against them, but to tell you the truth, he'd do the first thing that came handy to him. He's a shocking old gammon. We'll be hunting down their end to-morrow, and God send we find a fox. It's the most wonderful bit of country ; banks there you'd get up out of your bed in the night to jump them. Here we are, now."

We drove up a steep and rutted lane-way that was hardly an avenue, and stopped before a large and grimly imposing old house. The cold grey granite that built Cloneen Rectory came from the rough low hills at its back, dark wet heather and the sombre green of gorse battling up their flanks among the steep slabs of granite. Just below, a little dilapidated church snugged itself, cringing for shelter, against the hillside. I saw that a young horse and a hungry-looking heifer had found a gap in the wall of the church-yard, which allowed them to feed among the tilting tombstones.

"How do you do, Miss Pulleyns? Well, Dick how are you?"

Mr. Fox belonged to the generation of younger sons of the gentle Irish who found livings, if not exactly vocations, in the church of their country. He was tall and stooped, and, in his black-caped coat, surprisingly monkish-looking. When he smiled his false white teeth seemed as square and as numerous as the notes of a piano.

"You came to see the little horse?" he said to Willow, who walked beside him (hands deep in the pockets of her almost ragged brown tweed riding-coat) down a slimy, evergreen, shaded path, that led to the stableyard before venturing uncertainly onwards in the direction of the sorry little church.

"I'm so glad you did. You can see the brown mare I was telling you of, too. I *know* you'll like her—oh, a rare sort. Major Countless" ("that's our M.F.H."—Dick threw away a much-sucked butt of Gold Flake as he told me this) "was mad about her. He'd only bid me one-fifty, though. She's not going under two hundred."

"I thought Tony Countless told me he had the mare bought if she passed the vet." Willow said it out of the corner of her mouth. She walked as far away from Mr. Fox as the narrow path allowed. And I perceived that at some sacrifice of personal dislike I had been brought to buy a horse from this reverend gentleman.

"Well," said Mr. Fox with slightly less suavity

of manner, "that's *just* where Major Countless is mistaken."

"Oh!" said Willow.

"Look, Oliver," Willow said to me as Mr. Fox disappeared into one of the many good boxes in the untidy stableyard. "Let Dick get up on this horse and ride him a little school over banks to see what sort he is. The old fellow has him schooled silly over the furze hurdles and the wall out there. Let Dick take him out in the country if he gets the chance—then we'll find out about him. You know you have no feel about a bank. Well, Tommy, how are you?" Willow greeted a dark-faced, active-looking lad who came across the yard with a bridle in his hand. ("That's the best fellow in the country to ride a race; he alway's rides Fox's horses.")

We stooped under the iron cross-bars of the stable door, and I had my first look at my prospective purchase.

I had dreamed of a horse just made to carry thirteen-seven. Here he was. A big little horse, measuring just 16 hands. Well ribbed up, deep in his girth, standing on short legs (and such a set of limbs, too), a shoulder raking right back, and the gamest blood-like head. He was so close coupled I wondered (hating the doubt) if he could quite gallop. Well, an ideal hunter, and good for a point-to-point, perhaps.

"Pull him out, Tommy," said Mr. Fox, his

silence more eloquent than praise. "By Dustman," he said in answer to my question, "and Dustman was by Desmond and out of a Scotch Sign mare. There's breeding for you."

"Four off. Am I right, Miss Willow?" Willow, who had looked in his mouth, said nothing. "That? That's nothing—only the scar of an old cut he got as a three-year-old. Walk him down there, Tommy." Mr. Fox's eyes luxuriated on him as he was led away. "I *can't* take me eyes off him," he said. "Jog him up, Tommy! There's straight action."

"I'd like very much to see a saddle on him," I said.

"Put my Whippy saddle on him, Tommy," Mr. Fox ordered.

"You'd like to see him ridden, too, I suppose? Shall we walk on down the avenue?"

Willow, who was sitting on the mounting-block, lit a cigarette slowly, and offered the yellow packet to her host.

"Strip the sheets off the brown mare and let's have a look at her," she suggested. Obviously she shared my desire to see the shape of the little horse's back with a saddle cold upon it. Her manner was an imperceptible shade more friendly than it had been ; and faint as was the shade of warmth, it served to induce that delay which she purposed, although we did not get so far as the mare's box ; neither had we left the yard when

Tommy led the little horse out with a back up under his saddle that made me sigh with relief that someone else was to climb on to him before I did.

"Looks as if he'd go off *bang*, doesn't he?" Dick grinned unkindly. He had just come from round the corner of a straw rick; a dead rat, bloody-mouthed, swung by its tail from his hand. He held Flicker under one arm, her filthy feet pushed against his coat, her long fine neck straining back whence they had come. Sue trundled like a little white sow through the dirt beside him. Without comment Dick threw the rat on the manure-heap, where a vulgar red cur-lady, with no pretensions to gentility or sportsmanship, seized and shook it savagely.

"Good, Meg—goo' dog!" her master encouraged her.

"And when there was one kick left in it she wouldn't go near it." The expressions of his own two white ladies as they preceded us, three-legged (after the manner of all good terriers), down the dirty farm track to the fields were a veritable echo of Dick's disgust.

Tommy meanwhile had jogged on down the slushy lane and turned off through a deep trampled gap into a field in which black circles were cut out where horses had been lunged, and a stone wall, a pole and a furze hurdle succeeded to each other in the distance. I could not see the little horse and his rider, as the lane-way was sunken down so low, but Dick, who had climbed to the top of the stone wall that fenced it, reported proceedings with a hoarse chuckle. "He gave One—*Two*—THREE—and only Tommy caught his ear he was gone," he announced, dropping into the lane beside us, and helping himself to a cigarette from Willow's packet. "Where's my Flicker? Flicker! Flicker! Flicker!" He would not let either of the two dogs out of his sight for a moment.

In the field now, where a wind like a knife whipped through us, we stood in the comparative shelter of a line of Scots fir trees and watched Tommy gallop the horse towards us.

"Puts his toe right out," Willow murmured to me. She stretched an expressive arm and wrist. "He can go along a bit, Oliver, mind you. Look, Oliver—get up on him and take him over those fences backwards. Dick'll meet you out in the corner and slip off for a little school till you see what sort is he really."

Whether or no Dick should approve or Willow decry him, I knew I must buy that little horse. When I got up on him and walked off, feeling for the next two holes in the odd pair of leathers, I knew it. He rode green, of course, as what unnagged Irish horse does not? But there was the right and only feel about him, and he fairly laid himself down to gallop. The field we were in was flat, but a gap let me into one where, down the length of a fair slope, he made good use of that raking poem of a shoulder of his. Back in the training paddock again he pricked his small ears and nipped over bush fence, pole, and stone wall in a style that spoke of much schooling ; no mistake about it, he had a right pop in him.

Dick changed places with me at the corner of the field farthest from where Mr. Fox and Willow stood. Before he mounted he gave me his two white ones coupled together by a silk handkerchief. "Don't let them get away on you, Oliver. Mind that now, it's important," and he was gone, and back towards me again, jogging slowly. What straight action he had, that little horse ! He turned from us again. Yes, and his hocks well under him, too.

I joined my own handkerchief as a lead to the couples, and walked back to meet Willow and her black-coated escort. The Rev. Mr. Fox did not appear to be in the best of tempers.

" Is it your brother or your cousin is buying this horse, Miss Pulleyns ? " he asked, and his laugh was not particularly pleasing.

" Indeed, you wouldn't know but I'd buy him myself in the end," Willow answered with the complete evasion of her race. " Put him out there, Dicky," she said, and as Dick rode towards the place in the big solid bounds fence that his sister indicated, a spasm of acute anguish crossed Mr. Fox's face.

" Oh, *no*," he said, " don't jump there, my man. You wouldn't know was there a harrow out the other side."

However, Dick put the horse at it ; he jumped it, on and off clever, and away went Dick, and, as Willow said, we never clapped our eyes on him after that. At the end of five minutes, during which I strictly evaded Willow's eye—

" Oh *dear*," said Mr. Fox, " where is he ? "

" Oh *dear*," he said a little later on, " he's jumped him into a plough."

" Oh, *dammit*," he said.

" And he a clergyman," Willow murmured.

" He has the horse destroyed on me."

It was at this moment that Dick came jogging quietly up from the road. He gave up the horse to Tommy without a word. Mr. Fox, having satisfied himself that there was no visible damage done, and restored now to affability, bade us return to the house for tea, for drinks, for the warmth of the fire, for any and every reason hospitality could suggest.

" Ah, we don't want the tea," Dick said, as he took the little dogs from me, " but we want to see will the horse jog out sound after a half an hour in the box."

I raised my eyebrows. " Well ? " I asked, the only question that mattered.

" A champion," Dick said briefly. " You buy him, Oliver."

Through an incongruous glass porch, in which pots of unhealthy chrysanthemums languished neglected, we were ushered into the stately and stuffy red plush of an immense drawing-room, where I was introduced to Miss Fox, a lady of almost paralysing refinement, whose hair was built upon her head in a manner as remarkable as it was complicated. Willow discoursed with an ease and fluency which I was to envy passionately as I sat beside her during the rich and lavish tea to which we presently addressed ourselves.

" *Well*," said Dick an hour later, as the giant shafts of our headlights clove the darkness of the narrow roads, " *I* never saw a fellow do himself as well as old Fox. No, but, Willow—damned if I ever ate such a feed in my life as what we had. Oh, listen, Willow, till I tell you—I had him wild when you and Oliver went back to the yard to see how would the horse jog out. God, Oliver, I think you bought that horse very cheap—what's this I was saying?—oh, he was *wild*. ' Now, Mr. Fox,' I said to him, ' you're a clergyman and I *know* you cannot tell a lie, so will you tell me the rights of this story I heard about you the other day?' I said. ' What's this?' he said. ' Well, the way I heard it was, you were preaching a sermon in one of these churches and you took for your text, ' Do as ye will be done by.' I'm not exactly very great on the Bible myself, but I know that

was the text. ' Do as ye will be done by,' says
you, when a fella in the back o' the church got
up and, ' What about that horse ye sold me last
week ? ' says he. ' Now, Mr. Fox, is that a fact ? '
Well, Willow, he caught me by the arm and, ' That
poor man is dead now,' says he ; ' he was killed
just shortly after that sermon in a—in a hunting
accident.' " Dick sat forward to light a cigarette.

" Well, doesn't that beat out ! God, that was
a murderous rogue of a horse." Willow changed
gear with decided efficiency. I did not seem to
remember any hill so steep as this, and when we
took a sharp right-handed turn I knew we were
bearing in the wrong direction for home.

" Right again here," said Dick. I caught his
profile against the cheek of the night sky, and I
knew we three were for adventure now. I knew
it in Willow's silent obedience. It was told in
her quiet hands on the steering wheel.

" Left, I'm sure," said I, determined to be out
of it no longer.

" Ah, we're not going home at all." Dick gave
me a sudden agonising dig with his elbow. " *Oliver*,"
he said, " d'ye know what old Fox has in his outhouse ? "

" What ? " I said. " I *wish* you hadn't done
that ! " for I was dazed and in some pain.

" He has a *fox* there," said Dick, a raptness of
horror in his voice, " tied up in a sack, a bagman
to turn down before the hounds to-morrow."

"Before Anthony's hound's to-morrow," Willow echoed.

"But why?" I asked, "and how do you know?"

They were kind to my little wit.

"The old cod," they said, "he's playing in and out between Devereux (that's the fellow who has the Spree Harriers) and Tony Countless (that's our Master); he has Tony codded he's preserving foxes for him, and all the time he has Devereux ruxing out the coverts and butchering foxes every day in the week—Anthony won't believe it."

"Oh, he's English, poor man," said Willow leniently.

"As English as he is, he's getting a bit suspicious when he has two blank days running. That's the reason why old Fox had this gentleman provided for to-morrow. Three *would* be a bit steep, and in the nicest end of his country, too. Straight through this cross now. Willow, mind yourself—that's a wicked turn."

"But——" this intrigue was too thick for me.

"Oh, he's no fool." Willow was driving slower now on the shiftless uncertainty of this least of roads. "It's handy enough for him to be able to school his horses every day in the week with Lar Devereux's harriers, but Anthony and his friends from England are a right market for the horses once they are schooled. He's not going to be out with Anthony if he can help it. Oh, that's a right artist. Dick, Oliver and I had a look at that brown mare when we went out. She's a *nice* mare."

" Why wouldn't he let us see her in the afternoon, after all his chat ? (Be good now, my Sue.")

" Ah, she has a leg on her. I made Tommy take the bandage off. It's only the prod of a thorn. She's just Anthony's sort."

The road climbed steeply up ; we were, I thought, at the back of those hills that cupped Cloneen Rectory. Before we quite reached the top, Willow reversed the car into the narrow black gulf of a lane-way. She switched off the headlights and lit a cigarette. We waited.

" No hurry," Dick said, " till the men down there are finished for the night."

" Dick, how did you discover the fox ? " I asked him.

" My Flicker," he said. " When Sue was hunting rats in the manure-heap, Flicker was marking her fox in the outhouse. And the reason I wouldn't let them out of my sight afterwards was, if old Fox had seen them near the outhouse he'd have smelt a rat and moved the fox."

Willow turned on the dashlight to look at her watch, and turned it off again. " Come on now," she said, groping for the door catch.

" But listen, Willow—Sue and Flicker'll raise the mischief if they're left alone with Oliver. If one passed up the road, they'd bark their heads off—you know they would."

"Yes, my God." Willow sat back in her seat again. "You go, Oliver." Without hesitation she abandoned the rapture of this adventure to the fulfilment of its cause. Heartily as I wished I might stay in the car, I found some chord in me echoing Dick's pitying : " Poor Willow, it's a *shame* she should miss this," as we climbed onto and dropped off a series of hideously loose-built stone walls. And the drop was steep down the hill, the landing a nightmare alternative of strong-growing gorse or soft and holding bog.

We slipped round the horseshoe wall of the graveyard, and struck out wide of the sunk lane-way to the yard. Dick was the lightest thing on his feet I have ever seen, and very clever over the fences. He sang under his breath : " Oh, me *father* was a tinker and me *mother* was a'—I d'know what. Mind yourself, Oliver ; don't catch your toe in that root." A turn sharp left brought us back towards the massed gloom of the stable roofs. In the murky, choking shelter of a rick of hay we waited while the long beam of a stable lantern travelled quietly down the length of the yard. We heard a gate open and shut, a key hesitate and turn in a rusty padlock.

" ' Oh, me *father* was a tinker and me *mother* was—— ' Come on now, Oliver——"
In the unthinkable dark of a foul outhouse I stumbled behind Dick, tripping headlong over a loose sack upon the floor. The strong exciting reek

of fox lay heavy in an inky corner. "Feel *that*." Dick caught my hand in the dark, pressing it down. I felt the curl of a small, strong body through the roughness of a sack. I felt it whip round, and may be forgiven for snatching my hand away.

"'Oh me *father* was a——'" Dick sniggered, stooping in the gloom, to which my accustomed eyes had now mitigated the darkness. "A nice stiff little fox this would be by to-morrow—poor fellow ; he wouldn't have gone two fields before they'd catch him." Dick's whisper was indignant. He shouldered the sack with immense care, and was making for the square pallor of the doorway when, with a racket and clamour hideous to our ears, the Reverend Mr. Fox's ginger cur-dog advanced malignantly upon us.

In a flash Dick, with his load, was through the door, and quicker than I could think he had shut it in my face. "Catch the dog," he whispered through to me. "Catch her and choke her if you can. She never stirs a step without old Fox." With that he was gone. And the dog—I have said she was a cur—fawned on me, slinking against my legs in the dark.

It was then that my idea came to me, my great idea, that was to ennoble me for ever in the eyes of Willow and Dick. And indeed I was brave. Each moment I feared to see the monkish bulk of Mr. Fox stand stooping in the doorway, and yet I groped my way with pitiable slowness to where I had fallen, tripping over a sack as I came in—I prayed God it was a sound one—I found its limp mouth, and catching hold of that suddenly reluctant cur, I shoved her in, head first, tying the top of the sack with half my handkerchief—filthied on the floor. The sack was roomy and the night cold. When I put her down in the corner where we had found our bagman, the ginger lady turned herself round and settled down almost complacently. Nor when I had stepped out of the door and pulled it to behind me did I hear so much as a whimper of protest.

" Oliver," Willow said, as the car slipped in neutral down the steep hill, " I'm *glad* you went instead of me, for I'd never have had the wit to think of that."

" I *had* to leave you, Oliver," Dick said. " I knew you'd hold old Fox in chat better than I would if he did appear."

" Dick," I said, " what *did* you think I'd talk to him about ? "

" No, but what I'd like to see would be Tommy's face when he shakes out that red cur to-morrow," said Dick, neglecting my question.

Half-way home we shook our fox on the edge of an inky sea of gorse, well out of to-morrow's draw. A fine dog fox, Dick said it was ; but I could not pretend to see more than a shadow among shadows, that was there and was not there any more. We

climbed the two fences back to the road in an exult-
ant silence.   Within the car the little dogs raved
against their durance.   Dick stuffed the sack down
a rabbit hole, because that terrible war-like smell
of fox drove his Sue nearly frantic.

We were more than a little late for dinner when
we arrived back at Pullinstown, not that it mattered,
Sir Richard said, as with poor James laid up, the
food was in any case unfit to eat at any time, so
what did an hour here or there matter ?   Certainly
it could be of very little account to Willow or Dick
whether their parent fed or starved, since they
could so far outrage filial respect as to buy a horse
from a man who had proposed his—Sir Richard's—
death so short a time as five years ago.

"But it was *I* who bought the horse, Cousin
Richard."

"More fool you."   Sir Richard tucked a small
travelling rug round his knees and drank his soup
plaintively.   "But it's those two *I* blame," he said
when he had finished his soup ; and, lacing together his thin hands on the edge of the table,
regarded his children across his knuckles.

"How is James, father ? " Willow asked.   She
was tired after dinner and knelt—sunken back on
her heels, slowly turning the wheel that blew the
turf fire to an exquisite frenzy of blue and rose
flame, and when she stopped turning the wheel the
fire dropped and glowed.   Her baby donkey

squeezed as near as it dared to the heat, its stilted legs folded away, its long moth-like ears terrifically disproportionate to the rest of its body.

Sir Richard, fed now to the point of finding his family once more endurable, settled himself comfortably, with the one reading-lamp arranged to illumine his book or paper, and his alone.

"James?" he said in answer to Willow's question. "He was a bit restless to-night, I thought. I sent Phelan up to sit with him while we were at dinner."

"Oh, Sir Richard! You know Pheelan will be the death of James, and after all the torment I've had with him." Willow stood up, and the donkey (I had thought it was asleep) scrambled with a faint clatter to its feet and stood swinging its ridiculous head sleepily in the firelight. "How could you let him in? I suppose he has James filled up with whisky now."

"Oh, nonsense!" But Sir Richard did look a little ashamed of himself. "The reason I let him in, Willow, was because I thought James was rather down in himself, and Pheelan could keep him amused telling him about the races to-day. Pheelan went, you know."

"Where's Dick?" Willow's eyes went round the hall.

"Gone out to feed the hound puppies," I answered her.

"Oh, well, come on you, then, Oliver. I'll

want someone to help me straighten up the bed."

I looked down at Sir Richard as we climbed the stairs—Willow, her donkey, and I—and saw him split the wrapper of *Horse and Hound* (it arrived at Pullinstown on a Wednesday, forwarded by a friend) and settle down to meticulous and enjoyable perusal of its pages.

Half-way down the long, scarcely lighted passage to James's door, a curious and then, all in a trice, a terrifying smell assailed us—a smell of burning. Willow ran. I fell over the donkey, then, recovering myself and a measure of sense, hurried back to where I had seen a Minimax fire extinguisher (ruthlessly bracketed to an Elizabethan chest, that was why I had remembered). When I reached James's door, the fumes of burning cloth that filled the room choked for a moment all my powers of observation. All I saw was Willow standing dangerously still, one hand on the door-knob, and with his back to her Pheelan bent over James's bed, from which the fearful smell of burning came with sickening insistence.

" Willow," I said, " go out, Willow. Fetch Dick." I couldn't bear the thought of this for Willow, or for Dick either for that matter.

" Pheelan," James's voice was very weak, " the way I am now is I feel it operatin' up undther me lungs."

" That's what'll crown ye," said Pheelan, in

tones of the utmost satisfaction. "Wait now," he said, "till I'll light another candle; sure the room is as dark as a bottle."

I waited behind Willow in the doorway. We could see James now that Pheelan had moved away. He was propped forward in the bed, his shoulders very sharp and his head very round, outlined beneath a blanket; and it was from under the blanket that the ugly stink of smouldering rags crept into the room.

"Pheelan!" Willow's voice was not raised, but the tone of it made Pheelan jump—he was cleaning the thick candlewick with a match. "Take that blanket off James's head *at once*," she ordered, "and what," she pointed to the rags that charred smokily in the bottom of a tin basin on James's shaking knees, "is the meaning of that —Mister *Doctor* Pheelan?"

Pheelan had ridden first jockey in a stable of chasers. There is hardly a steeplechase course in Ireland where he has not broken a bone or won a race, and his nerve with horses is still careless in its completeness, but under Willow's eye he was visibly shaken.

"Well, now, Miss Willow," he said, with deprecatory garrulity, "I'll bet ten bob to the sight o' me eyes, James'll be the betther o' this before the night's out. Sure I seen horses kilt with a cold, and that's able to relieve them, let alone a Christian. There's no germ wouldn't lose its life in that."

"No, and no man neither," said Willow swiftly. "I'll not talk to you, Pheelan. I'll not tell you what I think of you, for you haven't what wit can understand me. But Sir Richard will see you in the morning, Pheelan, and God help you then, Pheelan ; and if that old fool James lives till morning, God help him too. Now you can go."

"Oh, God deliver us," James's voice was shocked into a certain strength. "Don't be hard on poor Pheelan, Miss Willow. Sure what little he done, he done it all for a passion o' love——" and James fell back among his pillows exhausted.

Willow dealt with it all very well. Pheelan went flying for Dick and brandy. "And don't come back," she added with vindictive finality. By the time I had the window open she was holding a smelling bottle under James's nose, and had a dose of sal volatile all ready to tip down. Dick and I rubbed him with brandy, and presently in a wavering whisper he begged us to wait now for one minyute till he'd regain his conscious.

When he came further to himself, it was to ask, with a protesting sniff of horror, "Could we find nothing only the choice thing in French brandy to squander on his body ? Sure the Sir would only drink it oncet in a great rarity, and 'twould put him" (James) "to the pin of his collar to say, where was it gone when he would be asked where was the third last bottle in the bin."

"Be quiet now," said Willow. She put a rat-tailed spoonful of it into his mouth, and when we had packed hot water-bags round him the three of us stood and watched him slip quietly to sleep.

We sat by the fire then far into the night, I on a square padded stool from which brocaded cherries were peeling fast, and Willow and Dick on a love-seat which had boasted more legs in the days of Queen Anne. Now a log propped it precariously at one corner, but they knew its balance. We packed the fire with turf, and ate apples of shrivelled sweetness that Dick found in the top of James's chest of drawers; below them his Sunday suits were decorously folded. We blew out the candles lest they should disturb James, and from a far corner of the room a fat little fish of red light swam suddenly on the dark—James's lamp burning continually beneath a tawdry and dreadful picture of the bleeding heart of Jesus. We talked in whispers about my horse; about the numbers of snipe in certain bogs; about the number of miles Willow's Ford would do to the gallon; about the prospects of hunting to-morrow. It was a perfect night, neither frosty nor stormy, Dick told us after a prolonged stare out of the window. We talked about the villainies of Mr. Fox and our outwitting of the same—" and the reason why, because we can use our brains," said Dick. We drank brandy (and, indeed, it was a rare and beautiful brandy), drinking in turn from a wine-glass that squatted low and heavy on a wide base—Waterford I should

have said by the feel of it—and Dick poked the
fire with what I realised to be the missing leg of the
love-seat.

At one o'clock James was still sleeping quietly
and Willow and Dick insisted that I should go to
bed. Though they leaned away from each other in
angular attitudes of complete discomfort, their
heads nodding, so desperately in need of sleep as
only the very young can be, they would not think
of bed.

" Good-night," I whispered ; " it's been a great
day."

" Wait till-to-morrow, Oliver," Dick answered.
" To-morrow will be twice as good a day."

They nodded to me in a hushed and owlish
manner from the paling circle of firelight, and when
I looked back from the doorway Willow's baby
donkey was eating James's last poultice. But
Willow was too tired to interfere.

THE CHASE

IT was raining finely at Pullinstown when I woke on the morning following our day of horse-coping and scheming and our night of burgling and doctoring. No matter what quarter the wind might be in, I would almost have answered for its proving a good scenting day, and as I was to set forth (on a horse that my cousins assured me to be the very living best) for my first day's hunting in an Irish country, I was glad that the morning promised well.

Although my watch said no more than half-past seven, I had woken as completely as one always does wake in a strange bed and house. Lying there, I thought with early morning clarity of my two young cousins, Willow and Dick; of their guile and their simplicity; of their dangerous eventful days, with the lust of fox-hunting and the element of horsemanship bred in them both and fulfilled to the utmost limit of their young endurance. I thought of Sir Richard, slightly infirm in body but more than a match for his children in villainy and trickeries and in great kindness too. I thought of his dolorously handsome face, and remembered his concern for James, his butler of years—sick now, and the house all to blazes without him. " Take up me own brandy, Willow," he had said ; " he'll *think* it'll do him more good, whether it does or no." And I have heard James say to Willow, " Strive and behave like a lady should, Miss Willow, me dear child," yet he obeyed her with punctilious ceremony on all public occasions.

A somewhat flustered handmaiden brought me my morning cup of tea. " Miss Willow bid me tell ye breakfast is nine o'clock, and Sir Richard is within in the bath at half-eight, sir."

Appreciative of the warning, I got out of bed and drank my tea at the open window. The pulse of the warm mist beat away from the house. It was the gentlest morning.

" Mary-Josey ! " I heard Willow's voice in the corridor outside my room, " is that Mr. Oliver's shaving water ? Is it hot ? "

And the answer, " Put yer hand in that ; it's boiling."

" Well, why don't you bring it in to him ? "

" Sure how could I, Miss Willow ? When I looked in the door wasn't he standing up on his two feet on the bedroom floor dhrinkin' tea in his night-shirt."

" I'm doing nothing of the sort," I called. Really, such an insult to Mr. Beal and Mr. Inman's most sumptuous of silk dressing-gowns was more than I could stomach. I was very proud of that dressing-gown. I went out now to show it to Willow, who admired it suitably and said I might leave it to her in my will. She herself was wearing one of faded camel hair that Dick must have had at his preparatory school. Her deadly fair hair stood out in feathers round her head, and she looked brighter than I could have thought possible considering that she had sat up till five o'clock with James.

"He's grand," she said in answer to my question. "No temperature at all. I thought I wouldn't be able to get out hunting to-day, but now I think I'll go."

A whinneying bray from across the landing announced that Willow's baby donkey was up and about. It put its head round the jamb of her bedroom door, and seeing us came forward on stuttering feet. "Go back to your bed," said Willow, "and don't make that noise, or the Sir'll sell you to the tinkers. Off you go!" The absurd donkey obeyed her like a dog.

Dick came out of his door, yawning enormously; he passed us and went into my room, poured himself out a cup of tea from my pot, hopped into my bed, and addressed himself to Mary-Josey.

"Bring those hunting-boots down to the yard along with my own," he said, "and stand them by the stove in the study as soon as Michael sends them in. And listen, Mary-Josey. If I see the track of your black fingers on the tops, I'll—*I'll tell James on you.* Have you my good gloves washed?"

"I have, Master Dick."

"Take my silk hat into James's room, and Mr. Oliver's too, and the velvet pad (you'll get it on the high shelf in the pantry). He's the only one can get any good of a silk hat."

"Dick," I said, "I'll do my own." I really thought James was not quite fit enough for valeting.

"Ah, it'll do him no harm." Willow came in and sat on the edge of the bed. She took the last slice of my bread and butter just an instant sooner than Dick. "He'd fret all day if he thought your hats weren't a credit to the place. *Look* at my ass," she said suddenly. "It's out again and it upsets the Sir for the day if he sees it on his way to the bathroom." She was gone, and it was with the same narrow but sufficient margin of time that she allowed herself to eat Dick's bread and butter that she got into the bathroom before me, and—I may add—out of it before her father.

Dick came down to breakfast in his breeches and a tweed coat, long violet stockings and black pump shoes, which gave him a curiously Georgian air, like a very young buck of those days. Willow said, "I *can't* eat breakfast in a stock. My stomach is not strong enough."

"Little bees-knees ye have," said her father with restrained acerbity. Ignoring the reference to her stomach, he fixed disapproving eyes on Willow's legs—legs which could hardly be other than her bootmaker's abiding joy. He did them well, too. Willow contemplated her left leg with extreme—almost unctuous satisfaction.

"That hole in my knee was put there by God

to take the top button of my breeches. *Now*, Sir
Richard."

"Your mother was a fine-looking woman, so
was your poor aunt, Lucia Verschoyle. I don't
know what happened you to be such a little scare-
crow."

"Kind father for me," replied Willow without
even raising her eyes from her plate.

"Mind, now "—Sir Richard, accepting momentary defeat in the wordy combat with his daughter,
faced about on his son—" you're to have that young
horse back here in his stable by four o'clock—
half a day is quite long enough for him, and too
long."

"Yes, father," Dick answered with suspicious
meekness ; he was holding a length of bacon rind
just half an inch above Sue's slavering, insistent
nose. "My Sue," he said, "my sweet pig. My
only . . ." But Flicker, jumping off her hocks
with the spring of a travelling grasshopper, was on
the table and with her nose in his plate, to refute
that last. It was more than she could bear.

"Oh, God help me ! " Sir Richard rose to his
feet in a sudden helpless early morning spasm of
complete and unavailing fury. "Put that dog down,
sir ; do you hear me, sir, put it down. I'll not
have it. Do you know where your nasty ass was
this morning, Willow ? *In the hot-air press !* Yes,
in my own bottom shelf, lying on my own bath-
towel. What between dogs and donkeys, I can't

call my house my own ; I can't eat my breakfast without being disgusted by you children and your antics. Though, indeed, I notice "—he whirled on Willow with the pounce of a swooping hawk and a very venom of scorn—" that you're a great deal too fond of your own good hot breakfast—*Miss*."

" I am, perhaps," Willow agreed mildly. She poured herself out a large cupful of coffee, and covered it slowly with thick yellow cream.

" You are, perhaps "—Sir Richard thought about it for a moment—" you are, perhaps," he repeated with slow intolerance. " Well, *perhaps*, miss, you'll remove yourself and your impertinence and your breakfast, too, from this room and eat it somewhere else. Do you understand me ? "

Willow helped herself to two pieces of toast, four pats of butter, and a large spoonful of marmalade before she rose to her feet and picked up her cup and plate. " I understand you perfectly well," she said, " but are you *quite* sure you wouldn't rather I stood in the corner ? " But before her father could express a preference one way or other, her thin black match-sticks of legs had carried her out of the room, and the door had closed behind her.

Sir Richard himself broke the silence in which I had begun to wonder whether I should not follow his daughter's example.

" Dick," he said, " make sure Pheelan puts the twisted snaffle on Romance for Willow. She was quite tired out after riding her in the plain snaffle the other day."

"She only pulls you the first couple of fields," Dick said, "after that she settles down."

"Well, I see no reason why she should pull the child at all," said Sir Richard, "if I can help it. You must remember little Willow's not as hardy as you are, Dick, even if she *is* twice as good a jockey."

"Yes, father." Dick snapped his fingers to his two white savages. "I'll go out and see about it now," he said.

We were to ride on to the meet that day. I was standing in the hall lost in admiration of the superb sheen that James had imparted to my silk hat, when I heard Dick's voice, low and angry, under the porch outside.

"You know well enough you shouldn't answer my father before one o'clock in the day," he was saying.

"Well, who started him off? You and your nasty dogs." Willow's tone was guiltily careless.

"You know right well it was your donkey in the hot press annoyed him—and you admiring your legs at breakfast time."

"Where's my father now?" said Willow suddenly.

"He's gone round to the stables."

"Well, I'll go on and talk to him—find Oliver, you Dick. We ought to be off in ten minutes."

She was gone, and Dick came back into the hall for me.

I have always laboured beneath the vague misapprehension, fostered perhaps by the generality of Irish novelists, that an Irish gentleman, mounted though he may be on the best of horses, cares little whether he follows the fashions of this year or twenty years ago in the matter of turning his person out for the chase. I can only say that young Dick was a dazzling contradiction of my preconceived idea.

Surtees has described for our delight, and I expect for his own exact and particular enjoyment, every button, every double-lap, every waistcoat, brooch, and neck-cloth—whether plain or spotted—worn by his heroes when they took the field. Why should such a catalogue read less like an outfitter's advertisement yesterday than to-day?

Dick was very much on the leg, he was thin and hard almost to frailness. I shall remember him, standing there in the hall, his whip under his arm, the doubled-back lash still trailing, a square of morning light striking his shoulders from above, the motes in it turning his red shoulders to silver. His breeches and boots were exact exaggerations of rightness. The neck of his spur shot a star into my eye. Blinking back at this bravely, I was at once a helpless victim of the conviction that my own were worn too low down on my heel.

"Come on now," said Dick, "time we were off." As he stooped forward to light a cigarette there was a flash of pale colour from under his coat. He picked up two pairs of gloves, leather and woollen, from the hall table, and waited out on the shining wet gravel until I had collected my own gloves and my whip and an infinitesimal packet of sandwiches, hardly bulkier than a postage stamp, that lay on a plate among the whips and gloves and unopened letters.

"One thing I *have* taught the cook," Dick said as we walked round towards the yard with the stilted precision insisted on by a hunting-boot before it really warms to the leg, "and that is to make a sandwich that will go in your pocket without bulging it." Putting my hand into my own pocket I felt sure that he had indeed succeeded.

A feint of sunshine gleamed like a pale foil through the grey mist. It struck a sleek crescent of light in the ridiculous penny-bun of hair that Willow had tacked and firmly netted to her bowler hat. She stood with her back to us beside the two stone steps of the mounting-block. Her pale cord breeches were the twin of Dick's and her legs did them almost equal credit. Always I had seen Willow ride in a ragged tweed coat, or, as on the day she won her race, in a flash of silk ; but now she was sober in a black coat, very workmanlike, short as a man's ; that she had put up the hunt button some time ago was obvious from the faintness of the traced monogram.

Sir Richard, shrunken as the old seem of a

morning, was talking to her gently. " Mind that now, child," he was saying, and " You can pull the mare out, Pheelan."

Romance came out of her box, gay enough even on this warm morning. I have met Romance before, yet each time I see her it gives me a queer pick up at the heart ; she is, for her sort, such a perfect thing. Not made to carry much more than Willow's eight stone seven, the little mare has done that well for the last two seasons, and has won her four point-to-points and run into a place twice.

Sir Richard caught his daughter's upheld boot and threw her into her saddle (a little old favourite saddle it must have been—the flaps nipped in dark below the half panel). Willow ran the single plaited rein through her fingers and walked the mare off, while Pheelan pursued her, dusting the toe of her boot with pertinacious zeal. His blue jackdaw-like eyes were everywhere, and he was full of the imperative importance of a groom on a hunting morning.

" Mind, Sir Richard," Willow said, " turn the key of the saddle-room door on Pheelan while we're gone, and keep him there for the day. I'll not have him up in James's room. His doctoring will finish James."

" Indeed I'll have Pheelan's life ! " replied Sir Richard equably; " I'll beat him till he forgets his tricks."

Pheelan, who had disappeared into a further

loose-box, led my horse out now. This was School-master, plain but a great old sort and warranted foolproof. His legs were thick with the honourable scars of many winters ; he came out of his stable a bit dickey, but warmed up sound in half an hour. One eye was blind from the prick of a thorn long years ago, but the remaining one served him more than well.

" Keep your heels out of his sides now, Oliver," Dick said as I got up on him. Certainly that strong back was humped under the saddle in a manner that invited no liberties.

" Keep him walking, Oliver," Willow said quietly. " Don't let him stop."

" Well, indeed, the third he'll give'd put you or me either to hell out o' that too quick," Pheelan observed warningly as he let go his head and de-parted for Dick's horse.

" Ah, he's a gay old sinner," said Sir Richard, with the indulgence of those who are on their feet for the horse that is pretty sure shortly to add another to their number.

Four such portentous warnings succeeded in making me thoroughly nervous of my mount. I circled the yard gingerly, feeling much as though I was sitting on top of a large volcanic egg, balanced on the brink of a steep precipice. However, I succeeded in the not too easy task of keeping Schoolmaster moving, at the same time keeping my heels out of his sides, while I remembered with horror the six young horses galloping loose in the field through which we must ride to reach the road. One of us, I thought, seeing Dick being thrown up (obviously he would not risk a toe in the stirrup) on a big and bad-tempered chestnut four-year-old, would take it good and proper before very many minutes were over. There was decidedly too much white round that chestnut's eye, and I did not like to see his driving plunge forward, made almost before he felt Dick in the saddle. With his feet still out of the stirrups, Dick stopped him—quick.

" Cripes Almighty !" was Pheelan's only comment, " tighten yerself, Master Dick."

As I rode after Willow out of the yard, our horses' hoofs echoing rudely on the flagstones under the dark stable arch, I fancied that Dick was not the only one of us to follow Pheelan's injunction. However, during our progression down the long avenue beneath the wet architectural aisle of the lime-trees, Schoolmaster's back went down and my spirits proportionately up. The young horses grouped in the distance favoured us with a long stare, but they were so used to horses being ridden among them that they did not precipitate themselves disruptively upon us, as I had in my palsied imagination feared they would do.

A sprite of a child came out of the deep-roofed lodge to open the gates; he hid himself shyly behind the dark thin lace of the wrought-iron work, one hand fast in the scruff of a pale greyhound puppy, while above him the stone pillars, exquisitely reeded, swept up to hold their grey cups high. We rode through, and Willow pulled Romance round on the dark gravel sweep to speak to the child. The soaring, lovely gates lend their true and only balance to my remembrance of her and that blood-like mare Romance as I saw them on a dim and proper hunting morning.

"Johnny," said Willow, "did you give that pup the wormball I sent down?"

"Yis, miss," hissed the shy little boy. "It's after reducin' her greatly, miss," he added, with an enormous effort.

"I'll bring you down a good bottle of cod-liver oil," Willow promised. She had forgotten her horse, mad fresh from its stable. She sat sideways in her saddle, dwelling on the thought of that greyhound puppy. "I'll bring it down to-night, Johnny," she said.

The little boy curtseyed, nipping his quiff of black hair between finger and thumb. We started off down the wet beech-canopied road.

"Ah, *have done*!" said Willow to Romance, who, as we broke into a gentle jog, dived her head down quick and wicked as a bee. "I can't *bear* a fresh horse." Dick rode in silence, aware of what he might expect, and more than ready for it. My old horse had settled down now, for which I was deeply grateful. Nor was there an inch of tarmac road to petrify one farther on all the six miles we rode to the meet. Puddles in potholes were misshapen grey shields. The demesne walls and big fields of Pullinstown give way to farms fenced with smaller and more intricate carefulness ; banks were wreathed and blind in briars or faced up tall and solid with stones ; and scarcely a strand of wire did I see, even on the fences that bounded the road. We passed several coverts, gorse growing strong down the length of a wet bog, and a steep hill led us over the curving back of a wood that smelt bitter and shrill as wet woods do smell. The road ran its narrow stony shelf under the shoulder of a rock-strewn hill, darkly crowned with heather, and rich in the dead brown of bracken. Below us a fair hunting country dropped to a vale of grass and grass again, its miles across lost in the mist and shine of the day and the farther mountains were worlds away in faery.

" What's the name of this hill ? " I wanted to know.

" Corragrue," Willow told me ; " it's the other side of Cloneen, where we were yesterday."

" And that "—Dick pointed bitterly to the vale that dreamed of fox-hunting below us—" that priceless bit of country has every covert in it poached and hunted by our harrier neighbours, with the Reverend Mr. Fox playing fast and loose between them and our Master. Oh, they're a lot of *beauties* those Spree harriers."

" Do you see that bit of covert, Oliver ? " Willow indicated a distant strong patch of gorse. " That used to be a pet covert for us," she said, "a certain find. And Anthony has drawn it blank twice this season. That's where old Fox'd have shaken his bagman, eh, Dick?"

"That's the very place," Dick nodded. "That's where Tommy'll turn down the ginger bitch to-day. I hope I get a good view of her."

I thought of the red cur-lady that Dick and I had substituted for the proposed bagman. It was like a dream to me, the day before. Had I really visited that parson - *cum* - horse - dealer - *cum* - poacher—the Reverend Mr. Fox? Had I indeed bought a horse from him, the like of which is not often to be had, for the money? Had I, in company with my cousins, subsequently and in the depths of night raided his stable yard, substituting for a bagman which was destined to remove the slur of blankness from his coverts, his own ginger cur? Had I with my law-abiding English hands tied the mouth of a sack on her protests, and had I seen then a good fox loosed in the night, the night that belongs to foxes? I had in very truth done all these things. And for the honour of a pack of hounds I had never seen, and to the confusion of those who break the greatest law of fox-hunting, " Thou shalt not draw another man's coverts."

A big car slipped down the hill past us with every care for our horses, its off-wheels nearly in the ditch. It was driven by a very small man in a very large coat, and Willow and Dick called, " 'Morning,

Master—'Morning, Peter," as that car went by.

" That's his wife, Peter," Dick said—" a *star*."
I had only seen a grave profile under the veil of her
hard hat and the car was gone, its wide tyre-tracks
impressive before us on the little wet road.

We turned left below the hill, and our horses, a
minute ago peacefully apathetic, woke to the immediate realisation of a hunting day. Hounds'
close footmarks patterned the road ahead, and the
sharp print of hunters' shoes excited the morning.
Dick's big chestnut had seen the hounds three times
before this, so he knew enough about the business
to make himself obnoxiously unruly when that first
mad smell caught his nostrils. Dick was very quiet
with him. Old Schoolmaster stiffened his neck and
proceeded at a vulgar and unslakeable trot, and
Willow, with Romance nicely in hand, laughed at
us unkindly.

Two public-houses, a vast Roman Catholic
church, and a memorial to the year 1798—a
towering cement cross in which pikeheads had been
embedded as suitable ornaments—raised a lonely
cross-roads to the status of village (Mandoran was
its lovely name), and here the West Common hounds
met.

A useful, active-looking sort, the West Common
hounds ; and if they were not a very even lot to
look at, I did not mind hazarding a guess that they
would run level enough. There was not one among
them that did not look like galloping ; and if they

had not the exaggerated bone of the Peterboro'
stamp, they had the right shoulders, laid well back
and plenty of muscle behind them, for dropping
off these steep stone-facers. Even to my English
eye, accustomed to a big heavily-built hound, they
were the right type for this enclosed country. And,
no two ways about it, they *did* look fox-catchers. I
would love them in their work, I knew. The hunt
servants were well mounted, but on the cobby stamp
of cut-and-come-again horse best suited to the
country. They were well turned out, too, a useful
couple of varminty-looking fellows, I'd say. The
bloom on the hounds spoke a real psalm in praise
of their kennel huntsman. And when that Major
Countless, who had just passed us on our way, rode
up to them, their greeting hung clamorous and joyful
on the sulky air. He was fond of and cheerful with
his hounds, one saw. They told me he showed right
sport.

The field already gathered at the cross-roads
numbered more than thirty. Perhaps fifteen of
Willow's and Dick's breed, and the rest a good sort
of sporting farmer mounted on his own old reliable
hunter, and in many cases with a young son out on
a good-looking youngster. Midway between the two
breeds were a few representatives of the Spree
harriers, prosperous young solicitors and shop-
keepers from the nearest town. " Lar Devereux is
the only one among them that knows what he's
about—bar Mr. Fox," Willow told me. " Those

are two great big blackguards." She had Romance stuck up under a hedge, and was pointing out to me the notabilities of the hunt while she shifted her saddle and drew in the girths.

"That's Maeve Fountain"—the loveliest girl with a sad mouth and a smile in her eye was talking to the master's wife, who sat square and fair on her weight-carrying hunter; she rode with a long rein and a long stirrup, and her back was as straight as a die—"Rowley—Maeve's husband—ran away with another," Willow continued, "and she's not the better of it yet."

"Oh, *Willow*, what a pity!" There was a real queen among women, and she carried her sorrow like a gift.

"She rides a hunt better than any woman I know. Look! that's Toby Sage." A young man, with a charming twisted smile, raised his blue velvet cap to Willow. He was a neighbouring master. Beside his own horse a groom led a pony no bigger than a mouse on which Toby and a tall girl, who looked not quite sixteen, had mounted their young son with enormous pomp and care.

"Hallo, Willow," the girl said; she had a frail slow voice. "Yes, I'm on my feet. Thursday is Dominick's hunting day, and he *will*-try to follow me if I'm riding." She indicated the little boy whose bucket stirrups hardly reached to the bottom of his saddle flaps. "Now he's off to tell Anthony what he thinks of his hounds. I *must* stop him," and she went striding away in pursuit of her young. Prudence was her name. There were others to whom Willow introduced me with casual friendliness.

The women as a whole showed quality. Many of them rode astride, turning themselves out well— though no one quite touched Willow—but Dick, among the men, was not an outstanding exquisite. They were all well mounted, the horses showing as much quality as their riders, and they were all very kind to me : none of that disposition to ride round a stranger with their hackles up, so often exhibited by the star-turns of a hunt in my own country.

Mr. Fox rode up beside me just as the hounds moved off. His muscular bulk was well carried by a big bay horse up to sixteen stone, and made like a pony : a perfect model of a weight-carrying hunter, and with manners on him like a ladies' hack. And Mr. Fox had, for his weight, a wonderful-looking seat on a horse.

" Good-morning, Mr. Pulleyns." His voice was as suave and meaningless as ever and his eye as bland : most certainly our doings of the night before had not as yet come to his knowledge. In his old-fashioned, full-skirted black hunting-coat (with as many quarters in its back as there are in an orange) and his rather low-crowned silk hat, he appeared the essence of sportsman-like respectability. " Well," he said, " I had O'Conner—that's the vet—out this morning looking at a sick heifer, and

I thought he might as well examine the little horse while he was about it. Yes, he gives him a clean bill." He answered my interrogative silence. He's posting you the certificate to-night. I have a horse going on the midday train," he continued, " and I'll box yours along with him, if you will wire to the other end."

Dick said, " That's lucky," when I told him. " At that rate he'll be on the train before the old sinner guesses we had anything to say to last night's show. Anthony has two coverts and the hills to draw before he goes to Cloneen covert."

At this point we turned off the narrow lane up which the hunt had ridden two by two, passed through the unbelieveably filthy yard of a farmhouse where children hid, peeping out from between the spokes of cart-wheels, and curs barked and geese hissed defiance as the hunt rode by. Three fields below the house an attractive bit of gorse grew strong on the sheltered side of a little slope ; but although they went in as keen as wolves and drew up to the last bush in the covert, hounds never once looked like finding there. Anthony had a good voice, of which he did not make undue use, and his servants were quick and efficient. The long-drawn notes on his horn sounded sadly over a good covert drawn blank. " Vigilant's missing," I heard him say as we waited. " She's shy since she was jumped on the other day ; won't come near horses. By Jove, she was the best of this year's entry. That morning at Coolaphancy she had a line of her own, and carried it across a bank, and threw her tongue in the next field and put them all right. Here she comes now. I must go and meet her."

We moved off to the next draw, not, to my surprise, by a line of hunting gates or along a serving road, but by a short cut that necessitated jumping several most unpleasant banks and in the coldest sort of blood. Leaving the matter entirely to Schoolmaster's ruling, I found that they were not so difficult to sit over after all.

At three o'clock in the day, and with the gorse-grown hills blank behind us, the hounds were put into Cloneen covert. Mr. Fox had been riding up alongside a silent and possibly rather grim master. From the conciliatory set of his broad black shoulders one could almost guess at the respectful explanations which he wasted on Anthony's disgruntled unresponsiveness. Anthony did not even acknowledge the hope that here in the amiable parson's own covert a fox would be found to redeem the day. He was with his hounds every yard they drew, heartening them, while sore and angry that they should be so sickened.

Dick and Willow and I stood together, a close little band of conspirators. We saw Mr. Fox ride off down the outside fence of the covert, and we saw a young fellow detach himself from a group that stood in the gateway and go towards him. It was Dick who gave me his horse to hold, and slipped off on his feet down a cross-ride to hear what he might hear. He came back choking with laughter.

"The ride met the fence," he told us. "I just heard Tommy say, 'She went off from home like blazes.' Old Fox gave him one *look*; I didn't hear what he said, but Tommy's face went white. He whipped his horse round then, and away with him back to the road. We'll not find here," Dick said, slipping his arm through his horse's rein and lighting a cigarette with expert competence. Willow unfastened her tiny sandwich, squeezed up the paper and threw it away. She took her feet out of the stirrups and crooked her knees up on the tree of her saddle.

"Michael Beary," Dick said to her, and she nodded heedlessly.

We stood in the steep shelter of a tree-grown bank. Behind us in the thick little wood, Anthony's infrequent voice sounded the right music for the day:

"Leu troi for him. . . . Leu troi. . . . Push him up, me lads. . . ."

An old hound drew up to us where we were standing, and disappeared into covert again.

"That's old Priestess," Willow said. "I walked her; she nearly died of the yellows on me."

Silver for ash saplings and grey for sturdy hazel, and a stillness of green held the little wood quietly. The questing excited voice of a young hound clamoured for a second on the air, followed by a harsh rate in Anthony's strong angry voice, " *Wilful*, have care ! *Wilful !* "

" That Wilful's very free with her tongue," Willow said disapprovingly.

A young man came up the ditch towards us ; he was tall and dark, and his wild gentle face was one of the handsomest I have ever seen.

" Tell me, my lad," Willow accosted him, " is this a place where the foxes do resort ? "

" Indeed, there was pucks of thim in it a-Friday. Mister Devereux's dogs got a right chase out of it."

" So I believe, indeed," replied Willow, with conversational ease that took no account of Dick's snort of horror. " Will we get one in it to-day, do you think ? "

" Ye'll get one right enough if those is wary dogs and good dogs, and little thanks to thim that brought an old cur bitch in a bag to loose her out before them. 'Faith, 'twas herself legged it out for home in standing leps and no more about her." He spat with deft and fitting contempt. " There's a little vixen in it," he continued, " a right little pet. In the month o' Febroary every dog fox in the country would be in the covert afther her."

" Is that a fact," said Dick, with due and weighty appreciation. " Well," he pondered, " I wouldn't wonder now would there be as many as six in it."

" Six ? Sha ! *Six* ? *Twinty-ni-en*——"

He delivered the good round number at us with a solemnity that befitted the phenomenon. In the

face of such exactitude there was, I felt, no more
to be said save in salute to that fascinating vixen.

" I'd wonder you'd be able to count them,"
Willow suggested, with faint scepticism.

" Is it count them ? Didn't I see thim each night
in the week, and they bawling around the covert
and frisking in the fi-elds."

" Well, last February is a long time ago," I
hazarded. " You didn't see her lately ? "

" I did—I got the thrack of her nail in the burra'."

" Maybe that was the nail she had for nailing up
the door." Dick finished the Fox subject with
sarcastic conclusiveness. " Tell me," he said, his
eyes on a far glimspe of bog, " is that a real soft
place or could you travel a horse in it ? "

" Well, ye could not thravel a horse in it." The
young lad rose from the bank where he had been
leaning during his discourse and pointed a lean
middle finger. " G'out north the land where ye'll
see the black trees," he said. " Ye'll not get out
below."

My eyes dropped from the distance to the nearer
tongue of convert that curled out long and narrow
into the end of the field where we stood. Quite idly
I was watching, and then in one bold second of
time my heart shot up to the last pounding notch
of excitement. That almost insane shock of courage,
which the view of a good fox leaving a covert gives
one, rose choking me in its intensity.

Slipping along the fence with grim composure

was a big greyhound of a fox, higher on the leg than most of our English breed. No shirking stay-at-home, he was on top of the first fence of the covert like a big cat, took one quiet look about him, and set his mask for the open country.

With Dick's ear-splitting holloa still screaming on the air as, hat in hand, he rose up to stand facing the way our fox had gone, an unorthodox but equally soul-lifting bellow came from our young companion, who sprang upon the fence, his eyes blazing in a glorious madness of the chase.

"*Wirra—Hurry—Wirra—Hurry—Wirra—Hurry*! Almighty Lord God! What should keep yiz? What good are yiz for huntsmin? Where's the bugler-man to sound his trumpet? He crossed out the ditch before me and he tippin' it like a boy. He's as grey as a badger. He the heighth of a deer——"

"*Which way was he going?*"

Anthony, galloping down a close-grown ride to the halloa, had jumped the awkward fence out of the covert with as much carelessness as did one good to see.

"East the fince, yer honour."

"Ahha! Ahha!" as the hounds came crashing through the undergrowth all alive, tumbling out of the covert, flying like wild things to the doubled notes on their huntsman's horn. "That's the boy can blow a blast will lead hounds to a rapid hunt! Hulla! Hulla! Hulla!" as the first couple on hit off the line. " Thim's the reigning dogs of all ! "

Very much on the right side of the covert we were, Dick and Willow and I—the most designing could not have devised a fairer start than we had. No one has ever accused Anthony of slipping his field, but to-day his hounds settled to the line of their fox, and were running on hard over the second field from the covert before any one thought about catching us. This I have observed often to be the case in an afternoon hunt. After the many disappointments of a blank morning the keenest spirits lose their edge. And this was no day for picking up a bad start, for there was such a scent in the open as one does not often see, added to which hounds were not three minutes behind their fox leaving the covert.

Anthony's were a right pack of hounds. No head and tail with a string joining the two about them. They ran well together, their voices a tearing ecstasy in the evening, the best of them snatching it again from the best. Nor did they ever overrun the line by a yard. Such *quick* hounds I have seldom seen. I saw the leading hounds as they landed off a fence ; they seemed almost to turn in the air with the scent, and proclaimed it right down the edge of the ditch, where their fox had turned short for a gap on his left.

Anthony, Willow, Dick, myself, and the first whipper-in, a hardy fellow, had set our horses well alight and got right with them from the start. A bit of a trial on old Schoolmaster, this first burst, and indeed we were beaten for pace. But to counterbalance that, any place (in any fence) you turned his head he would have a real go. My judgment about Irish banks being of the greenest (to me they all look equally dangerous) I took them as they came, performing, I do not doubt, prodigies of unwitting valour ; yet, thanks to Schoolmaster's being the horse he is, with better results than I deserved. The going was all grass and rode light, and the banks, high and frequent, were hideously blind but fairly sound. How Dick on that chestnut undependable of his stayed there I shall never guess. I doubt if he put a foot really right the first dozen fences he jumped. There was mud on his nose and on his bridle, but he had not been down past recovery, and Dick had stayed with him somehow. Willow has the quickest eye for a country I have ever seen. No sooner in a field than she is putting on the pace for the best of all possible ways out of it, which others—slower witted—have not even seen. Anthony was a bit of an artist too, but he was mounted extra well, and his whole mind and soul so flung forward with his hounds that he had need to be well mounted. Judgment was more a matter of instinct than thought with him.

For fifteen minutes, without the semblance of a check, hounds ran " like the wheels of hell," Dick said afterwards. We rattled our horses along at the best pace we were able. I had the right feeling

about a bank now—the stop and lift and steep
drop off it, or the wise pause on top before sailing
out over a ditch on the landing side. And with that
glory and gratitude (which is second to no sensation
in the world) for the horse that had carried me the
living best I stopped Schoolmaster as we landed in a
field of plough, where hounds were at fault for the
first time. There was a farm a field ahead of us,
the main road on our left, and a little river below us
on our right. Anthony allowed his hounds full time
to display their genius before giving us an exhibition
of his own. Like a flight of living birds they swung
their cast across the field, tried down the river bank
and then up till, where cattle had made a way for
drinking, an old bitch threw her silver tongue.

"Huick to Truthful ! Leu—over—Bitch*ies* ! Leu
—over ! over ! over ! . . ." Anthony cheered
them across the river, plopping into the water like
pied fruit, straining and scrambling up the steep
bank on the farther side ; a minute's uncertainty—
the current has taken their fox to a landing-point
farther down the stream, and now they are at him
again. "Diligent has it, sir." The whipper-in
gathered his cobby horse together and rib-roasted
him into the flood.

"Forrid together, Bitchies ! Forrid—Forrid—
Forrid ! " Anthony chose the soundest-looking
take off, and was over the water with little enough
to spare.

"Follow Jim, Oliver ! Schoolmaster'll drop his

legs in it," Willow called as Romance stood back
and jumped it—feet to the good on the right side.
We scrambled in and floundered out. Dick had taken
a cold bath farther down, and was just pulling the
chestnut out after himself.

Hounds were hunting more slowly now with a
worse scent than they had had ten minutes before,
but still good enough to hunt a fox. A couple of
fields of cold plough did not improve matters, nor
half a mile of thick holding gorse growing down a
slip of wet bog. Our fox ran the length of it, holding
to its shelter from view, and here hounds were still
farther behind him. It was a place where they
might easily have changed foxes, too. Scent grew
worse again till they could own it no longer.

It was indeed my moment when I saw one and a
half couples feathering up the ditch that ran along
the uncertain edge of the covert, busy as bees,
every instant keener. They spoke to it at last, and
proclaimed their fox was on.

Anthony's " Have at him again ! " was as hearty
a cheer as ever lifted my heart or went like wine
to my head. His hounds joined like lightning
together ; one crash through the covert and over
the open again. They started to run on now, and
took a bit more staying with.

" He lay down in the covert," Willow said. " I
wonder we didn't view him out of it. They're
closer to him now than they've been since we crossed
the river." She pointed Romance's nose towards an

almost invisible gap in the corner of a most forbidding fence, and set her going again like blazes.

We were riding over a vale of grass, the fences that Willow would get out of her bed in the night to jump, our portion. Sound wide banks, faced low, and solid with stones. A gorse-grown hill ahead of us must be our fox's point. " He'll get in in the rocks," said Willow. " Come *up*, mare ! " It was a joy to see her ride into her fences. Romance took them faster than I would have liked, but hit them all bang in the middle, and made no mistake about the ditch on the landing side. Dick's young horse had had about enough ; he was riding up a lane on our right, for Dick had sense as well as courage. A field in front of us the fluting crash and gallantry of the hounds' voices ennobled the evening to a wildness of glorious endeavour. It was a sinking fox before them now, and they knew it. Godsend they did not overrun his line in their eagerness. But no, they held steadily on, inclining always towards that gorse-crowned hill.

Fence succeeded fence, higher and stonier, as we turned right-handed for the hills, and each was a bit more of a contest than the last for our tiring horses. Willow, a featherweight and riding blood, was, I fancy, the only one of our select band really to enjoy the last fifteen minutes of that somewhat grim battle.

Hounds turned short at the foot of the hill, and as I jumped off to open a gate into a serving lane-way, I saw Dick's lifted hat on the hillside just to our right—that hill thick-grown with impenetrable Irish gorse where the odds were all in our fox's favour, beaten though he was.

Anthony saw the lifted hat too. But he saw his hounds, mute now for blood, crash out across the briar-wreathed lane, and he did not interfere with them. (Nor could he have done so had he wished.) Up the hill they stormed—what heart and condition they were in, his hounds—turned short left again where their fox had turned and caught him up against a loose-built wall of stones, where he leaped for his life and fell back to a quick and gallant death.

An instant's silence in the heather and gorse—a moment from the evening that belonged to the death of a fox—before Anthony's "Who—Whoop!" rang out over as stout a customer as a good pack of hounds ever killed in the open after a stern chase.

Anthony's hounds broke up their fox as savage as a pack of wolves. Fifteen minutes later not one rag of brown fur remained on the hillside to tell of the proud end of a good fox, nothing but his mask hanging down from the D's of the whipper-in's saddle. Nothing but the warm stir which would live for us in our remembrance of that good hunt (sixty-five minutes and a six-mile point)—a fox's most fitting immortality.

The light was behind the edge of that dark hill

as I led Schoolmaster down with slackened girths
and his game old head dropped to my hand. Out
in the lane the hounds crowded close round
Anthony's horse, and the gladness in his eyes for
them was a new lamp in the evening. We had a
nip—each in turn—from Dick's flask, and walked
on down the little friendly lane towards the road
where Anthony's car had passed us in the morning.
The exaltation of effort fulfilled mounted within
us. We all talked—Anthony and Jim of individual
hounds ; Dick of his young horse's prowess ; I of a
country that surpassed all countries I had ever
known to ride over. Willow dwelt with pleasure
on the rage and jealousy of the field that had never
caught us. None of us listened to another, but almost
we loved one another. The dregs of the wine of
fox-hunting are the only dregs of pleasure that are
as golden and hot to the head as the wine itself.

" Those are Tarquin's two daughters," said
Anthony to Willow, when she ceased her babbling
of things that mattered not and turned her mind back
to the hounds. " They are as good as their father.
Oh, *Willow*"—he was pained indeed—" *of course* you
remember old Tarquin. He was my chief authority
for a fox——"

Down by a little house, one hooded window
already a square of yellow, the others darker than
sloes in the dusk, we got on our horses again.

" And what *you're* going to say to the Sir—you
that were to have that young horse back in his

stable at four o'clock," Willow said to her brother
with quelling righteousness, "*I* don't know."

"Never mind, Dick," Anthony laughed, "think
of me! Peter'll have my life to-night." He rode on
with his hounds and Willow rode beside him.

"Well, poor old Fox!" I heard him say in his
pleasant voice. "He had one there for us after all,
and a *right* fox, too. I think I'll have to give him
his own price for that brown mare he's trying so
hard to sell me."

"Listen, Anthony," said Willow, "would you
like to hear a story that would cheapen that
mare?"

I did not catch Anthony's reply nor the tale that
Willow unfolded, but well I knew the matter thereof.
At the cross where our roads parted it ended, and
Anthony's face was white in the dusk.

"I'm very much obliged to you," he said; "at
the same time you gave yourselves a lot of unnecessary trouble. *My hounds* wouldn't hunt a bagged
fox." His voice was as white as his face. "As for
buying a horse from Mister Fox—I'll never speak
to the blackguard again. I wouldn't have a carcase
of one of his horses for my hounds. Good-night."

"Good-night, master."

"Good-night."

"Good-night, sir."

Tired in the dropping dark, their day fulfilled so
well, hounds and horses jogged slowly out of sight.

"Well," said Willow, leaning forward to scratch

Romance's sweat-itching head, " aren't the English very queer ? Dick, I know that mare of Fox's is a bit above *my* weight. But I think we might buy her at our own little price all the same." She looked at me. " Oliver," she said, " I think you have a dash of Irish roguery in you somewhere—aren't we awful divils ? But, Dick, that's a *hell* of a mare."

LADIES OF TEMPLESHAMBO

" There's all the difference in the world," said my cousin Willow, " between a right-rogue and a Prime Rogue. Now, father," her voice dropped to a proper pitch of reverence, " is a Prime Rogue."

" I think he's only a right-rogue." Dick removed his boots from the coral-red eiderdown which had been my gift to his sister when, her spirit subdued within her under the joint influences of a cracked shoulder blade and an acute attack of influenza, she had taken to her bed.

" Mind you, Willow, the Sir has come very near being badly had more than once. Do you remember when Cousin Honour was mad for marrying him ? Do you remember that brown horse he bought from Billy Morgan ? Those were two very close calls." Dick got off the edge of the bed and went across to Willow's dressing table where he tilted the mirror and set himself to the eloquent and proficient re-arrangement of the blue and red handkerchief that intricately circled his neck.

" Well "—Willow twisted herself argumentatively in bed—" he got out of the horse all right and out of old Honour too. Oh, Sir Richard is able to mind himself, my boy. Don't you think so, Oliver ? You'd want to be pretty smart to best father—don't you think so ? "

" I do," said I, thus appealed to.

" What's this you have ? " Dick was prowling among the medley on Willow's dressing table. There were gold-backed brushes and dusty boxes of face powder, old spurs almost brass colour with age and a new pair bright as silver, jockeys and pulleys for her hunting boots, a tin of saddle-soap and a great many boxes, some unopened, of cosmetics.

" What have you found ? " Willow peered forward. " Oh, that's great for chilblains—— " An attack of coughing defeating her, she fell back dramatically exhausted on her pillows. I poured out a dose of her cough mixture and brought it over to her. Willow got the most out of us all when she was ill. She took to coughing again now while I hovered absurdly with the medicine glass in my hand.

" Chilblains, *Ha !* " Dick had continued his investigations. " Chilblains, my God ! Well, I never saw cavaire put on chilblains yet."

Willow's cough hushed itself abruptly. " That's there since my last sickness."

" The time you were concussed ? That's a long time ago. Would it be good yet ? Smell it."

" Smell it yourself."

" You smell it, Oliver."

" Must I, Willow ? "

" Here, Sue, here, Pig, what do you think of it, my sweet swine ? " On the end of an immoderately long shoe-horn Dick gingerly tendered a morsel to his loved little bitch. She savoured its bouquet for a moment before rolling in that richness. Not every day do little dogs find like smells to carry away upon their persons.

Hastily Dick replaced the lid and threw the pot out of the window into the heart of a rhododendron bush that grew below, its early flowers enhaloed with that air of adventurous fragility which celebrates such young daring.

" Is that what you thought, my tiny sweet ? " Dick washed his little dog's be-fouled shoulder before Willow had time to protest at such gross misuse of her sponge, and sat down to dry her by the fire. Flicker, on seeing this, jumped like a soured grasshopper from my arms to insist on her proper share of dear attention. Willow coughed wearily above the battle which ensued between that fierce pair, Sue and Flicker. Her donkey thrust forth its silly baby head from beneath her bed and swung it there, ridiculously draped in the lifted frill of valance.

Sir Richard, his knock unheard, stood in the doorway, a handkerchief redolent of eucalyptus oil held to his patrician nose. He dreaded the infection of influenza.

" How are you, my child ? " he inquired through the handkerchief, with stifled sonorousness. " It's a wonder you're alive at all with this damned menagerie you have in here." His eye included

Dick and myself in his disapproval of Willow's ass and canary, and the two little white dogs that glared at each other, one crooked in either of Dick's arms. "All I came to say was, I ordered lunch for one o'clock instead of half-past, because I thought of driving Oliver over to Templeshambo this afternoon—if it would amuse him—and we'd want to start early."

"Thanks very much, Cousin Richard," said I, and I observed the look that telegraphed so much more than words could ever say between his children, "I'd like to come."

"Well, we'll go then. It's a very pretty place. You should like that when you're an artist. Does Pheelan know how to put that stuff on the mare's hock, Dick? Plaster it on with a knife—keep your chest covered, Willow, my child. I must go and see he does it right."

"And the men at their dinners, every lad of them," Dick said, as his father shut the door.

"You might have saved him a walk if you'd mentioned that sooner."

"No. I wouldn't do that. He's twice as happy tootling around. But what's he going to Templeshambo for, Willow? Eh, Willow? I wonder why he's mad for going to Templeshambo? I heard him tell James to go with him and James had neuralgia in his face. He wouldn't go. That was why he invited Oliver to make the trip."

"Who lives at Templeshambo?" I asked, a

little damped perhaps by this unaffected inter-
pretation of Sir Richard's desire for my company.

"Cousin Honour and Cousin Beauty, and the
roof's falling in on them, but the two old outlaws
won't leave it."

"Is it a nice place?"

"When the Dukes of Westcommon were in their
prime, it was—great. But Honour and Beauty are
the last of that lot, and they're broke. All their lives
long every penny they could rap and ram on a
horse they did, and now they're ruinated. Dick,
remind James to put that salmon in the car for
them."

"Which?" Dick rose to his feet, dispersing the
little dogs summarily from his person. He slid his
hands into the pockets of his jhodpores and gazed
with reflective consideration at the excellence of his
legs. "I'm a bit doubtful about that fifteen-
pounder I got in the stake-hole last night. He's
all right, but he's an ugly divil."

"Yes, that's the one to send." Willow sat up in
bed. "Here's my lunch. Open the door for James,
Oliver. He's not able for tray and all. He's bet on
his feet and he's bet every way."

"Thank ye, Mister Oliver. Thank ye very much,
sir." Hooded together like a sick black crow above
the heavy tray with which he had toiled from the
dining-room, James, paused at the foot of Willow's bed.
His eye skipped from the covered jug of water on

the washstand to Willow lying in great beauty, for sickness becomes her stricken paleness.

"Miss Willow," said he, "did ye have a nice wash this morning?"

"I had a nice bath last night," said Willow, with guilty evasion. "Can't you let me alone? You know I'm in fearful pain if I move at all. And if no one but men come near this room to do a hand's turn for me, how can I wash?"

"O, fie! O, fie! O, fie!" James clicked his tongue in lively disapprobation. "What a way to talk indeed." He deposited the tray and advanced upon her with a bath towel, which when tucked below her chin gave her a look as of some exquisite choir-boy. Dick and I, standing on the hearthrug, watched mesmerised as he sponged her face. "Show a hand, now," said he, and obedient and star-fish like, it was produced. "Now the other. There's nothing is so horrid," said James, as he accomplished these ministrations, "for man or beast as to be dirty. And ye'll not see the colour o' food, Miss Willow, me child, till you'll brush your teeth."

"Leave her alone, now, James," said Dick, interfering suddenly on his sister's behalf. "Last time she brushed her teeth you could hear the bones in her shoulder rattling together, and that's no way to knit them."

"And the *pain*——" said Willow, faintly.

"Sure what's that pain to the way thim brats o' lads o' dentists would pluck hell out o' ye and they fast in a toot' and to drag ye around the room to pleasure theirselves is what they'd do. Yes, b'God, hither and over for their pleasure."

" *They would?* " Fascinated by the horror of this picture called up by James, Willow took the toothbrush he tendered and made a half-hearted feint of arresting dental decay.

"That's my good child." James straightened her pillows and arranged the tray with skill. " See now "—he swept off a cover with a becoming flourish—" that's what'll crown ye."

" That's not the fish Master Dick brought in last night, is it ? "

" Was it Master Dick killed that poor brute ? Oh, pity ? "

" Did you get those hackles dyed for me yet, James ? " Dick turned the subject with uneasy quickness.

"Well, I did not. Micky Roche have those few hacks to bring me still. He didn't get to drop on the right cock yet. Will I put that—what's this I'll call it ? —that *salmon* in the motor along with the Sir and Mr. Oliver to go to Templeshambo, Master Dick ? "

" Yes, that's a good idea, James. Do that."

" I will, Master Dick. Have ye all now, Miss Willow ? Eat the young rhuburb. That's great for the body. I'll hop the lunch in now before the Sir'll eat me."

As I surveyed the departing back of Sir Richard's possible alternative to lunch, I thought how well it was for Willow that James should hold over her still the authority he had wielded with nice tolerance since her earliest years. Dick, as we made our way down the long, cloistered darkness of the passage from Willow's room, echoed my feelings. "James," he said, "is the only one who can get any good of Willow when she has a sickness."

All along the passage lovely cupboards towered wanly upwards. I guessed dimly at the treasures of glass and china stored and forgotten in them, and an itch for adventurous discovery excited my mind. Such an interest would, I knew, find but short sympathy from my cousins, its only connection in their minds being skin-tight, greasy purple suits, packed as full as they would hold of hebraic gentlemen from Dublin, determined at any cost to obtain a view of these treasures of Pullinstown. My thoughts were interrupted by a scuffle between Willow's ass—which had followed us from her room, the careful small clatter of its black feet never far behind—and Flicker. Whose was the first rudeness I cannot say, but the kick that was planted at Flicker rapped home instead into the panels of an inlaid cabinet. "And if that ass has lamed herself," Dick said solicitously, "Willow will go out of her mind——"

Sir Richard was waiting in the hall for us to go in to lunch. "You're an unpunctual young devil." He said it to Dick, but I, too, felt the poignancy of the rebuke. "Put out those curs. Put the ass out too——" He led us into the dining-room and talked as we ate. Some of his remarks were addressed to James, some to those powers who had seen fit to curse him with such a son as Dick. A few fell my way, but in general his mind was on greater matters.

"Well, Oliver, I hope you'll enjoy these races to-morrow; the course should suit the mare, I'd say. She's a great lepper over ditches, but she's a bad lepper when it comes to a high narrow one."

"Well, she'll take all the beating she'll get, to-morrow"; this from Dick, his eyes afar off towards the mountains; from the south windows of Pullins-town you saw them across water stretched like a silver skin, its edges pricked through by the young piercing green of flag leaves. A swan nested there and none dared invade that holden quietness. Far to the left, the rim of the fox-covert showed, the rim of a gold cup now, for the gorse was in rich blossom; the country was veined by its narrow streams of gold, dammed into frequent wide still-ness, sleeping gold lakes. Beyond, the mountains rose from note to note of a strange music—" and if you want to know what *I* think," said young Dick, taking his eyes from these distances, " I'd say that brown colt out there was as lame as a dog."

James put down the dish he was carrying round the table and went over to the window. "B'God, he is," he admitted, after a prolonged stare, " and for why?" He picked up the dish again and pro-ceeded with his ministrations to our wants—" He was leppin' out of his body at ten o'clock this morn-

ing. Ould Schoolmaster was let out to him in the
field, and I declare to God he took a dhrive at him
and he belted a womp of a kick into his belly would
down a bull. He took a whee-gee away then and he
comminced to gallop and to play——"

"He hit himself a belt on a tendon, I suppose,
with his play." Sir Richard looked sourly on these
young antics. "I'll have some more of that pudding, James. I suppose it's whipped out to the
servant's hall, is it? If those maids would do a
stroke of work in the house instead of cramming food
into themselves and drinking tea, it would be a nice
change for us all. Look at the grate in my bedroom—
well, go and look at it. Full half-way up the chimney
with paper and empty matchboxes. No, I'll not
have any more pudding now. I'm tired waiting for
it. Are they ever going to send up the coffee? A
very curious thing, Dick, how that dash of a blister
affected old Schoolmaster. He went out through the
stable roof with it. And, mind you, that's supposed
to be a mild blister."

"How mild is it when Johnny Pheelan was rubbing
it in for half the day," Dick said, with his eyes on his
empty plate.

"Well, I hope it does a job on the poor old legs."
Sir Richard pushed back his chair. He leaned out
of the window to flap a napkin towards the young
horses. "Yes, that colt is lame, and very lame,"
he said, as they moved off. "Tell Pheelan to catch
him up this afternoon, Dick. Come on, Oliver, we

should be off. These horses would put you in the asylum. If a wire comes, Dick, open it——"

I have driven with Sir Richard before now and will, I expect, do so again. I have also ridden horses on which I have been the least exacting of passengers. Neither experiences is precisely sedative to the nerves, but, of the two, I think I prefer the latter. On some days Sir Richard is more strange than dangerous in his driving, on other days he is fresh in himself and a terror alike to passenger and pedestrian, and on such days it seems an unkind ruling of fate that his brakes should never be quite at their best.

"Will we get round?" he said to-day, as we neared a corner heralded as dangerous by every device known to the Automobile Association. "We will. Now we're right. It's nearly a straight road from this on. We may step on it. I think you never met my cousins—Woa-o. Stop where you are," as a nimble and tidy black hen arrested with commendable promptitude her preconceived flight across the road. "That's right. You did the right thing. Honour was a very pretty woman once. *And a divil*. But poor Beauty was always a delicate poor thing. There's a prime view now, if you like scenery. And that's wonderful land for young horses."

A river bent strong bows and sped silver arrows through the woods that stooped strong and seemly, measurely stepping down their gradual heights to its level. The purple of spring was on the birch trees—an enamoured bloom, and a frail lace was dyed new in green for the infrequent beeches. A hill was gold above the woods and, steeply built into it, was the smallest castle I have ever seen. It looked out proudly to watch the narrow way across its ford below, and the narrow way over the mountain at its back. Walls, as spread and ribbed as the wings of a little bat, dropped their height in a short, steep flight that gripped into the hill. We crossed the river by a curly hog-backed bridge, and taking one of the five small roads that met there, followed its leading to the distant stone gates of Templeshambo.

" Well, I can remember when this was one of the nicest places in the country, and the *fun* we used to have here." Sir Richard drove perilously up the rutted avenue. A little wood of those maiden trees the birches strove with frail persistence towards the hazel and gallant rhododendron across the way, as they tired, perhaps, of pale sister arms and sought jocund embrace and to know other loves.

" Ah," said Sir Richard, " those were great days. My uncle had a pack of harriers and the two girls used to whip in to him. Honour had a little grey mare called Tantrum and she wouldn't care where she went on her. Beauty was good too. She had very nice hands. But Honour was *so* fond of the hounds—did I tell Dick if a wire came from O'Hagen to open it ? He might have to send in to the five o'clock train to meet that young horse. I did, I think. Honour was a pretty girl, though you wouldn't think it now to look at her. Here we are now, I must look out for Beauty's pack of curs. This place is rank with them. I think I'll go down into second. Straight forward, I think, isn't it? B'God, I wish some of these inventive fellows would make you a silent gear change."

From this side the little castle presented a more domestic face. Snapdragons and wallflowers were pinned, bright brooches, to the winged walls; grass, laboriously maintained in some sort of order, as though a child with a toy mowing machine had worked on it once a week, held the woods at a lovely distance. The grass was speckled with chicken coops and creosoted dog kennels, and the flower border that ran its patched ribband of colour below the windows was only preserved from the depredations of dogs and fowl by stern fortifications of wire netting.

"Oh, Richard, isn't this nice? I was saying to Beauty only this very morning *how* long is it since Richard came near us? And who is this young man? I'm *sure* it must be twenty years since we had a young man to tea——" Old Lady Honour's laugh was the most enchanting, hurried affair. "Oh, *indeed*, I knew your father——. You wouldn't remember old Elflocks? I sold him Elflocks and he loved her. And you're so like him—isn't that extraordinary. Now it's an amazing likeness I must say. *Richard*, I'm out of my mind trying to work the incubator, I must fly back to it;

half the eggs are stony cold and the rest are hard-boiled, and *look* at the state of dirt I'm in——"

As I followed Cousin Richard and Lady Honour across the lawn and along a yew hedge, whereon carved animals and birds had long since relapsed into such strange shapes as to recall their legendary begetters, I thought how enchanting the lady— I thought how adorable the lady—so small and merry and sweet now, and once, I knew, so lovely. And still, I thought, so lovely. The quick, brave lines of her jaw and forehead, the dragged-down eyes, was this last memory of their beauty more exciting than their beauty had ever been? The structure of her body was as clear and emphatic as the unbroken skeleton of any sea-bird. Indeed, she was delightful. And most efficient over the incubator, paying very little attention to Sir Richard's talk as she put its intricate affairs in order. I dared say that few of those layered eggs would fail in their right fruition, she was so seriously careful over them.

" And now we must find Beauty and go and look at the horses," she said as we stepped up the hollowed steps and stooped out below the low door of that dark little room which was, as it might be, the great toe of a tower foot. She pulled the heavy little door to behind her and dropped the embroidered iron latch, waiting till it clicked carefully home. One hand shading her eyes, for she wore no hat on her short white hair, she stared down the length of the yew walk and past the castle windows. "There she is, I declare, walking up from the moat with the dogs. Beauty! Beauty! Hey! *Beau-ty!* Did she hear me? She did. Look, she's coming back now. We'll go and meet her."

I wondered why they had called Lady Eveleen "Beauty." I did not think she could ever have had quite that quality. At the first glance, one thought, a swan—so curling necked and breasted, and at the second one knew, alas, no, but a goose, romantically shaped, but never a swan was she. She was shy and gabbled a little in her talking. She had not her sister's quick living force of words. She whistled in vain for her fat, disobedient spaniels, and they, feathers flying, hunted the moat out with illegitimate fury.

"This is a curious old moat, isn't it?" she said to me. It was as though she tried a little desperately to make conversation. "Nobody knows if it's a burying place of the kings." All the brown and green shadows of the hazels and thorn that grew on that high mound troubled her eyes. "There's a glorious view from the top," she went on; "on a fine day you can see Poulshone Bay, through the gap between Mooncoin and Mandoran. *Aren't* those dogs naughty? Bundle! Doodle! *Here! Come here at once!* Would you like to go on with Honour and Richard while I wait for them? Oh, the monsters! Here they are——"

The dogs, subdued to contrition, coupled and on a lead, we walked on together round the strange moat. "They buried a lot of people here in the Bad Times," Lady Eveleen said. "Honour and I would hear them digging the graves at night. You know, if one of our family turns a sod on this moat they'll die before the year's out. Isn't that a peculiar thing? Indeed, I had a young cousin once—quite a nice boy, too—he went up here one day, he heard the hounds might draw this way, to stop the earths and, *my dear*, in six months' time if he didn't fall from the gallery down into the hall, a stone floor it was, of a house in Yorkshire, and break his neck. It was a large party, too, and of course that quite spoilt it—such a pity. And really a dear boy. So nice-looking."

"How frightful," I said. "How frightfully sad."

"Wasn't it? Terrible. And look at this queer old stone. We had a girl staying here once who was mad on archæology (the poor thing, she never got married), and she used to be very excited over this stone. She said it was the side of a coffin or a tomb of some sort. Indeed it must be very old, I should think——"

Looking at the flat graven stone tilted there among the rooted hazel and the grasping sod, I thought so, too. A serpent was carved thereon for Wisdom, and a wolf-hound for the Flight of Time.

"There are as many old *stories* about this place."

Lady Eveleen raised deprecating hands, flicking her wrists on the word "stories," and her gesture said "far be it from me to bore a guest by their recital." "We must hurry," she said, "I'm sure Richard will admire Honour's beautiful two-year-old. *Such* quality and *such* size. By a winner and out of the dam of winners. Oh, we hope she's going to be worth a *lot* of money."

Sir Richard and his elder cousin, when we came upon them, were standing in a shallow bay of the birch wood, where the field ran a green knife into its heart, and blue-bells lapped across the narrow wound for its healing. A brown two-year-old filly, a yearling that had not thriven too well, and a mare and foal were the subjects of their contemplation. "That foal," Sir Richard was saying, "will want to fill out a lot."

"Fill out?" Lady Honour's laugh was sharpened from its sweetness. "Fill out? Isn't he as thick as a ditch? What do you say, Oliver? Is he a nice foal, or *is* he a nice foal?"

"I'm an awfully poor judge of a foal," I had a look at him; "But I should say he was a *grand* foal. Great in his ribs. Big, flat joints, hasn't he?"

"*Great* big joints——" Sir Richard was peering sourly hockwards. "But I *hope* I don't see a curb forming there already. I do, I think; I'm afraid I do. Ah, a pity!"

"Well, since you're the only one who can see it, Richard, I'll not distress myself over it too much yet-a-while. Especially as I don't flatter myself I'll ever sell the colt to *you*." And this time there could be no doubt that Lady Honour, could, when she so chose, be most successfully acid.

"Ah, well, Honour, at any rate you have a nice two-year-old there." Sir Richard's eyes had dwelt but a pained and silent moment on the yearling. "Quite a nice one," he repeated in undeniable mild commendation, "she'll make a *very* useful sort of ladies' hunter."

"She will—or indeed she might do Beauty to hack about the place. That Doctor Kill-All of hers was been ordering her to take more exercise. By Bright Light—by Nightlight-out-of-Sunshine-and - Sunshine - was - own - sister - to - the - dam - of Starlight - and - bred - Candlelight - before - I - got - her." Lady Honour had whipped round on me and rapped out this distinguished breeding in one breath. "Tell me," she invited, "should she win races or should she not?" Not that she cared for my lowly opinion, nor stopped to hear it. "Talk about size," she went on, "talk about substance, talk about quality and *strength*—look at that—and hocks on the *ground*, absolutely on the ground."

"Oh, she's a nice mare all right. What sort of a mover is the divil?" Sir Richard, entirely undisturbed by Lady Honour's venomous denial of his opinion, flapped his handkerchief by its corner, and shouted till the three spoilt babies and their dam were surprised from their staring in-

credulity at such rudeness, and moved off at an
indignant jog—the foal jerking his little sweet
head and going at great gallop to keep pace with
his elders. Some fancy seizing their clumsy young
minds, the two-year-old and the yearling laid themselves suddenly down to go, and wheeled from us
towards the mountains and back to stand staring,
divinely excited into the bravest beauty that I
think there is.

" *Now*, does she gallop ? Does she gallop ? "
Lady Honour's head was tilted back very proud
and roguish on her bird's neck, her face was broken
and lit with excitement, she hopped from foot to
foot and smote her hands together, laughing upwards at Sir Richard, for she is no height at all.
" Does she gallop, tell me that ? Are her hocks
under her ? Is her toe out ? " She was madly
excited.

" Ah, and a great goer in it, too—Honour, that's
a nice mare." Sir Richard stooped and told her
this as though bestowing a valuable piece of information, and Lady Honour surprisingly accepted this
with meekness.

" Is she, Richard ? " she said. " Well, I *am*
glad you like her."

" Not that I couldn't crab her," he went on
guardedly, " because I could, of course ; but I
like her."

" Of course you could crab her." Lady Eveleen
had taken no part in the skirmishes up to this

point. " Doesn't every one know it takes two real good horses to make one perfect horse ? Shall we go in to tea now, Honour, while he thinks out where he crabs her ? "

We had tea in a room that looked down into the river, into its prune-coloured depths and blown gold manes of imperious water, for here the river was narrow, and stormed through the woods, impatient of their spring swoonings and slow passions.

This tower room was rounded and bulged out over the river in a way that seemed romantical and dangerous. The table was laid in the window. On the curving white walls, discoloured and stained to a lovely parchment, were hung a gallery of minia-tures and silhouettes, and on the tables and cabinets were cases of miniatures. Some of these were open, some closed. Some of the miniatures were framed in gold, some in pearls and some in dirty little garnets. Some were enamelled, some painted on chicken skin, some on silk, some were valueless, some were priceless. There were small and ugly likenesses, and small likenesses of a divine prettiness and exactitude.

The tables in this room were small and fine, too ; they stood on shaped, tapered legs, and their drawers were fitted with chased ring-drop handles. Two Hepplewhite chairs, their straight legs reeded and finished in exquisite thimble toes, their thin hard cushions covered in a brocade, more yellow now than green, stood one on either side of such an Adams fireplace as I shall not see again. Its lovely shallow urn, lidded so primly ; the swing of those thread-like leaf garlands ; the perfect relation between its graceful height and narrow width ; such were so fit and apt that their lines had better be unpraised for ever.

Lady Honour talked to Sir Richard still, and charmed him exceedingly, I think, with her quick burning way. She tempted him with young radishes and watercress. She took two hands to lift the wide silver teapot with a plump, pointed strawberry on its lid. Between them was a thin gold air as of Romance forgotten, but with a nip to it still as though it had wilfully been put from them, not out-worn and sick with sentiment.

Meanwhile Lady Eveleen talked to me. We ate bread and butter and honey, since those radishes were consecrated food, yes and watercress as a wafer. I found her low-voiced gabble delightfully illuminating now and a proper recitative for dramatic tales in it unfolded. As a fitting pendant to the story of that dashing young cousin whose end had been so unlucky and untimely in Yorkshire, was hung the tale of " an old cousin we had, a very rich old man. Well, he'd get his income in cheques of *five hundred pounds*, this old cousin would. And when one would come for him he'd sit back in his chair and drop the cheque on the ground and ' I *think*—I'll buy meself a box of French Plums,' he'd say. Oh, he was *very* mean—— Honour, are you and Richard going out to look at the filly again? I'm going to take Harry to see my dogs and the fairy Duke's Leap." (But Harry was my father's name.)

We played with the dogs for a time; they were as charming to us as only spaniels are, and before the last supper had been eaten I had purchased a lovely quality bitch that should furnish. She was eleven months old and came, Lady Eveleen told me, of a great strain of shooting dogs. " But you must see the Duke's Leap," she said, and we went down the yew walk, and turning left past its buttresses came to where a stone stairway leapt upwards to an arching window, all that remained of an older castle. " It's very curious, indeed," she said, " but He rides up those stairs on a little chestnut horse and *out* with him through that window——"

" What's below? "

" The drop down to the river. And then He'll gallop round to the forge at that little crooked bridge you came by to-day, and tell one of the O'Sheas to see to his horse's shoes—you know the O'Sheas have made shoes for the Templeshambo horses I'd be frightened to say how long. And I'll tell you another very queer thing. That little horse is silver-shod, and the luck of this family goes up and down with the thickness or thinness of those shoes.'"

" When was he seen last ? " I asked her. No bird sang in those dark yews nor was there any sound, but a shrillness in the air, and a strange old smell of sour sod and chill stone. " When was he seen last ? " I asked her again, and she said : " In my father's time. He once saw Him leap out there, but when he went down to the forge next day to ask O'Shea about the shoes—*they were nearly worn through*." She whispered, and her head, on its long curling neck, wagged at me. I was a little frightened ; she was so simple in her acceptance of these eldritch certainties.

" Listen ! " she said, " there's Richard blowing his motor horn for you. Imagine—they *have* been quick. I'm afraid they can never have dealt in that time." A quick shade of annoyance passed over her face at that admission. " And a good thing, too," she went on without a stagger. " I told Honour she was out of her mind to think of selling that mare. We should keep her. She'll be worth a lot of money in three years' time."

By the car Sir Richard and Lady Honour were standing, still in converse—there was about them a look of guarded and careful amiability as though perhaps each thought : " I shall do better out of this affair if I keep careful watch on my words, tell nothing and absorb what negative information there is to be extracted from my opponent's silences or evasions or questions."

Lady Honour flung towards us as we came,

Beauty and I walking sedately down the sloping lawn. I stopped to help her over an entanglement of wire netting that crossed our way, and Lady Honour burst out laughing. "You might *be* Harry," she said, and glanced at her sister naughtily as she said it.

"I don't see the likeness so plainly as you do." Lady Eveleen looked both annoyed and abashed, I thought.

"Well, I only hope he's as good a jockey as his father, because I've just heard young Morgan has broken his collar-bone schooling this afternoon; and Richard says Dick is riding Romance as Willow is laid up, so I'd like to offer Oliver the ride on Surprise in the open race to-morrow. Will you ride her, Oliver? You'll have a nice safe ride anyhow, and indeed you might come near winning it."

"Thank you ever so much." I said. I was more pleased than I have often been by the offer of a very unknown quantity in the way of a mount in a point-to-point. "But I'm not a star, you know."

"Has he ridden over banks at all?" Lady Eveleen struck in; she looked very put out, and I felt that whatever the result of the race, she would crab my riding to hell. A sour old goose, I thought, rudely; and I was pleased when Sir Richard said :

"The children tell me he's very good."

"Still, he can't have much experience of riding

point-to-points in this country—he may be a champion over fences." Lady Eveleen was obstinately against my having the ride. "I'd like to *flay* that young Morgan for going schooling to-day." She was not far from angry tears.

"If it was young Billy Morgan you had riding the mare, I think you're very lucky to be out of him." Sir Richard stared at his cousins for a moment. "That's the boy-o would have done you dirt somehow. I wouldn't care to bet about your chances with Romance in the race to-morrow, but if you had any, that's the lad for a nice easy fall out in the country. No, give Oliver the ride. He's a good boy, mind you—so the children tell me. Where is this great race horse, Honour? How quiet you kept about her. I suppose it's that thing you had a boy out hunting on before Christmas, is it? I wouldn't like her, I must say."

"Well, really, if I'd known you were coming, Richard," Lady Honour's voice was a study in sweetness, "I'd have let her walk the twenty-five miles to the course to-morrow rather than miss your opinion of her, but as it is I'll have to wait till to-morrow to hear it, because, unfortunately, I put her on the nine o'clock train at Kilanna this morning. I hope she's at Tinahinch by now."

"With the Morgans? Honour, you're mad, I think. I think you're cracked. My dear girl, if Billy Morgan isn't riding her, he'll see to stopping her all right. A couple of buckets of water in the morning," said Sir Richard portentously, "will do the thing nicely."

"I have a good boy with her." But Lady Honour was not quite quick enough to hide the change that passed a little broken ripple over her face.

"What? Not your old Jerry Brophy?"

"No, a young lad, a right boy. Indeed, if Oliver wasn't riding I might put him up."

"Well, whatever else you do, you can't do that." Lady Eveleen gabbled angrily.

"Why not?"

"When he's ridden under rules?"

I wondered if Sir Richard saw the look that blazed for an instant only between the two ladies. The look that said on one side: "I'm a fool!"; and on the other: "No, but a d—— fool!" I don't think he did, and it puzzled me exceedingly. He climbed slowly into the car and sat there behind the wheel, an amiable and sly old falcon, his elbows so spread upon it.

"He may bring a bag with his things to the races, anyhow, Honour?" he asked. It seemed he was not going to let her off that offer of a ride to me.

"Oh, he may come dressed to ride." Lady Honour flirted her head away from her sister like an angry little bird. She laid her hardy scraps of hands on the half-open window of the car, and looked in on us sweetly. "He'll ride the mare.

It's the third race," she said to me, " will you meet me at the entrance to the saddling enclosure before the horses go out for the second race ? "

" I'll be there," said I, and seldom have I trysted more warmly or gaily.

" Well, good-bye, Honour. I'm sorry we couldn't deal. Good-bye, Beauty. Clear your dogs out from under the car like a good girl ; thank you. And Honour——" Sir Richard had the car in gear now, " Put a dash of a blister on that bump above her fetlock—it's as big as a box——" He let in his clutch and was off before she could do more than shake her doubled fists at us and laugh.

Before the first bend in the avenue hid them from our sight I looked back and saw them standing there, Lady Honour and Lady Beauty, at their castle door. Lady Beauty protested—I saw her hands. Lady Honour explained, exclaimed, was patient, was furious ; I saw her foot—lifted and stamped. She whirled round from her stupid sister and whipped in at the castle door. But Lady Beauty stood on the steps still ; I saw her there as Sir Richard turned a corner that seemed to last for ever, so unbalanced was his steering. " Poor old Beauty," he said as we drove out of the gates, and he laughed inconsequently. Afterwards he said : " B'God, you *are* like your father." And laughed again.

At the bridge where the five roads met I looked for the forge which the fairy Duke chose for his horse's shoeing, and there it was, little and hunched below the road. Not much custom, I thought, went there now. An elder tree grew stoutly from the centre of the quartered wheel stone ; there was neither glow nor smoke, nor the rough smell of horny hoof ; a pile of rusted horse shoes forged long and long ago, were grown over now by nettles tall and grey. I thought of the hunters that had been shod there, and the race horses, and the carriage horses ; and I thought of those silver shoes that had worn thin as paper.

Sir Richard was strangely silent for the first mile or so of our homeward way ; his mind was back, I thought, in the lively past, and indeed I thought so rightly, for he looked at me and said suddenly from his silence :

" D'ye know, Oliver, when I think back now over all the dear hunts I've seen, and all the dear girls I've loved, and all the good horses I've bought cheap, d'ye know, I can't regret one year of my life. Well, I'm sixty-five years of age and—B'God, sir, will you keep your own side of the road, sir, will you sir, please sir. Do you think the whole road is made for you, do you ? Do you ? "

That the road was, in point of fact, wide enough for both cars was lucky ; but the battered old Ford that had turned a corner so untimely to interrupt Sir Richard's reminiscence, had definitely the worst of the encounter. That her near wing, crushed against the left bank of the road in her avoidance

of our car, should be her only casualty, was a matter
for congratulation. The congratulation did not,
however, come from Sir Richard. He drove on,
leaving the two men who were in the car to extricate
it as best they could from the ditch. As one of
them had an arm in a sling I thought it strange of
him to ignore my suggestion that we should help
them.

" Many's the one that laddo has slipped into
a ditch in his day, *and will again*. He cut the nose
off Willow at Coolbawn last year. Yes, landing over
the double, but she came up on the inside, he couldn't
stop her, and she walloped him. Ah, and he was
riding a horse he thought would beat the Lord
himself if he came down——" Sir Richard slewed
his head to me suddenly. " You didn't know either
of those fellows in the car, of course. Well, the
wounded hero was Billy Morgan who should
have ridden her ladyship's mare to-morrow, and
I'll put a name to the other fellow in a minute.
I've seen him before, I know ; wait, now——"

We drove a further mile in silence while I sat
enchanting myself with thoughts of that smallest
castle and its ladies ; of the silver shoes worn thin
and smooth as paper ; of the painted china door-
plate and handle in that room where we had tea ;
of young horses wrought about in splendour and
promise, and of the mist that must rise from the
river and lie at night about the castle. But now,
as we drove along, the bitter dreaming of turf

smoke was blown sometimes about us, and fawn-coloured goats stared wall-eyed as they pursued their lean activities upon the roadside banks. The gorse burnt with a sullen flame in the evening, for the sun had gone down quietly and not in splendour. There was, in fact, a cold feeling of rain in the air, an uncertain presage.

" I have it now," said Sir Richard suddenly. " Woa-o, boy—terrible hold some of these cars take. It'll make us late for dinner, Oliver, but I'm going down this way to Myross Station."

He laughed once on the way, and once he said, " That's one's as cute as a pet fox," but he did not enlighten me further as to the reason for his sudden departure from the road home.

At Myross Station he climbed laboriously out of the car, cursing his sciatica, but firmly intent on prosecuting his own inquiries (whatever they might concern) within the station. I was about to get out of the car, too, but he looked at me firmly and said : " Stop where you are, Oliver. I don't like the look of some of these fellows about here." As the station yard was at the moment empty of any human occupation, I took the hint and did not offer to accompany him.

I had not sat there many minutes before Life was manifest about me. It was, I think, the hour of the evening train from Dublin, and such an arrival created a suitable stir about the station. Another of the immortal breed of Ford car, which, in Ireland, survive through changing fashion to priceless tried antiquity, drew up beside me with a rattling of her life's breath ; was turned and stopped with a stilted precision and dignity that her younger sisters will never know, and died under her driver's hand in an obedient throaty gasp. The driver, aged I should have said not more than thirteen years, dismounted from those heights whence he controlled her, and leaned against the door in arrogant ownership. Presently he was joined by a porter, a clerkly young gentleman, and a very old man with a cough and a large hole in the knee of his trousers.

" Eh, Jimmy," said the old man, " did ye dhrive that motor up to Dublin a-Tuesday? Did ye, eh ? "

" I did," said the mechanical child (and now I thought his arrogance pardonable). " A man should be very hardy," he continued, " to dhrive through Dublin thraffic. He wouldn't want to be foolish-going at all."

" Well," the clerkly young man had a superior and jaunty way with him, " if that car o' yours met a thram-car—it was gone."

" If the biggest car in the world met a thram-car—where was it ? " The child's retort was un-delayed and delivered at speed and with an apprais-ing eye divided between his companions and Sir Richard's Bentley. " See here," he went on in fluid narration, "there's three owned this old yoke before ever I had her. There's Doyles and Redmonds and Whelans owned her, and I tell you they have her going the roads hither and over this eight year. 'Twas Whelan should leave her above on the crown of the Crosses Hill, and she went lashin' off with him one night. A-ha ! And so——"

" Was that the night——"

" And so of course he went to take the clutch out, and she should go twice faster then, of course." The mechanical child completed his story undeterred by interruption. The old man's laugh finished in a fit of unpleasant coughing, which he seemed rather to enjoy than otherwise.

" Was that the night," he prosecuted his inquiry, " Whelan left the crowd above in the public house, and the only one he took in the wind up was Mrs. Connol ? "

But much as I would have given to hear what had befallen on such a night, I was never to know, for Sir Richard came out of the station at that moment and disposed himself in the car once more.

" Home now," Sir Richard said, " and we should hurry." He was very thoughtful. The gates of Pullinstown were shadowy in the evening as we waited there, blowing our horn for one to come out of the dark lodge and open them to us.

" Look here, Oliver," he said as we waited, " you needn't say anything to young Dick about

our going to Myross ; no, nor to Willow either.
Those are two right young divils for minding other
people's business. What the blazes were you at,
Mrs. Pheelan, that you couldn't come out to the
gate a bit quicker ? I'm here ten minutes very
nearly, wasting electricity blowing for you. It's a
right puzzle," he continued, as we drove up the
avenue, " to know who to put in a gate lodge.
Breeding long families is all they're good for.
Look at the hare—ah, if I had my old bitch, Truthful, here, she's the one would hunt that fellow."

But I thought, as the hare loped out across the
avenue before us, of the saying about a hare bring-
ing bad luck to the driver of whatever vehicle it
may cross in its path, and I looked at Sir Richard,
and wondered very much if this was a saying worthy
to be believed.

"You've walked the course, I suppose," Lady Honour asked me, and I nodded. Indeed, Dick and I had but just completed the three miles in time for me to meet her in the throng that seethed (quite irrespective of owner or jockeyship) in the saddling enclosure before the horses went out for the second race.

We had been late in starting from Pullinstown that morning. James, who was staying behind to minister to the wants of a bedridden and sulking Willow, had not, I think, quite put the spur on his underlings in the matter of lunch, or at any rate not to the extent he would have done had he himself been in a fever to see the start of the first race on the card.

"Ah, what matter the first race," he said in answer to Dick's protests, "that confined race is no race. And for walking the course, Master Dick, that'll hardly delay ye any length, for it's a course needs very little improvement."

I was still pondering on the true inwardness of this statement when the car, mercifully driven by Dick, got under way. We had not, however, proceeded very far down the avenue before our attention was attracted by a rook-like squawking from James and steam-whistle yells from a young member of Pullinstown's domestic staff, who at the same time pursued the car at a pace that did equal credit to her legs and lungs.

Dick reversed impatiently to meet her, wondering volubly as he did so what dire necessity of the day James had forgotten to pack into the car.

"A limon, Master Dick," she breathed in his ear, thrusting her empurpled face in at the window, "would ye bring a limon from the town, if ye please, and a couple o' round o' Reckett's Blue; and would ye leave the bets in with Miss Doyle." She handed several mysterious little packages through the window.

"If Bridgie Hogan," said Dick swiftly, "hadn't broken down the bicycle with the weight she is from taking no exercise, I'd say she could ride it into the town herself for her lemons and put on her own bets. As it is, she can go in on Shank's mare and out again. You may tell her that from me."

"Oh great and merciful God——" The young messenger clapped a hand to her mouth and subsided in giggles, so we drove on and left her.

"Those divils," Sir Richard observed negligently; "how much work will they do to-day, I wonder."

"Drinking tea and passing rude remarks with the stable boys," Dick commented. "By the way, father, did ye tell Johnny to put that blister on Goldenrod?"

" I did, I think. I think I did. I wonder, Dick, would it have been wiser to have had him fired ? "

" I wonder, would it ? " Dick was never very committal with his father, I had noticed.

" I have had nothing but worry with that horse since he came into the place," Sir Richard pondered grievously. " I was really *hurt* when Lady Duncannon sent him back to me. You know she's a suspicious sort of woman—*very*. She wouldn't believe my word it was only splints he was lame on—all the same I'll never buy a horse again that's back of his knees, they always go on their tendons. Mrs. Pheelan is out pretty smart to open the gate this morning, I notice. I think she kept Oliver and me waiting half an hour last night."

" I suppose she thought you and Oliver were stopping out the night at Templeshambo—I know we did." Dick shot a look at his father in which was as much censure as he dared combine with raillery.

" Ah," said Sir Richard, " we walked the soles off our boots looking for those young horses of your cousin Honour's. They might be anywhere in that place."

" So they might. It's a great range for young horses. I hear she has a very nice two-year-old—out of the old mare. Is that true, father ? "

" She has a very nice foal there, and not a bad

sort of a yearling at all. I didn't think much of the two-year-old—she's a leggy divil, but, of course, the old ladies are cracked about her."

" Out of their minds, I suppose." Dick let the subject drop. He had no more curiosity in it. At this, indeed, I did not wonder, for I had myself unfolded to him and Willow every circumstance of our doings at Templeshambo, not omitting Sir Richard's secret visit to Myross Station.

" I don't know what he's at," Willow had commented. " He has me puzzled." And neither could Dick throw any light on Sir Richard's perplexing behaviour. " It might be nothing at all," Willow had said, " or it might be *a bit of a plan* " ; and there was as much dark secrecy in the way she said this as to fill my mind with a hundred suppositions of possible roguery.

But to-day I could not think why anything should be wrong. I was glad to be having a ride round, and very glad that the ride should be Lady Honour's horse. Unlikely, I knew, that I would beat Dick on Romance, even though he was giving me a lot of weight. Still, they say Dick is worth a stone to any horse he rides. There were other good things in the race besides Romance, for this was the end of the point-to-pointing season, which meant a fairly hot class of horses in an open light-weight race. The possible stars that had crowded the fields earlier in the season had now waned in their owners' estimation. They ran them no longer. Lady

Honour being, I suppose, an exception to this, as
to most other rules.

"Tootle around and enjoy yourself," had been
Willow's parting advice to me. "Try not to take
a fall, because falls hurt. Barring accidents, Dick
should win it, though I'm a bit frightened of that
horse of old Colonel Power's. I think he'd have
beaten me at Lisgarry if he hadn't fallen, and he's
receiving 7 lb. from us to-day."

"Ah, he'll tip up again——" Dick had been
optimistic.

"Well, if he doesn't, Dick? It rained a lot
last night and the going will be deep. Romance
isn't too fond of the mud, and the 7 lb. might just
beat her. D'you remember that awful day at
Kylemore? Ah, that race went *through* the mare;
absolutely went *through* her." Her voice was frail
and vibrant at this suffering memory.

"I don't know. I'd be more afraid of something
unknown in the field, such as Oliver's ride, for
instance. D'you know, I think I'm giving him
21 lb.—it's a divil of a penalty."

"That, my dear? A four-year-old and I never
liked her lack of guts. She was a good lepper,
though, for a young horse. All Honour's horses
lep like dogs. She has them following her round
the country on strings like dogs—that's why. Well,
I hope you enjoy yourself, Oliver, and collect all
the chat for me," Willow had said.

And we had walked the course, Dick and I—

three miles over a very fair country it was. Banks with ditches mostly to you, a few stone walls, and not a twisty course either. "All the same, mind you, this course walks a lot nicer than it rides, I always think," Dick told me. "I don't know what it is about these banks. They'd all meet you right if you were going the other way round. As it is there's always a lot of clouting and falling here."

In the shelter of a gorse-blown bank we lit our cigarettes, the loud, small flutter of a white flag in our ears. Far and away blue shadows were painted wet and heavy on the mountains, and nearer fields of young oats were square-cut tour-malines in the flowing bright air—thickened to honey and burdened by almonds this loving air. But beyond any loving, far and unto itself, the little flame of a lark's song burned against the sky.

Dick took a walk out across the field and came back to me. "I wonder how much ground you'd save if you did that," he said, and stood considering the matter, his head sunk, his hands in his breeches pockets. "You could jump the wall there instead of the bank, and not miss a flag at all. I do think that'd be the shortest course to go, Oliver. We'd better go back to the car and eat a sandwich now, I suppose. And you have to meet your owner." He grinned unkindly : "I'd rather ride for the devil himself," said he, "than ride a horse for Cousin Honour."

But I found her still enchanting. When we had struggled out of the throng in the enclosure and through the mob that surged about the bookies' stand, she went straight as a bird to the spot where her car was parked, and this was a position which had (in addition to being not too far away from the weighing tent) the advantages of combining an excellent view of the course and an easy exit from the car park ; this she told me on our way thither. "And," she said, unfolding her shooting stick, spearing it into the ground and seating her person thereon immediately before the dirtiest and most demure of the old, blunt-nosed Morris cars, " Let me introduce you, Oliver, to Mr. Billy Morgan ; Captain Pulleyns—Mr. Morgan."

" Very pleased to meet you," a preposterously good-looking young man shook me by the hand. He gave me his left hand because his right arm was in a sling, and he gave me three parts of a glance out of his navy-blue eyes that surprised me. He was tall, Mr. Morgan. Yes, and dark, and handsome. Only his legs were vulgar, although he had taken some pains about them, for his brown field boots were by an excellent maker. His voice, too, was as preposterous as his looks, and there hung about it the same rich comeliness. My cousins, Dick and Willow, frequently speak in a strange brogue, and indeed express their meaning more coarsely than did this young man ; nevertheless their voices cannot be compared. Theirs never lack a certain quality. His never attained that certain quality.

"What bad luck about your collar bone," I said.

"Wasn't it—rotten! Lady Honour's very cross with me," there was a certain charm about him, "and Lady Eveleen won't speak to me at all."

It was only now that I perceived Lady Eveleen seated in the car—on the seat beside her was a vast blue roll of cotton wool, neatly rolled white bandages, a saddle and a weight cloth. She looked as important as any priestess at any other altar.

"Good-morning," I said, taking off my hat. "Good-morning," said she, and that was all. I could not help disliking her still evident displeasure in the prospect of my riding. After all, how did she know I would not give the horse a real good ride. Lady Honour, though very sweet, was a little strained, perhaps a little silent. I wondered if they could really be having a good bet on their horse, but thought it unlikely. Mr. Morgan only was happy, confident and friendly. He stood upon the step of the car, his glasses to his eyes, and kept up a running commentary on the horses going down to the start.

"God, that's a common divil of Hanlon's. Do you like that mare of Johnny Kehoe's, Lady Honour? You know she's bred fit to win races. I like the way she goes, too—near the ground and doesn't take too much out of herself. She should stay. Look at young O'Brien now, having a preliminary. What's that—black and a cerise cap—a chestnut horse. Is it Bonny Judy? They're all down there now, I think; twelve starters, that's not a bad field at all to go out in a Farmer's race. Johnny Kehoe can't get a pull on that mare; look at her shaking her head, she'll gallop into the bog-hole if he doesn't watch himself—that's a shocking soft bog there on your left, mind, as you go down to the start. Keep in beside the fence—— They're off—they're not; false start. God, he could have let them go, this isn't five furlongs. Now they're off—there's some wicked riding the first mile in this race, I tell you. That thing of Johnny Kehoe's is jumping very ignorant—Johnny went out between her two ears. I thought he'd never meet the saddle again. Wait now, this is a straight one they're coming to. A horse very rarely meets it really right. I think there's not a big enough ditch to you for the height of it. They get under it somehow. Furlong's down! Well, the *welt* he hit it. Bonny Judy's down and there's another down. I can't see who it is. Johnny Kehoe's taking them a good gallop. He may quieten himself now—this is a real soft field and so is the next. That thing of Hartigan's is going very easily—he's jumping well; I wouldn't wonder if he beat Johnny."

"What's leading, Major?" An incredibly old

man, balancing on the fence beside the car, grasped
my hand to pull me up beside him.

" I'll tell you in a minute." I had found them
again now. " Kehoe's horse is leading still ; Vain
Lady second ; and a chestnut horse third."

" A chaisnut horse ? Is it Tommy Hartigan is on
him ? "

" I couldn't tell you."

" It must be them spy-glasses is no great good so.
God knows ye'd nearly see that much with the
sight o' yer eyes."

I ventured after this to read the race aloud no
more, and indeed the horses were but four fences
from home, so we could see them plainly. The
chestnut horse had gone up to the leaders now,
and something of a contest was in progress.

" Come on, Hartigan ! *Come* on, Hartigan ! "
The old man clung to me for his balance, and we
swayed together on the bank in an ecstasy of excitement. " Aha ! Aha ! He have John Kehoe
bestered. Look at he sweepin' home. *God, he's
off*——" as the chestnut horse, in landing over the
last fence, made a bad mistake and a grand
recovery. " He's off ! He's not ! He's not,
b'god ! Only for he to be so great a jock and so
constant he was gone——"

Tears streaming from his eyes, and the wind
blowing his long hair and beard upwards and backwards, this ancient votary of sport clasped both my
hands and would for very little, I think, have kissed

me as a salute to speed and young courage, and to
the emotion of dangerous endeavour.

"Bedam, he was as wise as a dog," he said,
"I'd have to cry to see the poor bastard so cour-
ageous. 'Tis for a passion o' love I'd cry, or for the
like of a horse race I'd rain tears from me two eyes.
Did ye remark the way Hartigan did was to foster
Johnny Kehoe always. Did ye go nigh him at all
till he come to win his race? He did not. Did
he ever let him more than a couple o' perches
out before him? He did not. Ah, Johnny Kehoe
puts great conceit out of himself to be a real up-to-
date jock, but—be the Holy Seaman—young
Hartigan have him bewitched, bothered and
bewildered." He whipped round on a dreary
young friend who up to the moment had simmered
unnoticed beside him, and recommenced his mas-
terly analysis of the race. But the time now being
more than come when I should struggle again towards the weighing tent I picked up saddle and
weight cloth and accompanied by Lady Honour
(her hand-bag full of spare lead), regretfully parted
from my old companion.

"See here, Oliver," said she to me as we clove
our way through a party of young girls who had
chosen the only gap in the fence as a suitable spot
in which to drink pink lemonade and sport with
their loves. "Don't pay *any* attention to *any*thing
Beauty says to you about riding the mare." I
looked down to see two deep triangles of carnation

in her cheeks, and tears, I think, excited her eyes. " I don't like to say any one is a fool," said she, and the tears snapped back from her eyes, " but I think poor Beauty's *dull*."

" She's not far out in thinking me a very inexperienced jockey over banks," I put in guardedly.

" My dear boy," Lady Honour was indeed in earnest, " provided you don't actually fall off the mare the race is a gift to us. The mare's fit, she won't fall down and she has the legs of the lot of them ; what more do you want ? "

After which encomium of confidence I felt that any blame for defeat would more than certainly be laid at my door, which, since my mount was a four-year-old and this her first time out, I felt would be manifestly unfair. In fact, Lady Honour's unbridled expression of confidence in her horse depressed rather than cheered me. Almost I found myself at one with Lady Eveleen in wishing Mr. Billy Morgan and not myself had the honour of the ride.

But that was before I had seen Surprise, for such was the name of Lady Honour Dermot's brown mare, four years old, to whom almost every other horse in the field of ten was giving a stone and some so much as 21 lb. I think only two of the entries on the card were at level weights with us, and I knew one of these did not run. In my opinion Surprise looked like giving weight and a beating to any horse in the race, although as a four-year-old she was so justly entitled to receive both. That she was indeed, but four off I found it difficult to believe, such muscle and such condition are not often carried by a young horse. I have seldom seen anything fitter run in a point-to-point, or look more like winning one.

Lady Honour and Lady Eveleen quarrelled outrageously over the saddling of their horse, a task with which Mr. Billy Morgan and an astute-looking lad in a purple coat and trousers proceeded undeterred by the commands and suggestions of either lady.

"Put a pad under the saddle," Lady Eveleen insisted. "Can't any fool see it will cut the withers out of the mare the way it's down on her back?"

"Do no such thing; leave the saddle the way it is. Take up that girth, Jim. Willy, you put those bandages on beautifully in spite of your arm. I never saw bandages better put on, even by you."

Mr. Morgan, very quick and certain in his way of saddling a horse, accepted the compliment in silence.

"All the same," Lady Eveleen was almost in tears, "I can't bear the mare to go out with the saddle like that on her."

"It's not down on her, Lady Eveleen. Really, it's not," Mr. Morgan found patience to tell her.

"Are you sure? Oh, did you *see* that poor horse that came in after the first race. Did you *see* its back?"

" No, but Beauty, did you see the jockey's boots ? "
Lady Honour included even the lad in her exasperated witticism, " they were oozing blood ! "

" Now get mounted, please. Get mounted,
please. Come on now, jockeys, get mounted,
please." An impatient steward made his first
effort to get the horses out of the saddling enclosure
and down to the start.

" *Oliver*," Lady Eveleen hissed in my ear, "you
go up to the front and stay there. You'll keep out
of trouble and interference."

" *Do no such thing*." Lady Honour's angrier
hiss overrode her sister's whisper in my other ear.
" Let young Dick make the pace. That mare of
his won't stay two miles in this going. Goodness
me, she's tied to the ground with that penalty on
her. Come away from him the last mile, and don't
go winning the race before that, mind."

All Mr. Morgan said, as the boy led my mount
out of the enclosure and clove for us a path through
the mob outside was : " You can fall and win the
race. So don't let her go from you if you do fall."
And with such instructions I set out on my lone
(lone at last) adventure.

" Thanks, thanks very much. *Would* you mind
letting us through ? We *rather* want to ride our
horses——" It was Dick in the crowd behind me ;
Dick sitting on top of a packet of lead and Romance
shaking her game little head and laying the ears
back at the crowd. And there were others ; the

lad with the ankle-length boots and spurs two inches long and his breeches worn over his stockings, riding a savage of a brown horse that had killed one man and frightened several so badly that they never wanted to ride again ; an M.F.H. with a face like one of his own dog hounds and a very pretty sort of hunting seat on a horse. An old man of a curious brave fragility. " Many happy returns, Colonel Power," Dick said to him. He told me afterwards that this was a sixty-fourth birthday party.

But we were out of the crowd now and riding our horses down a series of three small, bare fields, their grass eaten low by sheep and geese, and through a gap where a wall had been summarily knocked down to let us out into a lane and back into the country again through another gap of the same nature. The mare fidgeted and pulled me as we went, her head carried low, her back up under the saddle, she was, I have no doubt, switching her tail in a way that would have frightened me worse could I have seen it. As it was, I felt miserably nervous. A cold wind turned knifishly on my cheek and made fun of the jersey (royal blue and a yellow sash, Lady Honour's colours) which I wore. I was the strange victim of that unhappy lack of feeling, in which state one belongs neither to oneself nor to one's horse, but to a chill blankness in which habit and instinct take the place of reasoned action.

Dick, riding up beside me, looked as strained and as paper-thin and as anxious as he always does look when going out to ride a race ; keyed to the moment so that should one but gently touch him one might think he would thrum like a fiddle-string. He looked at me now and at the mare. " Oliver," he said, " I'd say you'd beat me if you stand up. I never saw anything come on like that mare. I don't know her at all." He looked puzzled for a moment instead of strained. It was then, I think, that my feeling of blankness and nerves fell from me. I was warm again and knew what I was about. I felt the mare's mouth and sat forward to canter down to the start, and it was when she felt me take hold of her that she jumped off after a fashion which might have told a sillier man even than I am that she had been ridden in work at least. I wondered ; and I dropped my hands to her, and she stopped like an old chaser who has had plenty of it might do. And then I think, had I been wise, was the moment for me to decide on a soft fall out in the country or such palpable missing of a flag as could not but be ob-jected to. But I am seldom wise though often lucky. Besides I had felt the mare's low, powerful stride, and the strange lust that comes on men to ride a race was on me now. Which is an emotional way of stating that when the starter let us go I was quite as mad to win my race as though no feelings of doubt had ever plucked at my reason as to whether or no my horse was qualified to run at all, much less to win.

This course doesn't ride as nice as it walks, Dick had said. Neither, he had said, did the fences meet you kindly. But if the fences did not meet us right, we met them so well that I would not have faulted them in any respect.

Never shall I describe my ride on Surprise that day. I may say that in the matter of riding to instructions I obeyed Lady Eveleen's to the letter, for after we had jumped the first fence blinded, and saved a fall how I knew not—I thought there was something in keeping out of trouble, and sent the mare on with the first three. Before we had gone a mile I knew without any doubt that I had the legs of the lot of them and a couple of stone in hand. The course rode heavy enough, and a field of plough followed by two with pretty deep going, brought Dick and Romance back to us all right. It was then that I sent Surprise into the lead, for, I thought, Dick won't want to lose me altogether, and the going and the weight between them will beat him here. Four banks in a nice straight line from us, the last one jumped on the down-hill and I went on at them. Dick stuck to me ; I think he was right, for he knew now my mount was unlikely to tip up, and he could see she was going very easily ; it would be difficult for him to make up ground later. The course turned pretty sharp left after the fourth of these nice banks, and Dick

as he landed in the field beyond fairly cut the nose
off me. "*There's* a rudeness," I said to him as his
sister Willow might have done, and terrified lest
no nicer considerations should prevent his either
pushing me off or tripping my horse up, I took a
frightened look over my shoulder and went away
from him like a scalded cat. We were less than a
mile from home now, and I think Romance was
stone-cold. How Dick sat still on her and held her
together I do not know, but game and honest little
bit that she is, Romance was giving us more weight
than she could have done, even on top of the
ground. We won very easily. Dick was not going to
kill the mare when he saw he could not win. He
finished third. The gentleman who was celebrating
his sixty-fourth birthday second, and not a feather
out of him. He was very fit.

It was Lady Eveleen (surprisingly enough)
who detached herself from the crowd and beat her
sister by a short head only for the honour of leading
their horse in to unsaddle.

"My dear," she said, "you gave her a great
ride and I'm so *delighted* we've beaten Richard."
She was looking back at me and talking, her face
very gently radiant, not minding at all where she
was going or leading the horse. But I thought it
unkind of Lady Honour to snatch the rein from her
sister with a biting comment. But Lady Eveleen
refused to be shaken off, and so conducted by them
both I dismounted at last and departed with my

saddle towards the scales, while they alternately assisted the boy to scrape lather off the mare, and turned from their task to receive the congratulations of their friends.

Any man who wins a race, whether point-to-point, steeplechase, or on the flat is, for that brief moment, a hero and a good jockey. Let him be beaten by a better horse and a short head when riding the race of his life, and his stock is down at once. No one but can put a finger then on some gross error in judgment on his part and there are few among the commentators unconvinced that they (or almost any one, indeed) could have ridden the race better. To-day I was in the former and more enviable position, and enjoyed it to the full as I sat on the step of Lady Honour's car eating salmon sandwiches (Dick's salmon was all right in sandwiches, anyhow) with a whisky and soda, half a horn tumbler full of port and a rapidly cooling cup of coffee ranged on the grass beside me. The arrival of Mr. Billy Morgan interrupted the praises and the questions of my two owners, which I was enjoying almost as much as their food and drink.

"Well, didn't I tell you you'd enjoy yourself," he said to me by way, I suppose, of congratulation. "But isn't she a great mare? A different class from the ordinary point-to-point horse, isn't she? I think indeed it's a pity for Lady Honour to knock her about in point-to-points at all. That mare should be winning chases this minute."

"Will you have a bun, Mr. Morgan?" Lady Eveleen asked him, and her manner was more than repressive.

"Thank you, but I don't care about sweet cakes." Mr Morgan accepted a salmon sandwich and a cup of tea, and we all ate comfortably, our anxieties so happily over and the glow of success so close about us.

"Do you know anything, Lady Honour," Mr. Morgan inquired suddenly, "is good for the nerves?"

"Goodness knows you're not troubled with nerves, Billy," Lady Honour was both surprised and amused.

"Ah, no, not in regard o' horses I wouldn't be," Mr. Morgan reassured us. "But," he went on seriously, "when I'd be readin' a book—when I'd get to the excitin' part I'd have to t'row it down. I'd accuse it," he added thoughtfully, "on drinkin' tea." And swilling the dregs of his cup three times round he aimed them with great precision at the nearest gorse bush.

"Has the mare started for home?" Lady Honour asked, fitting the lid on to a sandwich box with quick dexterity.

"Yes. I sent the boy off with her at once." Mr. Morgan put his cup away in a basket and rose to his feet; whether or not he had seen Dick an

Sir Richard's approach, he took his departure
without undue delay.

"Well, Oliver, you brat, that was a noble victory,"
Dick smiled at me. "Wait till Willow hears you
defeated the mare—she'll tear you. I must con-
gratulate Cousin Honour," he said, and did so
with all politeness. Sir Richard, too, expressed
himself delighted that the race if not his should then
be hers. "Were you satisfied with Oliver's riding,
Beauty?" he asked Lady Eveleen, but did not
embarrass her by requiring an answer. "I'm
coming over to you to-morrow to look at that filly
again," he said to Lady Honour. "I must get
the car out now before the last race. Some of these
cars will be here to-morrow morning." He gathered
Dick and myself to him with a glance in which
appeal and authority balanced each other, and so
we left the ladies of Templeshambo. But before
we had gone Lady Eveleen caught awkwardly
at the elbow of my coat and "come to-morrow
with Richard, Oliver," she said. She was earnest
and without charm, but there was a steadfastness
behind her nervous face like a light beyond lantern-
glass. When Lady Honour laughed and told me
not to waste my time visiting two old women, I
said that I would like to come, but would not
trouble her since Lady Eveleen had promised to
look after me.

"You'll have Honour and Beauty at one another's
throats," Sir Richard said to me a little later as

we seated ourselves in the car and proceeded to repulse the army of mendicant guardians of its safety who swarmed for alms about our departure.

" 'Twas I minded the car, sir——"

" No, 'twas I, yer honour—any looked near it I belted hell out o' them, and the young lad of a son I have pasted them also."

I gave the young lad two shillings. Sir Richard disposed himself in the car beside Dick. " Be off, now, the lot of you."

" Sure, that's not my son, your honour—the lad with the locks is my son." But Sir Richard wound up his window, immovable to further petition.

In the back of the car I turned up the collar of my coat, an even simplicity of delight about me, the limber glow that succeeds striven effort, the level mind that follows on success were mine. I lit two cigarettes, one for Dick and one for myself, and handed him his when we had lurched, our engine racing, out of the field and down the rutted lane towards the main road.

" Thank you, Oliver." Dick leaned forward to set the windscreen wiper working, for a shower of rain lashed bitterly towards us from the mountains. The day was turned suddenly to indigo and silver, darkly changing behind the sloped spears of rain. I thought of the fire in Willow's room where Dick and I would sit making toast and telling of our doings. I thought of little rivers rushing low and dark beneath blackthorns and hazel, and the hewn wings of a gull brought a pale greyhound bitch to my mind, I had called her Sally. But Dick was talking:

"Twenty-one pounds was a cruel penalty to put on that little mare. She was tied to the floor. I couldn't stop you coming up on the inside, could I, Oliver? Ah, she was stone-cold going up the hill. I knew I couldn't do it, so I thought I'd finish without a fall. Would I have done it if we'd been on top of the ground, Father. I wouldn't?"

"You would not," said Sir Richard suddenly. "You did what five steeplechase jockeys out of ten can't do, and nine point-to-point jockeys out of ten can't do—you sat still on her and you kept hold of her head. And I'll tell you another thing, Dick, you wouldn't have beaten Oliver to-day at level weights either."

"What? And that mare only four years old—well, five now. Oh, Sir Richard!"

"Four years old?" said Sir Richard. "A four year old? *She is?*"

"What d'you mean, father?" Dick asked him, but he would not tell us, switching into another topic with the disconcerting independence of mind that was particularly his own.

"That lad," he said, "that Honour had with the mare—do you know where I saw him last? In Tommy Redmond's stables. And as tough a place as Tommy's is—they didn't keep that beauty long in it."

" Who is Tommy Redmond ? " I asked.

" Tommy ? Oh, he trains horses. He's a sort of relation of Honour's and Beauty's. Well, in a kind of a way, he's one of the old Lords. And a horrible fellow. There's no villainy or trickery or roguery he's not up to it and he runs his horses about as straight as a ram's horn."

" Oh," I said, and a lonely blankness settled now on my spirit. Coldly and slowly the pieces of a difficult and sorry business fitted into their places in my mind. The memory of my ride was distant from me now, apart from its heat and effort it would seem to have been but a nasty ramp. But I had not known. How could I even now be sure ? I must wait and see what would follow. There was no cohesion in this villainy. Any key there might be to the matter was in Sir Richard's canny grasp. Somehow I felt that there would be suffering yet over this, and it was not Honour who would suffer most for it but that poor Beauty, poor stricken goose.

And the weight of this doubt stayed with me heavily, disallowing Willow's generous congratulations and Dick's assurances that the Sir was never without a bee in his bonnet over any horse that was good enough to beat one of his own. I would have liked, I think, to talk the matter over with James, but since the neuralgia he said was stitching in and out through his poll like the devil's needle, I could not think the evening opportune for the discussion of my own trivial affairs.

The afternoon of the following day a strangely solemn and silent Sir Richard drove me over to Templeshambo. Sometimes, as we drove, I saw his lips move, and I knew he was rehearsing to himself the speeches of his set part in whatever piece this was which presently he would stage. I wondered how my own part was cast and I felt, indeed, a soured and unwilling puppet. The more so when I saw the airy nonchalance of manner which could not quite disguise the shifting anxiety in Lady Honour's eyes as she greeted us.

" To see you three days running, Richard, it makes us feel quite young and silly," Lady Honour was naughty, not sentimental, " and *Oliver*, my dear, Beauty will be mad with excitement "—here was malice.

She went on before us down the long narrow dark hall, her little head poised back, her narrow shoulder blades knife-sharp under her coat. She had a peculiar way of walking, sliding her feet very evenly past each other like a little fox. When she turned her head to smile round at us, I thought I saw again in her the vixen and forgot how yesterday her bird-like charm had ravished me.

" We are sitting in here to-day," she said, opening a door at the end of the hall, " because one of Beauty's puppies has the yellows and as she insisted on lighting a fire for it I thought we might as well have the good of it too."

" Well, after your win yesterday," Sir Richard

said swiftly, " I should think you might light fires all over the house and hang the expense, eh, Honour ? "

" Indeed, if we had only backed the mare we were right," Lady Honour answered regretfully. " But poor Beauty has no courage. She wouldn't let me do it. Well, I suppose she was right, really. What did we know about the mare except that she could lep and we *thought* she could gallop ? But a four-year-old and running in such good company— wouldn't we have been very silly, Richard ? Don't you think so ? We would have been, wouldn't we ? "

" Well," said Sir Richard, with undue weightiness, " circumstances, of course, alter cases." He sat himself down on a minor inquisition in the shape of a sofa and added, " My dear Honour." I sat down on a chair near the sick puppy's basket, wishing very much that I might be bidden to take myself off for a little walk in the garden, rain it never so hard ; failing this I could only look about the room and pretend I was not there. And such a room, as different as it could be from that room of fragile adventure where yesterday we had drunk our tea in the glamour of a Perhaps that Never Was. Here was Time Past ; and rightly so, I thought, my mind petrifying in its contemplation of case upon glass case of stuffed birds, gulls of every variety, their beauty betrayed forever to clumsiness ; hawks primly hovering, jays and mag- pies perched for ever ; two white owls, in all the

sulkiness of their unspread wings, squinted forbiddingly down their crooked parrot beaks. A
stuffed fox was curled woodenly in a chair, and a
badger lay for a footstool beneath a distant writing-
table—his back was worn nearly bare by the feet
that had rested on it so often. And there was (this
startled me) a little monkey stuffed, and for more
ghastly realism chained to the corner of a book-case.
The curtains in the high windows and all the chair
covers were dark red and every inch of woodwork
had been painted dark brown. The rain lashed
forbiddingly against the windows and the sick
puppy rose waveringly from its basket. I wished
very much that Lady Eveleen would come in.

"And so you see, Richard," Lady Honour was
saying, "as the filly's really as much Beauty's as
mine, I have very little say in the matter. And you
know Beauty is wickedly obstinate."

"I see. And I suppose Tommy Redmond has a
share in her too?"

"What do you mean?" Poor sorry little fox!
A thin, frightened shadow passed, it seemed, right
through her. Now she was indeed beset.

"Well, the fact is, Honour," Sir Richard said,
"there's been a certain amount of talk about the
running of your mare yesterday, which puts me in
a very difficult position as a steward, because I
happen to know what I would a lot rather I didn't
know, and that is, the mare is not yours at all but
Tommy Redmond's, and what's more, she's a

winner under rules, and she's unqualified to run at any point-to-point meeting."

"And may one ask how you came to that interesting conclusion?" Lady Honour was game.

"Well, there *are* such things as consignments of the boxing of horses to be seen at railway stations, if a person has the wit to go and look for them, eh, Honour? That was a silly mistake you made, you know. She should have gone in your name from Killanna Station instead of being booked in Tommy's from Myross. It was only six miles farther to walk her to Killanna, that's where you should have ordered the box. No, if there is any fuss about it, I'm afraid——"

"If there is any fuss about it, the best thing *you* could do, Richard, would be to keep your mouth shut." Such complete and sudden acceptance of the matter on Lady Honour's part fairly surprised me, nor was I less taken aback by Sir Richard's answer.

"Now, Honour, if there is any inquiry, I don't see how I can help saying what I know. Some one might know I knew it, you never can tell."

"You can't do that, Richard—a nice mess you'd get Oliver into. However satisfactory the explanation of his part of the business is, you know yourself that any one mixed up with Tommy must put up with the reputation of being fairly hot."

"Too hot to touch." Sir Richard looked over at me sourly. I could feel that in his imagination he already saw me in the part of a willing accomplice to the ramp. " What a lucky thing for you Billy Morgan laid himself up," he said. " It looked a lot better for Oliver to have the ride. I suppose you thought I'd keep quiet about it all rather than see him in a scrape. B'God, Honour, you very nearly brought the thing off nicely. I'm sorry about Oliver ; I wish now I'd never allowed you to give him the ride. I encouraged the idea in my inno- cence." He looked sadly from one to the other of us. " Poor Beauty," he said, " will be very upset," and as he said it I saw her going past the windows in a mackintosh, carrying a bucket of dogs' food and leaning towards its weight and into the rain.

" If you won't mind," I said, " I think I'll go out and help Lady Eveleen feed the dogs while you and Cousin Richard think of some way out of this difficulty. I really feel so shaken by all this——"

She was not with the dogs, Lady Eveleen, but I found her in the tower-foot room regulating the incubator. " I hope these eggs are all right," she said. " We forgot about them yesterday in our excitement over the point-to-point. I hope they'll be all right. Honour and I never seem to have any success with things like chickens. By the way, Oliver, I had a fiver on the mare for you yesterday." She said this so sadly as she pushed in a drawer of eggs that I wondered whether she knew what had brought Sir Richard here to-day. She would not look at me at all and then I saw why. She was crying, poor Beauty in distress—I saw her tears—they were helpless and foolish and how they grieved and shocked me I never can tell. Back and forth went her awkward hands over the tidy drawers of eggs. The light in the little room was almost none, the white sprouting of potatoes in a corner illuminated the darkness. Her pale, stooped neck another moony thing.

"What is it?" I was saying. I took her arm and sat her down on a dishevelled chair. I put my handkerchief in her hand, for hers, I observed, she had used to wipe tears from her eyes and from the eggs with indiscriminate carefulness for the latter's welfare.

"Honour and Richard are so *unkind*," she whimpered at last. "Honour is such a dreadful tease. She goes on and on and on, until—oh, *please* don't mind me, I'm a silly disgusting old woman to cry like this. It is very shameful."

"Why do they tease you?"

"Oh, for no reason—it's just my stupidity." She was incoherent; a cruel colour blazed down her long neck. And when I turned and saw Lady Honour laughing in the doorway and Sir Richard, blue and beaky in the rain behind her, I was almost staggered by the strength of my pity for my poor goose.

"Come in, Richard; come in out of the rain." Lady Honour would suckle him still to her with sweet, twisty ways, I thought. A turn in her voice and a light in her eye, alike they said, "Escape me, never!"

"See, Beauty," she addressed her poor sister, "Richard has bid me within twenty-five pounds of the price you put on the filly. Will you deal?"

"I will not," said Lady Eveleen. She was calm now and passionately determined. "I won't sell that mare for one penny less than I said I would."

Sir Richard from the doorway gave her a very dark look and said he: "Well, indeed, my dear Beauty, I came here to-day on a very different matter, but as Honour seemed anxious, and rightly so, to get out of the mare, I made her my outside bid for her, and neither will I go one penny beyond it."

"And what did you come for then?" Lady Eveleen held on to the seat of her chair and faced them both with the unanswerable gallantry of a goose at bay.

"Oh." Sir Richard jerked his head, the fine tilted bones of his face were drawn with sudden impressionistic beauty against the dreary light. "Honour has persuaded me to say no more about the matter I came for, and though I hate to tell a lie "—his hands on his stick before him crossed and knotted, Sir Richard appeared for the moment the very epitome of aristocratic impeccability—" though it really *hurts* me to tell a lie I think, b'God, it would put you all in a very uncomfortable position if I told the truth. And when I think of poor

Oliver. You know I loved his father"—here he
waited for a moment and I could feel that indeed
he spoke the truth, without a doubt he had loved
my father, and while that love would never straiten
him in any present convenient betrayal, nevertheless
it was a truthful emotion—" and more for his sake
than any of your sakes I've agreed to keep quiet
about this matter, do you see, Beauty?"

"*Well*, Beauty?" Lady Honour's voice slipped
exasperatedly into the silence that fell when Sir
Richard, having said his say, waited for some answer.

But Beauty made no answer. Her pale un-
focused eyes sought blindly from one to the other
of them. One saw her mind groping helpless in
its stupidity for some telling weapon wherewith to
strike at them, and finding none, I feared she would
weep again. I was angry because they had made
of me and of her sad memory of my father a twice-
knotted stick with which to beat her to submission,
angry and ashamed for their unkindness.

"I leave it entirely to you, Honour," she said at
last, "whatever you think best——" She gave us
all a queer, stricken look, grotesque in its youthful-
ness, and slipped out into the rain to feed her dogs.

"I'm too kindhearted," Sir Richard said, as
down the avenue to Pullinstown young horses
advanced swooping and stopping, upon us. "That's
the worst of me. You know, Oliver, I should *never*
have bought that mare from the old ladies. This

place is rotten with horses as it is. And I'm not really fond of the mare, you know. There are several things I don't like about her."

" Then why did you buy her, Cousin Richard ? " I asked curiously.

" Ah well, it's not a bad thing for Honour to have a good fright now and again. That was a shocking thing she did, you know—running that mare yesterday. I must say I was surprised at her. And she thought she had me nicely cornered if she gave you the ride ; I couldn't say a word about anything then—she must think I have very little regard for the truth—that's what hurt me. That's what shocked me."

" Anyhow," I said, with the graven and crude condemnation of my age, " between you, you twisted poor Beauty's tail till you got the filly out of her for your own price."

" Oh, I gave Beauty her price in the end." Sir Richard's excellent manners entirely ignored my rather rude speech. " You see, I had a tenner on the mare when you won yesterday—I could afford to give her another twenty-five quid. But I gave Honour a good fright too." And he added, with almost sentimental satisfaction, " The prime little rogue ! "

STRANGER

THE month was June, and all sporting activities were far from my mind, very far indeed. I gathered lily of the valley in the walled kitchen garden of Pullinstown. Willow had brought me there to help her and left me there to work alone. So while she ate radishes in a distant border I bent my back over the lilies' weedy bed, and groped in the steep icy dark between their leaves for those strong stems—my fingers stiff and wet, my cuff dripping through the monotonous pluck and quiet yielding as the stems came up from their roots again and again and many times again in this dark forest, where only my hands could see. And their scent on the cold, rain-cleared air—among all the birds' songs, one sang the sweetest and would be heard, so with this scent—so strong and pure. A branch of cherry blossom, its paper whiteness drowning in bright rain, is no less a stranger to the vulgarity of flower shops and sick women's rooms than is this scent in the chill garden.

Willow came down the straight greened path to join me. Now the sun struck yellow on the path and silver on her hair. She hiccuped—as full of radishes as a thrush of currants—and stooped to work beside me. She is an honest and quick worker, and soon we have stripped the bed empty of flowers so that a hand brushed through the spatulate green discovered no further flowers.

The sun shone upon the garden for a brief and radiant interval. It had rained, and would rain again before long, but in the meantime there was warmth in the air and a light as iridescent over everything as the lining of a river mussel. We sat upon the edge of a water tank, Willow and I, and smoked our cigarettes in silence. For a little while we sat there, and then Willow said :

" And what do you think of Dick's young girl-friend ? "

" I've hardly seen her, have I ? Only at luncheon to-day. I thought she was your girl-friend, Willow ? " I was cautious in comment or inquiry.

" Well, I was the fool that brought her here, no doubt "—Willow quenched the end of her cigarette viciously on the path—" but Dick," said she, and here was venom, " is the fool who keeps her here. And the Sir—he's mad about her too. Yes, and James—oh, they all think she's a lovely girl."

" So she is, Willow. *Lovely*." That much was undeniable.

" Yes, and dam' dull. *Deadly*."

" Is she, Willow—dull ? "

" Oh, *yes* ; she always does everything with every one. Fishing with Dick and walking round the horses with Sir Richard—till she must be nearly growing a horse's tail out of her own body—and driving James to the town in her car. When she hears you're an artist, Oliver, she'll want to go sitting in the spring ditches to paint the mountain scenery with you."

I rather liked the girl; but how to make her tolerable to Willow? I hated her to dislike any one, for I remembered what I had suffered when I first came to Pullinstown. So: "Could you rob her? Is there any way you could rob her?" I suggested. Better the intricate process of a robbery than the distant lengths of Willow's dislike.

But, "No," said Willow, after a moment's further thought. "I wouldn't even rob her." After a silence she said drearily: "Dick's mad about her. He has the gramophone worn out playing it to her."

"Oh, you wouldn't mind Dick," said I, "he is but as a child. Nineteen? Twenty?"

"No, I wouldn't mind Dick," said she, "but you know, Oliver, I think what this girl wants is *love*. Not a doubt but she's in love." This statement Willow produced with an undeniable sad conviction which silenced me, and silent I remained, pondering on this new complexity in the relationships at Pullinstown, until the garden gate opened far down the straight central path, and Dick and the girl walked into our solitary retreat.

Down the long path they came between the straight perspective of the espalier apple trees, and indeed she was lovely. Very tall and nearly as fair as Willow, but with a prettier, more curled and kept fairness. For her short hair was like many,

many young gold vipers, and her mouth curled too ;
it was painted as spring-like a red as a young radish,
and in her cheeks was a colour as faint and changing
as the wild apple-blossom is. I liked her bright
green clothes, her wing-like eyebrows, her charming
legs, but I did not like her ugly, much manicured
hands, nor her one-toned, enthusiastic voice.

" Dick and I are so *exhausted*," she said, sitting
down beside me and picking a radish from the
bunch Willow had gathered for tea (" a little rabbit
food "—I felt Willow's shudder). She cleaned it
in the box edging and popped it in her mouth. " So
is James—he's been teaching me to fish a prawn
and we've had such *awful* over-runs and buzz-fuzz's
to disentangle. *Terrible*. All the same I've fished
the Tinker's Stream and George's Pool and Lennon's
Flat since luncheon, and I'll run up after tea and fish
a fly down Grey-sands. After dinner we'll go dry-
flying in the reservoir, shall we, Dick ? "

" We will," said Dick, but his enthusiasm, it
appeared to me, was rather for the lady than for the
sport. I did not blame him. I cannot bear these
intensive fishers myself. Nor did I wonder that he
stood behind her, so best could one see the stooped
back of her neck and those adder-like clusters of
hair.

" And run five miles before you go to bed," said
Willow, looking sourly down between her feet ;
" then you really might call it a day."

" My dear—you're such an *idler*——"

" Idle ? Me ? " Willow was indignant. " Picking flowers and radishes half the afternoon," she said. " Besides, if I didn't rest my body in the summer months I'd pass away."

" *You* would——" Dick was derisive.

" I would——" Now was Willow near to tears as she snatched her radishes from that greedy nymph and departed at speed from the garden ? I, following with a bride-like bouquet of lilies in my hands, wondered very much. For Willow and Dick have for each other a curious importance ; a love and a meaning which seldom exists between relatives, and in which no third person may have any ultimate connection. It is not clear to me quite what this is but I have seen it and know its presence and its power. While Dick derives some entertainment from Willow's skirmishes with men, his own friskings with the opposite sex have never till now been of a nature to cause Willow one moment's consideration. But now, as I have said, I wondered. I was not unimpressed myself by this girl's exciting beauty.

At tea-time she sat in a tapestried chair and sported pleasantly with Sir Richard, her glib, smooth talk running on through Willow's purposeful silence and Dick's silent watchfulness. Sir Richard teased her, his pleasantries occasionally bawdy and often really witty ; and she fell headlong into the conversational pit-falls he digged for her, and laughed with him at herself. She had a pleasant way of laughing, of really shouting with laughter, that was delightful

to hear. The embroidered chair in which she sat
was like a green wood behind her, and the sun came
flooding in at the window, drowning her hair in
light. Now she must tell of an affair she had with
a sailor, and now she talked of fox-hunting with a
tense ability and a sort of gathered knowledge that
showed her a long way from any true interest in
the chase. But Sir Richard listened to her with
polite and serious interest now, till Willow pushed
back her chair, saying : " Well, thanks be to heaven,
the dangers of the chase are gone from us for another
couple of months——" And when the girl quoted :
" Races are won at home : foxes caught in the
summer," I did see for a second what Willow meant
when she had said " damned dull." Insufferably
sporting, I feared.

" Are you going down to the river again ? "
Willow asked. She had put her favourite tune on the
gramophone and cast her body down in her favourite
chair before any could forestall her.

" Oh, *yes* ! I must have a fish to-day just to annoy
Dick. He swears we won't get one till there's some
water."

" Well, it's a grand thing to be a hard-working
girl——" Willow turned her face into the cushion
of her chair, only her straight, chiselled hair could
I see.

" Oh, that's *nothing* ! " The girl's eyes grew wide,
surcharged with memory. " Once, when we were
in Scotland, I caught two fish before luncheon. I

rushed home and got my gun and shot a brace of grouse ; rushed home and got my rifle and shot a stag before dinner. I did call that a good day, I've never forgotten it. It was wonderful."

"Once," said Willow, suddenly rousing herself, "I shot a black-and-white Tom-cat up in a tree. Well, if I did, he went away with himself like blazes and I loosed off the gun again and I *killed* him."

"Oh," said the girl, "oh, really." She was seeking for some apt and encouraging remark, I know, but before she found it Dick arrived to summon her on to fish.

"Well, such a girl——" Willow was roused to angry concern ; "what Dick can see in her I don't know. What is it, Oliver ? "

"Oh, she's *lovely*," I murmured foolishly.

Willow gave me a very dark look. "You're like all the rest of them," she said. "Even James is on her side."

After this I walked awhile through the spring fields with Sir Richard ; he ground the tender thistles under his heel—" Die, you beggar, die." He stood and regarded a watery ditch and a labouring man who delved therein. We stopped by the young horses : "That's a nice filly——" "That's one of the horses that really disgusts me——" We gathered up the stones that interfered with a wooden harrow at its ribbon-making on the grass (the growth of which we applauded) and so down the

Long Pasture and home, gathering the dogs to us as we went.

"Shall we go round by the brood-mares? " said I.

"Faith, I'll take my oath we won't! We'll go into the house and take a read."

"We will."

"A read at the paper."

But before we reached the house he asked: "And what do you think of this girl of Dick's? "

"A *lovely* girl! "

"Yes, I call her a grand girl. Now do you think she'd suit Dick, Oliver? "

"Well, it's absurd. He's so young. Why he's only just come up to Oxford."

"Oh, I mean in time, I mean in time. I don't see why it wouldn't be a very good thing. Willow is very provoking about the whole affair, though she's very fond of Dick, I know, but still she might think of his future. It's so suitable, you know ; a charming girl, a lot of money, fond of sport——"

"Yes, *indeed* ! "

"Fond of Dick," Sir Richard continued, un-staggered by my interruption. "Loves hunting. Besides I *like* the girl—what could be more suitable?"

"Nothing," said I.

"Nothing in the world," said he. "She's a very nice girl. B'God, I must give Pheelan that blister in the morning for Goldenrod. Remind me, Oliver. I suppose it must be about time to change for dinner now."

Dick and the girl came in very late for dinner, unbathed, unchanged, and sovereigns in the calm following on their day's endeavour.

But in the light of that summer night I saw everything through the turbulence of Willow's unhappy vision and indeed I felt for her, preposterous and useless as I knew her attitude of mind to be. For the first time I saw her touched past any power of her resistance or dissembling ; fighting for her hand, and her hand was Dick, against curious odds.

I could not tell what Dick's mind might be. He was quiet almost to gentleness and through the evening concerned himself as much with Willow as with this lovely girl. But that untroubled secrecy that I have always known between them was disturbed and wanting now. For dreadful moments they were polite to each other ; again they would be bitter and distant, and once I thought had nearly come to blows. And through it all I feared I saw a sort of smug supremacy manifest in the girl, or again that beauty which will not be hid which is love flowered terribly about her.

Softened from the ghastly activity of her sporting day she sat empty-handed by the wide, warm, open window, waiting, it seemed to me, with a certain security of purpose, indefinite yet safe, gentle and enormously obstinate. She had such good manners, very sweet manners. She talked to me of Pullinstown and its beauty with real excitement. And of artists and their work with the same tense ability wherewith she had discoursed on hunting. She had seen pictures of mine in exhibitions, yes, and even knew a man who had bought one. Now she felt this to be a picture she could really *live* with, she told me, and many such kind things. I thought of Willow's unkind words on the subject of this versatility and knew them true in part. This creature must be intolerable to Willow.

Dick came and sat himself on the floor beside us. The hour was charged with Love and Melancholy— very sweet. Willow, wrung and tormented, sat by herself outside the circle that even the two dogs had joined, and played a quiet, harsh little tune upon the gramophone again and again and yet again.

The night flowed quietly out into the evening till at last day was no more than a drowned face under green summer waters, and the mountains— the distance between us and them gone now—were as flat as mountains are in an eastern picture.

"Let's go out and kill a rat," said the girl, who had been dissuaded from her late evening fishing.

Dick turned his head towards her and murmured, "*No.*" He was quite sure about this although had I been he and the lake so bright a mirror I must have gone, I think.

"I must catch a fish to-morrow," she said then. "How are we to catch a fish to-morrow?"

Dick gathered himself up and went into the hall, returning with a black tin box full of flies. "These are the Sir's," he said. "He'd kill us if he knew

we looked near them, but there's a great pattern of
a little fly he has in here—somewhere—— If we
could find it we were right. James could copy it
for us to-morrow."

"Not *that* !" The girl took it from Dick and
held it up between her finger and thumb, towards
the last of the light, screwing her eyes upon it in
disdainful inquiry.

"Yes, that's it." Dick was as nearly excited as
I have ever seen him ; "I knew he had it tucked
away somewhere. If only James is in good form
he'll tie us one of these lads to-morrow and you
shall kill a fish."

There was a lover's promise indeed. Both Willow
and the girl saw it as such. The one grew suddenly
less. The other was crowned.

Dick put the fly carefully away, and shut the
box. "I must put this back," he said, "they're
the Sir's things. I'll ask him for it in the morning."

"Why don't you keep it out and give it to James.
He could tie us one of it when we're riding."

"Well, the Sir's gone to bed. I can't ask him
now," Dick explained.

"Yes, but give it to James, and tell him afterwards."

"If my father knew I was standing here with this
box of his flies in my hand—he'd destroy me."
Dick was entirely solemn. "He goes clean out of
his mind if any one touches his fishing things. He has
them what he calls ' arranged,' and though he'll

hardly wet a line the season through, he'll go fiddling about with them and playing with rods in the attics. He knows where he has everything, which is more than any one else does. I couldn't touch that fly for five pounds——"

" I wouldn't care to be the one to put five pounds down in front of you," Willow interrupted, with bitter sarcasm.

" Well, I'd like to see you the day you'd interfere with the Sir's fishing tackle. A grand change for bravery would come on you that day." Dick retreated before the argument could proceed further. In a short time he returned, looking very upset. " My father *hadn't* gone to bed," he said. " He met me putting his flies back. And, Willow, he's lepping."

" He is ? " Willow, too, was overcome.

" Will he let us have the fly, though ? " The girl's voice was hard and acquisitive.

" And do you think I asked him ? " Dick was very nearly impatient. " I tell you he was very annoyed with me."

" Oh, you are a coward ! *I'll* ask him——" But even her hardy maidenhood sank back in her seat abashed by the frozen horror with which this suggestion was received. " Oh, *well*," she said, " I don't see why you're so frightened of him. I think he's perfectly sweet."

Nor then did they answer her. Dick gave her a bedtime glass of water and stared at her as she drank it, reassuring himself, I think, in her evening beauty, for what she might lack in certain grace of understanding. He stood at the door as Willow and she went up to bed. " Will you ride out a horse in the morning ? " he asked her, and her assent was eager. I began to tire of this never-failing vitality, and Willow's dreary, " I *suppose* I'll have to——" was its necessary contrast.

" Will you, Oliver ? "

" Well, if there's a nice quiet horse," I murmured weakly, " so that I can enjoy the view."

" Oh, I adore a difficult ride "—this girl's enthusiasm *was* never-failing. " I was schooling a four-year-old for a man the other day ; he gave me nine falls, but he was such a *grand* horse. I loved him. He's going to give me a day's hunting on him next season."

" What a kind man ! " Willow murmured acidly. " You *are* a lucky girl."

Dick came back to me. " That was terrible about the Sir," he said. He drank a glass of water in silence and in silence we went up to bed.

Early, very early the next morning, Dick summoned us each in turn to rise from our beds and ride out. I always think it is unnecessary of him to exercise his horses quite so soon after cock-crow, but he has his reasons for it, no doubt.

There were three young horses in process of subjection during the summer months, and Willow's show-jumping cob which she rides round the jumping competitions at near-by agricultural shows, deriving therefrom an obscure excitement which she would rather die than admit. I believe she has a theory that Goldenrod enjoys his show-jumping successes. She may be right.

I rode out on him this morning and a pleasant and docile cob he is. I did not envy anybody else : neither Willow, silent and careful, nor Dick with his eye not quite happy on the girl who was not yet on the kindest terms with her mount. Least of all did I envy her, for although certainly able, she was one of those tutored, unsympathetic riders who are so often meeting with undeserved disaster. As we rode up the fields towards the avenue gate I must say I thought the disaster might prove imminent. Nor was I deceived. Sourly and unkindly, his ears laid half back and switching his tail, that good-looking young horse proceeded, ready at the smallest provocation to make himself as objectionable as possible.

The provocation arrived in the shape of a galloping ass—Willow's baby donkey turned out now in the summer months and as undeniably affectionate and annoying as only a late pet can be.

Two consecutive eel-like plunges the girl survived most creditably, but at the third, and the brute whipped round and dropped his shoulder for he really meant it, she was gone—and no shame to her either.

Leaving Dick to comfort her, Willow and I

pursued and captured her horse, but when we returned it to them I learned with horror Dick's intention that I, and not his tender young love, should mount the brute again.

She was angry and hurt and most bitterly ashamed. She persuaded. She protested. She scolded. But for once adamant, Dick insisted that it should be as he had said. So nearly in tears, the poor proud girl was thrown up on Goldenrod, and I, also nearly in tears, gingerly mounted that horrible horse. However, his gallop round the field having taken the first edge off his morning humour, he proceeded now fairly kindly.

" I'm really sorry for that girl," Willow said, riding up alongside of me as we turned out of the avenue gate, its shadows blue, dewy pillars on the gravel in the early light. " She won't get over that now for a long time. She'd rather lose ten pounds than that should have happened to her. I know these outdoor girls. They'll take a thing like that to heart and really distress themselves about it."

" Only because she thought she looked silly." I was not feeling too kindly disposed towards her with my nice quiet morning's ride gone from me.

" Well, nobody enjoys looking silly," Willow said kindly ; " you wouldn't enjoy yourself one bit now if I hit this horse you're riding one belt with this little stick I have."

" Don't, Willow, please don't. You know I can't

ride one side of him as it is. My only hope is to keep him quiet."

"Well, you're a cowardly divil, Oliver."

"Yes, I know."

So we rode on together in an amiable silence, Dick and the girl following behind. We rode along a narrow lane that threaded faithfully past every turning of Pullinstown's demesne wall. On the other hand were small fields, the shadows of their stone walls lapping half across them ; and open stretches of bleached bog, with deep waters hemmed strictly about by tall sharp flag leaves ; and sudden patches of green, quick green that took the eye like a flame. Soon I knew we should come to an old castle where jackdaws swooped importantly through the dead windows, their distracted shadows passing on the grass, and cattle sheltered in the silent heat of summer, and here we would leave the lane and take to the country, presently leaping what was known as " the small bog double " (an obstacle which always frightened me). So through a gap and a gate and out into the lane that still girdled Pullinstown, a little stony way very low and dark below the wall and the belt of unfrequented wood behind it. But in another hundred yards or so the lane would turn left-handed and the mountains bloom forth on the morning, to be my song and my delight in the morning.

And so it was. I could not have borne it if they had been a lesser blue or less deeply grained in shadow. Nor to have them farther away. Nor at a closer distance. They were as I knew them, their blind lovely shapes the same, and I ask no more of anything.

We turned in at the farm avenue gate and rode back towards the house, the mountains behind us now. The lake was shining on our left hand and the sunlight was bland and enduring on the house. Such a gay morning, so sweet and so bright.

The girl rode up beside Willow and me. She looked nice on Goldenrod, confident and less mannered, and her jhodpores were most lovely.

" I'm trying very hard to buy that horse from Dick," she said to me. " I love that horse. I love him. Such a *delicious* shoulder." But what enthusiasm.

" You're *not* ! " Willow's incredulity was un-affected, not rude. " Well, I'd go a long way before I bought a dirty brute that threw me on my back on the hard ground."

" Oh, I don't mind about that." (This valorous girl.) " It was really my own stupidity. If I'd only remembered a tip Major Seymour taught me I wouldn't have parted."

" That must be a great idea " ; Willow was still quite kind. " I know if a horse really gives two good ones with me I leave the saddle *very* light and airy."

" Oh, one *shouldn't*, of course. . . . I *was* so annoyed with Dick for not letting me up upon him again ; I can't bear to be defeated about anything."

"Well, if that's the reason you're buying this horse," Willow said, "I advise you to keep away from him ; he's a nice enough horse, but he wouldn't suit everybody, for there's no doubt he's a difficult horse to ride."

"Yes. I think he'd suit me very well. I think he'd be a great horse in Warwickshire."

"Yes, he's a bold horse all right," Willow admitted almost grudgingly. "*And* he gallops. To tell you the truth, I'd an idea of winning a few point-to-points with him myself next season."

And this was the horse of whom I had heard it said that he was as slow as a man ; could not, in fact, go fast enough to warm himself. And I had heard him abused for a cowardly devil and a dirty tempered brute. Well, no one could say that the case had been understated to his optimistic purchaser. She had even had very practical proof of the sort he was. Though I remembered how Willow had said she would not even rob this girl, I saw no reason why she should not pluck a fool as well as another. But whether Dick would permit that this horse should be sold to his love—I wondered.

In the yard, Pheelan's concern over the mud on her back upset the girl again, and the more provoked she was at the memory of her mishap the more eager she grew to own the cause of it. She departed at speed for the dining-room, determined to enlist Sir Richard on her side.

"Sell her the horse, Dick," said I. "If she *wants*

a brute she'll easily buy a worse one from somebody else."

Dick looked at Willow doubtfully, but if it was counsel that he wanted from her he failed to get it. She walked through the hall in distant silence and on to breakfast.

There was no Sir Richard in the dining-room ; the maid who brought in breakfast said that he had gone to a fair with James, and left word that he would lunch out on his way home.

" Oh," said the girl ; she turned scarlet with annoyance and *would* talk although her mouth was full of scrambled egg, " but what are we to *do* ? What are we to do about it ? " She could have cried.

" Why, about what, my pet ? What is the matter, sweet ? "—so kind Dick was. And Willow stared at her in blatant wonder, her fork in the air, her face hard and blank with surprise.

" Oh, Dick, you are so *awful*—about that dreary fly, of course."

" James isn't here to copy it for us in any case," Dick pointed out.

" Yes, but I know Sir Richard'd have let me have it. I know he would."

" Well, you may be a great success with old men," Willow walked over to the sideboard to pour out a cup of coffee, " but one thing I *do* know, the Sir wouldn't give one of his flies, not the shadow of one of them, to the most *lovely* woman in the world "

—and I saw a fleeting vision of beseeching beauty as Willow said this—" not if she asked him till she was sick asking him."

" You'll just have to persevere with the prawn," said I, unkindly I know. The thought of perseverance with a prawn makes me nearly sick myself, the skill required to fish it with success being so far beyond me as apparently it exceeded even the girl's enthusiasm.

" I hate, and loathe and detest prawning," she said, now in a perfect storm of despair, very lovely with her Fury's viperish hair and her hands shaking with anger and her eyes screwed together to keep back tears. " You *know* what a miserable day I spent prawning yesterday, and I was so *good* about it—I tried so *hard* and I was so *tired*, and now when I might catch a fish at last you won't let me have this one dismal little fly."

" Oh, don't be so *silly*," said Dick and Willow in the same breath, and Willow tried to look as though she had not spoken, above all had not spoken in unison with Dick : never again in unison with Dick.

Little they could know, either of them, how genuine was this storm to her—poor, tired, defeated sporting girl. For to her I saw any event such as this morning's simple catastrophe was a bitter defeat, a real shaming of herself to herself. And how hard she worked to catch a fish. For a week persistently she had fished and fished with the water nearly hopeless. If James and Dick could charm them out of the river an odd time, why not she? Poor silly girl, how should she know the guile of old river secrets which James and Dick, knowing the water as they did, exploited almost unconsciously, but could not for all their willing helpfulness have imparted to another. She was one of these who must have success or die and will die, too, in their striving for that end. All strife and effort this girl's sport to her ; the serious talk of it was hardly exaggerated. In this temperamental moment she could suffer crudely and really. She was of that stuff they made lovers of thirty years ago, those silent lovers who resolved their unrequited passions in the desperate pursuit of BIG GAME. Should she live and should she suffer, I knew in my very bowels that her consolation and assuagement would be secured probably upon the horns of an *Ovis Poli* or some creature equally difficult to find and pre-posterously difficult to slay. And she was so rich she could do this sort of thing—and so lovely it was a pity that she should.

But here she was now, tears falling on the honey in her plate, and Dick and Willow staring at her with the intense and cruel pre-occupation of two children. If they had been on better terms with one another, I know they would have winked and laughed at her together.

"You *shall* catch a fish," said Dick at last. "My darling, I promise you you shall."

" And will you sell me that horse ? " she asked.

" *No*," he said. Perhaps her tears had made his love more tender and strengthened his resolve.

Willow rose and stood beside her chair. " Do you want lunch for two, Dick ? " Her voice was frozen up inside her, small and unkind. She could not endure even such a mild expression of his passion as his refusal to sell this horse betokened. " I want to tell the cook."

" For three, I think." Dick was lighting two cigarettes, one for himself and one for the girl ; he thrust it into her mouth as a mother gives her child a chocolate to stop its complaining. " Oliver is coming with me to carry my things about and to carry her fish up to the house when she gets him."

" Oliver is going to draw pictures," said I weakly.

" Pictures ? Pictures of what ? "

" Pictures of Oliver sleeping. Pictures of Dick carrying his own gaffs and bags and beastly fish about——"

" For three then," said Willow, in the impersonal voice of a waitress booking an uninteresting order. " And I'm going over to Templeshambo to school a horse for Beauty, if any one wants to know where I am." She left us then, unfit we knew for her further consideration.

The morning was too bright. Too bright for fishing, too bright for painting, too bright for grieving. Too hot for walking, too hot for working, too hot for thinking. But quite right for lying and dreaming in great beauty, in great peace, in that happiness which is mine at Pullinstown—that clear unfrustrated happiness. Now I lay on a steep bank where nut trees grew and aged grey rocks tilted their hoary sides to the sun and laid their split dark shades behind them. The last fires of the gorse burnt sullenly about me and beyond me. I wished to see some graceful foxgloves, but it was too early for them yet. I made a square window of my arms and looked through it up the river, up to where a thin spinsterish bridge stepped its five steps across the river ; and through my window I sniffed that delicious smell, old and fresh, of a river ; and through it I saw the girl flogging away at the rough stream below the bridge—the most taking place on the water this was. After a minute I saw Dick too—his clothes were so much the colour of the bank, I could only just see him. He gave her last words of wisdom and walked away up the river. Two brilliant white dots preceded him. The dogs, no doubt. He had not gone many minutes before she sat down upon the bank and changed her fly. I still gazed through my window, but now I was looking at a fire-crested wren, a very matronly one, the mother of nine or ten I don't doubt. Rhymes are so true. But now my poor window was grown tired, so I laid my arms along the ground and laid my head along my arms, thinking all the time of that Blessed Damozel, but since I could not remember her poem at all correctly, I slept.

I awoke to hear that sound which anglers rave and write and talk of endlessly—" the scream of an outgoing reel "—and, leaping with creditable promptness to my feet, I beheld below me the Crown of Perseverance and Effort Rewarded. For the girl was without doubt in a fish at last. The rod was bent and her shoulders leaned backwards from the strain of keeping its point up, as she played her fish. When I arrived, full of goodwill, she was nearly screaming with nerves and excitement.

" *Look*," she said, " he's off again ! Get below him—get below him—quick ! If he gets me round the Bull Rock I'm done. I tell you he'll *break* me ! "

And the fish indeed was off downstream in as determined a rush towards the sea as ever I saw. Down the bank I ran towards the fatal grey saddle of the " bull rock," and, the distemper of excitement well through my blood now, plunged into the river, splashing and waving my arms and grateful as for a major clemency of Heaven when her fish retreated upstream again.

" Half an hour at least I must have had him on," she gasped. " *Oh* "—she almost screamed as he jumped clean out of the water—a flashing bar of —alas ! not silver as in the best fishing stories, but gold, red-gold and very red indeed. Alas, indeed, poor girl, was it for this you wept and laboured sore ? But she did not seem to take it in—" thirty pounds," she breathed—" he *must* be——" And ten minutes of steady and careful pressure brought him lashing to the surface. A little longer and he came in to the bank.

"Gaff him," she said. "Now—*Now*, you fool! Oh, *Now!*"

On the bank he lay kicking and flapping in all his ugly glory—a very old red cock, diseased too.

She looked at him for an exhausted and rapturous second before it dawned on her. Then: "He doesn't look too good, *does* he?" she asked in pitiful doubt.

"No," I said; I did not look at her. "He's better out of the river anyway." I hit him a couple of cracks that stilled his flapping and took out a little battered fly (he was well hooked) and gave it to her. "What is it?" I asked.

"Oh, a—one Dick gave me, a Slaney something, he calls it." She would cry, I knew she would in a minute. It was all too sad.

"Wait," said I. "I'll put this in the wood. Dick can bury it afterwards. I'll tell him. I'll have to go up to the house and change, I think."

"Oh, yes. You were so kind to go in. Don't catch cold, will you? And don't bother Dick about it. He's so sweet he'd probably come back here to comfort me, and I'd much rather he went on fishing."

So I left her, sitting sad and solitary on the bank, her hat beside her on the grass. He lovely head was bent in distress. I went up from the river and laid that ugly fish out of sight in the wood—and uglier each moment he grew. Then I proceeded on up the bank and met Dick and told him, of course, when he was filled with a great pity.

"The awful thing is, Oliver," he said, "I put her there because it's the best stand and the easiest to fish—and look——" Yes : the authentic silver of a nice fresh little fish, so wholesome and beautiful to look at after that monster, flashed up from the deep grass. "Isn't it terrible ? " he said. "And if you really are going up to the house, Oliver, would you mind carrying it up. The sight of it might grieve her."

"But the weight of it may grieve me," said I. Yet, although I hate carrying heavy weights about, I gathered this up and went on towards the house with it. For the distress of Beauty was still more grievous to my mind.

As I went into the hall, which seemed to sweat icily after the heat outside, I encountered James.

"Aren't you back early ? " I asked.

"We are, Master Oliver, we are. Ah, there was no prices in the Fair at all and the Sir got vexed and he come home then."

"He's not the only one who's vexed," said I, mysteriously. I have learnt the value of mystery and circumspection in telling a tale at Pullinstown. Now I had James's attention. I told him of all the morning's doings. He laid Dick's fish on the floor at our feet and listened closely.

"And the one I pity," he said at last, "is poor Miss Willow. Well, I knew this time must come,

but she's very fond of poor Master Dick. Poor
Master Dick, he must go courting some time. ' Keep
on courting, Master Dick,' I used to say to him,
and he a young lad ; ' if ye don't court ye'll never
marry.' And the poor young lady's greatly knocked
about over the poor bloody fish. Well, well——"

From this distressful little summary it may be
seen that I had succeeded in conveying to James
some of the pathos and the pain of the morning.

"Listen to me now," he said, "I'll tell you
what we'll do. The Sir have a great little beggar
of a low water fly some place in his fly-box. I
can't rightly recall the dressing of it on the minute,
but I'll ax him for the lend of it, and I'll tie one for
the young lady. 'Tis a noble little pattern, and
she should surely kill a fish on it to-night with the
water the way it is at the present. She vexed
herself yesterday with the prawn, the poor
child——" He picked up the fish and departed
with it towards the back regions while I went up
to my room to change.

But when I went down again towards the river
I brought no fly with me, only the promise of its
forth-coming, for Sir Richard was out about the
fields and James, no less than Dick, was aware
of the gross offence involved in meddling unbeknown
to the Sir among his fishing tackle.

"Well, I don't give a dam one way or other,"
said Dick with sudden and ugly temper, rude and
unexplainable to my mind, "whether she catches

a fish or not. Where's Willow," he said. "Did you see Willow in the house?"

"Gone to Templeshambo," I said. I was staring at him with my eyes and with my mind. What strange perversity was this? Had he proved over-fond or over-bold in his comforting? Had she turned on him and rebuffed him? Why this clear and sudden change?

"I'll just fish these last three casts down to the end," he said, "and then I'll go and look for Willow. Keep an eye on the girl till lunch time, will you, Oliver? James can mind her after that."

Here was a matter for me to gape at in wonder and secret alarm. Looking at Dick told me nothing. He wore that expression of resolute blankness with which either he or Willow can mask their minds from any of us. But Dick added to it the brutal impenetrability of a schoolboy. I could not tell if he was hurt or shocked or sorry or glad, I only knew that he would do as he pleased in this as in any other matter. I left him then, and feeling but a "slight and unmeritable man meet to be sent on errands," I went on down the river towards the hazel grown bank where I had left our food and beer to drink.

The girl ceased her fishing when I called her to come and eat, and came walking slowly up from the bank.

"Where's Dick?" she asked me with would-be carelessness. But her voice was too still and cold.

" Dick—he went up to the house. Something he'd forgotten to tell Pheelan, I think."

I sat there and gave her food to eat, which she did not eat, and beer to drink which she did not enjoy. About her there was a desperate sense of unhappiness, a wild and silent complaint. I pitied her very much and wished for her sake that she could tell me what had happened, for this was no sporting disappointment. This was young love stricken ; I felt it and knew it. And Dick, if he was minded to deal forth an unkindness in love would do so with an elementary venom that came from the very bone and core of his savage youth. For there was no kindness in him as yet, only strength and charm and wit, and sometimes a gentleness. But how could this poor girl know ? And if she loved him she was the more insecure towards him for that.

Sitting there with her in the wood she had all my pity and, seeking to comfort her, I told her how James was even now trying for her sake that killing fly on which a fish should surely die. But when I told her this she grew even more distressed. A clear red colour filled slowly under her skin up to her eyes and down her neck and left her pale and fevered when it passed. She fidgeted painfully, breaking little sticks from a hazel branch and opening her mouth to speak, then uttering some trivial thing far, very far from the word in her mind.

" Be God, Master Oliver, what a nest ye have !
I declare yer as snug as a thrush——" It was
James, his head surmounting a bush like an old
satyr of these groves. I was glad to see him, for
all this dumb distress was becoming slightly em-
barrassing. He knelt on the grass to show her the
fly he had tied, holding it to the light the better
to praise the colour in its hackle.

" Mind you, I'll not say 'tis the exact pattern,
for we couldn't come at it, 'twas whipped from the
Sir's box, but 'tis very near the spit of it. Look ! "
James scrambled to his feet and stood before us a
narrator of dreadful things. " Look ! The Sir's
after belting hell out of poor Master Dick over the
loss o' that fly. 'Twas pitiful. ' Go from me ! '
says he to him. ' The world is wide,' he says, ' and
may I never see your face again.' "

" Oh, James, you *know* he didn't ! " I could
not endure this.

" Well, he was greatly vexed, indeed," James
admitted my moderation of the tale, " for he recalled
he cot him with the box e'er yesterday. ' Ye little
tinker,' he says to him now, ' yer no more than an
ugly little grievance to me,' he says. ' Between
yerself and Miss Willow I'm not able to lay any
little article aside out o' me hand but it's whipped.'
Master Dick was as knocked about—the poor child
—only for it to be such a good little divil of a little
fly he'd never have looked next nor near it. Well,
the Sir is very passionate when he'd be vexed.

He's roaring meal-a-murder around the house now
and the devil himself wouldn't content him."

I was so absorbed in the drama of the tale that
I never noticed the girl at all, and when she said :
" I think I won't fish any more. I think I have a
bit of a headache. I think I'll go back to the house
and lie down——"   Her bruised, tired voice
stirred me far more keenly than James's elaborate
tale of woe had done.

" The poor child," said James when she had gone,
" she'll do no good with Master Dick. He's very
stiff and he's very bitter."

" But why, James, why ? What has the poor
girl done ? "

" 'Twas she whipped the fly out o' the Sir's
box," James told me with tolerant disapproval,
" and when Master Dick come up and cot her
fishing it she allowed 'twas a fly she had from a
fisher in Scotland. What a fool she thinks he is.
'Twas partly that disgusted him, and 'twas partly
he was vexed. . . . Well," James hesitated, " 'tis
a rudeness in me to say it, and my place is well
known to me, Mister Oliver, but 'twas not a lady's
part to do a thing the like o' that."

" No, James," I said. " But oh, I am so sorry for
her."

And I was—wildly sorry for her. Poor, jealous,
lovely, sporting girl. This morning she would have
given the earth to catch a fish—their withholding
of that fly through which toward success her mind

was set, was to her a vain and silly scruple. Why
should she not have taken it? How quickly she
could have wheedled Sir Richard into amused
tolerance of her theft—had he discovered that little
loss. But, alas, to her undoing it had been Dick
and not Sir Richard who had made the discovery.
Dick with his harshness and his lack of understanding for this desire, that rode her to find success
in sport. For he and Willow are entirely devoid
of jealousy or of systemised endeavour in the pursuit
of game. They will hunt a rat with their terriers
with as diligent an interest as, were either a huntsman, he would hunt a fox. They have no knowledge
of pomp or jealousy within themselves, and to
find this a veritable lust within another, and in a
nearly beloved, must have given Dick a disgust
which he made no effort to conceal. "I will
find my own kind," he had thought at once, and
said: "Where's Willow?" and gone to her.

Again I thought of the lies wherein he and Willow
so often and so shamelessly enmeshed themselves
with regard to the buying and selling of horses,
yes, and in other matters, too. Why should this
little foolish lie of hers have created so much unkindness between them? The difference lay in
their reasons for lying. For to have schemed a
little scheme, and gone softly and taken what was
held with good reason as sacred, and to have insisted then in a stupid denial—that was a horrid
matter. I could not wonder that Dick should see

her now as apart from himself and Willow—a flatterer of old men, a pretty sneak—not to be trusted with any large truth or untruth. No fit partner for crime or for love. And James could see this, too, I knew. " Did Master Dick tell you about it, James ? " I asked. We were down on the river bank now, and I watched him casting a prawn with that simple precision experts use, so that it went where, and precisely where he pleased.

"Well, he did, but he was annoyed ; he was vexed." James could apologise even for Dick's having told him of it, that was how they would look at the matter. " I'd rain down tears this minute," he said, " to think o' the child, but her and Master Dick could never agree. And to see them," he added sadly, " ye'd imagine all could be so nice——"

On my way back to the house I met with her again. She came hurrying towards me, her valiant young beauty dim and fugitive beyond her tears.

" Could you," she said, " would it be a frightful bother to you—or *could* you lend me five pounds ? I'm just going away," she said, " and you see the banks are shut now and I can't cash a cheque, and I shall have to buy some petrol for my car."

" You're not going away ? " I said, " just like this—you can't be."

" Yes, I am. I'm going now."

She meant it. She took my five pounds.

She got into her car in the garage, stuffed the

note into one of its pockets, for she had waited
neither for bag nor hat, nor luggage. She backed her
car out of the shadow of the house and departed
from Pullinstown, I knew, for ever. And in this
one wild unpremeditated act she was nearer to
them—to Dick and Willow—than she had ever
been or would ever be again.

Sir Richard could not understand it. He was
distressed and grieved past measure. All that
evening he lamented her departure, and tried by
any means to discover its cause. Willow, he guessed,
had been unkind and Dick had shown some rudeness. But James could not enlighten him, nor could
I, as to the reason of her going, and as for Dick and
Willow—a brick wall had compared poorly with
their blank reticence. They knew nothing and
they were incurious. The only discussion between
them which I was privileged to hear on the subject
took place after dinner in the school-room.

"You'll have to sell her that horse now, Dick,"
Willow said, pausing in her selection of a record for
the gramophone.

"I will, I suppose," Dick answered easily.

"Yes." Willow wound up the gramophone.
"You'd hate to hurt anybody's feelings unless
you had to—wouldn't you, Oliver?"

I PRAISE NOT

AGAIN to be in Ireland and again at Pullinstown; in these happy circumstances my spirit is alight and afloat. To be with these Irish cousins, their kindness mine and the quick fire of their interest changes me strangely, I think, so that all safe known values are gone from me and I am theirs, giving myself with a great abandon of delight to the furtherance of such schemes, moral or otherwise, as may for the moment torture the course of their lives.

I see them : my cousin Willow, pale as a candle with hair plated like a thin metal cap upon her head and a light burning so far within her, so small and still, that one may never see even the edge of its flame. I see her brother, Dick, with his rakish seventeenth-century looks ; his manners and speech a simplicity of delight ; his thoughts his own alone ; his actions unpredictable ; his love Willow's—strongly, entirely and only Willow's. He would never know even pity for another, man or woman. And then Sir Richard, Sir Richard Pulleyns of Pullinstown, who shall tell of his mighty deeds past in the making and breaking of horses, of his great present wit and wisdom in buying or selling the same ? I have told all these things as I

heard and saw them ; along with his ruthlessness
and kindness, his love and his hating, his base
expedient and ready forgiveness of such measures
in any other. For I am dismayed at his villainy
and his charm disarms me ever.

Horses, many horses ; horses past, present and to
come ; horses good and bad ; hunters, point-to-point
horses and race-horses (I have learnt, God knows,
the difference between these two classes) ; all
these bright, dangerous horses, never one forgotten,
forge a chain of memory, speculation and future
event which holds these three, Sir Richard and
his son and daughter, to one another ; or, con-
trarily, drags them each to a point of passionate
difference that must, one would think, cause them
to forego for ever any illusion of family unity or
kindness. And yet, the chain will rend and part,
and bind again closer than before.

They are alike each other, in face as in speech.
Sir Richard, the flesh burnt away whitely from his
arrogant bones, his hair now a thin grey wisp on
his skull of a poll, has been as insanely fair as Willow's once. And Dick, though not yet so haggard
and never so handsome, is his father again in
narrow, meagre bone. But there is more than this
animal likeness between them ; there is an incor-
porate, inescapable affinity holding them together
past any power of hating to undo. Nor is it Love,
except, I think, Dick's for that Willow.

"Willow, Willow, what are you at?"   Sir

Richard went fidgeting through his tall, cold rooms, for the ceaseless, unpitiful rain of August beat down, teemed and beat without, so that work must cease and with this ceasing, so must his harrying of labouring men. Even the engine which in these cursed days employed three idle beggars cutting wood, had failed, and Dick was gone to the town with a part of its vitals. So, "Willow," he called peevishly, "Willow, where are you?"

"Put that coal under the sofa, Oliver," said Willow to me, "before the Sir sees it. I'm here, father"; she raised her harsh, small, crow of a voice, "I'm lighting the library fire."

"*Fires* in the month of August," Sir Richard came in and sat himself down as closely as possible to the incipient blaze. "Is there any coal in that fire?" He bent, peering crossly, for to burn coal and wood together is an extravagance uncountenanced by Pullinstown's lord.

"Divil a coal," said Willow. She cast her body down the length of the sofa and picked up a book called *What Katie did at School*—she has been reading this book off and on since I have known her.

Sir Richard rose and wound the gramophone.

"For God's sake, Oliver," he said a minute later, "stop that gramophone. That's a cursed cod of a yoke. That's an awful tune."

"That's what I'd call a prime tune," Willow yawned uncombatively.

" *You* would ? "

" I would."

" Well, take it off, anyway, Oliver." Sir Richard stretched out an arm towards a heap of illustrated papers on a near table. I think I saw Willow's face change a little.

" There is no doubt," she said pleasantly, " my dad is a holy terror to God on a wet day. He is— a divil. Give me *The Tatler*, Sir Richard, if you don't want it."

" Can't you see I want it ? I'm reading it. You children have no manners." Sir Richard settled himself determinedly to its perusal. " That's a very shocking picture—I wonder they allow such things—there's a proper beauty of a jockey— look at the horse's head loosed out—such a way to ride a finish——" and, " *oh*," said Sir Richard, and fell silent.

" Well," he said a minute later, " that was a very interesting paper." He handed it over to Willow, " and a great glimpse of your social life it gave me. I must say it's most gratifying for a man to see a picture of his daughter on such very friendly terms with a buckeen of a bounder like Mister Billy Morgan. May I ask since when you've taken to going racing with that officer ? May I ask how you hit it off with his Uncle Joe ? May I ask if you were on Golden Fleece the day they won at Leopardstown with him at eight-to-one ? I needn't ask whether you backed him when they were pulling the head off the horse every time they ran him this summer."

"When did they pull him?" Willow asked, without heat.

"At Mellick, for one thing——" I thought Sir Richard wavered a little.

"Were you at Mellick?" Willow put a finger between the pages of *What Katie did at School*, and sat up very straight on the sofa. "Well, did you see him jump that last hurdle? He staggered going into it. He staggered over it and he staggered four times when he landed—and people will tell you the horse was pulled." She lay down again and opened her book. A watery beam of light made a truthful arrow in silver on her gold hair. Her face was in shadow and sullen.

"He improved surprisingly since Mellick," Sir Richard jeered.

"He improved enough to win a maiden hurdle race in very moderate company the second time of asking. I'm glad he did." Willow settled herself composedly. "I had a fiver on him at eight-to-one."

"Which went on with the stable money, I suppose." Sir Richard looked like having the last word here.

"Well, I don't know." Willow gave him a very level look. "It was your old girl-friend, Cousin Honour, who did it for me. It was with her I went racing that day, as it happens—if that's any relief to your mind."

"Honour seems to have taken a strong fancy for her strange relations these days."

"Relations? I didn't know Joe and Billy were any relations—they can't be." Willow had yielded to that eagerness for gossip to which the young so often betray their dignity.

"Well, they are—in a sort of a way——" Sir Richard was confused and portentous. "A way that's better avoided," he concluded lamely. "Not that that's anything against them," he went on. "If they hadn't every roguery and cleverality known to man, or if they'd ever been known to run a horse they owned or trained straight. No. I tell you what, Willow, I'll not have you going about with that lot. I forbid it ; do you understand me ? I entirely forbid it. And while you live in this house you'll do as I say. Yes, I'll speak to Honour about it. God knows she ought to have more sense than to let my daughter be seen about with Billy Morgan —a motherless girl like you, too——" Sir Richard's very real dislike of this intimacy was netting him surely in a tangle of Victorian clichés—but Willow, I guessed, knew quite well what he meant. However, before she could continue the argument, the door of the schoolroom opened and Dick announced that his father's presence was required immediately in the engine shed.

"Blast them ! There's not one of them can do a hand's turn unless I'm standing over them." Sir Richard rose to his feet, rearing himself slowly to

his surprising, gaunt height. He was not dis-
pleased to avoid for the moment his parental duties
and to apply himself to other more blessedly kind
and concrete matters. " Did you bring those bolts
back, Dick ? "

" I did. I left them with Michael." Dick
seated himself in his father's empty chair and produced a damp bag of peppermints from the pocket
of his coat. It was a long-skirted tweed coat of a
very beautiful colour, full of age and character,
and smelt of ferrets and turf-smoke on a wet day
like this. He put a peppermint in his cheek, thus
ruining his profile, and said he at once : " That's
a cod of a fire."

Now "cod" is a word that means a great deal.
It may mean a poor fire, or a disappointing gramophone record for which one has paid four-and-six.
Or, used in another way, it may mean a good joke
—one " cods " with a friend, or " cods " about the
town—or again (involving usually the practice of a
wicked deceit) one " cods " an adversary up to the
two eye-balls. And yet again, a poor and talkative
fool is best described as an old cod. It is an impossible word. I believe Shakespeare found it
useful and descriptive, and so do my cousins
Willow and Dick.

While they were extracting small pieces of coal
from the brown paper parcel under the sofa, and
artfully concealing them in the heart of the fire,
I opened *The Tatler* for which I had been itching

during the past ten minutes, and searched its pages
for this photograph of Willow and a squire that had
so excited Sir Richard. I saw it with the little
passing shock dealt one by photographs of one's
friends. " Miss Willow Pulleyns. . . . Miss Pulleyns
is the only daughter of Sir Richard Pulleyns, Bart.,
of Pullinstown . . . rode the winners of six point-
to-point races this season. . . . Mr. Billy Morgan
who rode that eight-to-one winner, White Tag, at
this meeting."

Mr. Billy Morgan, I saw him again, so tall, so
dark, so handsome, with his empty coat-sleeve and
his bright sling, saddling that horse of Lady Honour's
on which I had enjoyed such a pleasant and successful ride at the Lisowen harriers point-to-point.
Mr. Billy Morgan, the brains, no doubt, of that
profitable little ramp to which I had been a very
helpful and unwitting party. And here again I
saw him, impossibly good-looking, the belt of his
overcoat straining his hollow middle as near as
might be to his hollow back. He was rolling his
whip between the palms of his hands. His profile
was as clear as a nun's against the dark shelter of
his coat collar. He was looking at Willow and she,
propped on her shooting stick, her back against
some rails, stared past him and away beyond,
with that dim intensity which only means that her
thoughts are very near at hand—on a horse, or her
next meal, on a bottle of beer—charming creature
that she is. This time they may have been on the

race he was just going out to ride and not unlikely, with a fiver in balance on the matter.

But who was this who stood beside them, her hips square as a box ; her sparse legs out-bowed with riding of horses ; her face glum to another square—a pretty face, a sad mouth and eyes that yearned too sadly towards Mr. Billy Morgan. The paper did not tell me, so I asked Willow : "Willow, who is this poor girl you have supplanted ? "

" That's Joe's daughter, Biddy. She loves Billy Morgan with a great girlish passion."

The best of asking Willow a direct question is that one quite often receives a direct answer. But indeed, gazing again on this picture, I had to admit to myself that she would hardly have been so foolish as to deny the obvious.

" There's a car," said Dick, " coming down the avenue. It's Cousin Honour," he said a moment later. " Sir Richard'll have a good crack at her now about that photograph."

" If he speaks to her at all——" Willow got up from her sofa. " I must open the avenue gate," she said and was out through the window before I could say, " I'll do it, Willow."

" Never mind her, Oliver. Leave her alone. Honour'll be in great humour when Willow goes out in the rain to open a gate for her." Dick leaned his back against the mantelshelf and smiled a faun's inhuman smile to himself. " Sir Richard's not one bit pleased," he said irreverently, "with this cursed fashion she's taken for going to Temple-shambo every other day and being so friendly with Honour. And now if Honour takes to coming over here——"

"But Dick——" how helpless one was to read them, or to translate those silences which alone may betray them. "I thought he liked Lady Honour. Well, *liked* . . . I mean they're very old friends, aren't they, as well as being cousins?"

"They can't let each other *alone*," Dick grinned again, unkindly, but this time he seemed to be honestly puzzling for some reason to tell me. "If you call that friendship. You see, Oliver, the Sir'll have a crack at her one time, just in case she gets too big for her boots (and indeed she was always a bit under-shod), and then she'll wait months perhaps to get a good crack home on him, do you see, Oliver? She hasn't paid him out yet for that fright he gave her over the mare they ran in Lisowen —that you rode, you know."

"Indeed, I know, but go on——"

"He had a real wallop at her then, and the best of it was, he got nothing out of it for himself in the end."

"Except that three-year-old——" I suggested.

"Yes. But he gave them their own price for her. No, all the satisfaction he got was to show them he was a long way too cute for them—but that satisfied him. Willow told him it was a dam'

shame for him. She told him he'd meet his Water-
loo one of these days for annoying poor Beauty,
anyhow."

"And she's been playing round with Honour
all the summer since? Dick, I do wonder what
she's up to?"

"I don't know," said Dick, suddenly defensive
and unfriendly. "Why should she be up to anything? Perhaps the Sir annoyed her. Anyway,
if she likes to cod about with Honour she can, she's
able for six Honours." He went over to the gramophone and put on the tune Sir Richard had lately
reviled, thus abruptly breaking the thread of confidence on which I had leaned too much weight.

It was then that Willow came back with Lady
Honour. Lady Honour, smiling her shining, dim
smile, rain in her white hair and hollow drops of
it on her little grey hat. Her ringed hands were
small and wet and cold, and her voice enchanted
and excited me as ever before. It tilted to such
sweet and easy notes. It was stayed low and halting
for sympathy, and tuned to a charming pitch of
roguishness. She was delighted to see me. I knew
deeply and with enjoyment that, indeed, this was
so. Although a moment later I wondered if her
greeting to me was not contrasted almost too
sharply with hers to Dick. "Well, Dick—how's
poor Dick?" This was offensive and difficult to
parry—this "poor."

"He's warmer than poor old Honour anyway."

Dick dropped that frozen, stiff little hand and kicked the fire together into an obliging blaze. "There's no day," said Dick, "so cold as a wet day in August."

"And I was changing a wheel," said Lady Honour. "*Fancy!*—in all that rain. Don't you *pity* me, Oliver? And not a soul to help me. Yes, and two white Wyandotte chickens of Beauty's were tied in the car, and if they didn't escape and *away* with them through the country—how could I catch them?"

"Beauty'll have your life." Willow looked up from *What Katie Did at School* to say this.

"Oh, Willow, darling, always *reading*—I wish I had your brains——" I was startled by the sincerity with which this was delivered. "Ah, but they'll find their way home all right," she pursued the subject under discussion without a falter. "They're very like hounds, you know, always go back to their kennels no matter where they are. I thought on the way here I might tell Beauty that —*oh*, but will she believe me?"

"*I* believed you," said I in an honest Briton's voice, and she laughed so high and clear, there was something imperishable in her laughter. "But really," she went on, "that wasn't what I came to talk about. The thing is this, Willow—can you ride a horse for Joe in the Tincurry Show to-morrow?"

"Well," Willow hesitated, "does Joe think he'll win in his class?"

" He does. He thinks he'll win the championship with him. He's a smashing horse."

" It's the brown Sandstorm horse, isn't it ? "

" Yes."

" Well, why doesn't he put Billy up, or Biddy ? "

" You *know* Biddy's no good to show a horse ;
and last time Billy rode him the horse was too full
of himself, don't you remember, he kicked one of
the judges off in the ring ? But that was before
Joe bought him from Tom Brien, and now if you're
riding him it's quite probable that they won't
remember the horse ; he looks a lot better since
they whipped the mane off him," Lady Honour
concluded, pensively.

" Are they the same judges ? " I asked.

" One of them is ; the one that was landed,
unfortunately. And he'll give the horse a much
better ride if he's not expecting to be kicked off
if he looses him out of a jog—you see, Willow ? "

" And very nice I'll look when the Sir sees my
picture in the papers riding the champion of the
Tincurry show, won't I ? " Willow did, indeed,
seem rather shaken at the prospect. " Prime state
I'll be in when my dad sends me off to earn my
bread as a governess—he's forever threatening it
on me. If he knew I could read and write as well
as I can, he'd have done it long ago."

" He hates Joe ? " Lady Honour dwelt with
gentle questioning on the subject.

" Isn't he right ? Joe's a rogue, and that Billy—

he's too hot to touch even if he is such a lovely man." Willow was not tender in her admiration. "They're a nice crowd," she said, "to have a young girl like me airing herself round on their horses—a right young Miss I'll be after this."

Lady Honour's smile was gone into laughter in a moment. "Willow, aren't you splendid? Thank you so much. You know, I almost promised poor old Joe you'd do it. He'd have been so upset. . . . Then shall I call for you to-morrow morning? We can tell Richard we're going on to look at a horse—so true!"

"No. Thank you very much all the same, Honour. I'll get myself to the show. You wouldn't have room for Oliver and Dick."

"But you'll never get there in your old car, my *child*!"

"Oh, yes, we will—Oliver's a great mechanic. If he only sits up in a car it goes off with itself like the wheels of blazes." Dick delivered himself of this in a tone of firm intention from which I gathered, more unalterable than his praises of myself, the fact that he was bent on attending his sister on this laurel-gathering expedition for another man's horse.

"Well, that's just as you like," Lady Honour let be lightly. "And if they judge the championship before lunch," she said, "we might go racing in the afternoon."

"Go racing, where? Ballymotey?"

"Wouldn't it be fun? The entries are great.

Will we go? We will—or to the sea," she amended.

"We will," said Willow, and there was an end—or a start—of the matter.

Sir Richard was sitting in the hall waiting when we left the schoolroom fire to seek our tea. He looked down sourly at the floor, through the long bow of his hollow thighs, and his fingers beat a steady flight on the razor-edged crook of his knees. The rain swept in against the glass of the hall windows and his face seemed as a nearer part of that strange light that hangs behind rain. His was the face of an angel betrayed, its lines taken from Beauty and sadly carved in white wood, the glimmer of these lines like rotted wood in the near dusk. Willow, his daughter, has this look of his— this forsaken look as of a spirit burnt away long ago, no more than shadow-thick for good or evil now; malign and humorless, briefly and terribly generous, as tender sometimes as loving children might be unrestrainedly tender, and as cruel and as cold as only children can be in their level unkindness.

"Well, Honour," he said now, "you must have had very little to do at home to take the road on such a day as this. Nothing doing in the Racing World to-day, either, I suppose?"

"You wouldn't see me cross the road to go to a race meeting on a wet day, Richard."

"Not even if there was money to be made?"

" Well, it would want to be the biggest certainty in racing."

Sir Richard grunted. He was looking at Willow who was pouring out tea in withdrawn concentration, but he did not give me the impression that he would now recall to angry life that incident in the schoolroom. In fact, he chid her almost kindly :

" Look at Willow, pouring out tea—you're not pouring beer, Miss. Why can't you pour out tea like a lady ? "

Willow said : " Oliver's the only person who can do right in this house—here, Oliver, you pour out the tea——"

This was not kind to me. No one wishes to be made the darling of the senile. Although I love Sir Richard I cannot be embarrassed on his account. After tea I followed him into his own room, ashamed of my faint embarrassment, and read a paper there till presently the rain ceased and there came to us that strong and idle sense of warmth and beauty that comes from flowers unseen and satisfied after rain. I particularly observed the rich, close scent of laurel blossom—flowering out of due time.

" Are you going out, Cousin Richard ? " I said, when he set a dog down from off his knee and stirred uneasily in his chair.

" I must go up and see if the tank in the attics has overflowed with all this rain," he said ; so I followed him up steep, mean stairways to the tropic regions of the attics. Here a strange hollowly shaped heat was stored beneath the slates, and water dripped with that particular quiet insistence that invests water, even the most domestic, with a solitary dignity—especially in unvisited places.

Here then, in the hot solitude, Sir Richard leaned his body in strange, long angles above the dark water tanks, and I wondered and waited and observed, bearing him company.

" What lovely field boots," I said, spying three pairs, never worn, I think, standing stately and exquisite upon their trees.

" Those are mine," said Sir Richard, with dimly kindling pride. " Ah, what a leg I had for a boot —you *might* say. I bought those just before I gave up the chase. Dick can't wear them, and Dick's leg is not too bad. Could you wear them—— No ? How well the divils whipped the laces out of them even if they couldn't squeeze their legs in " ; he removed his sour scrutiny from those past glories and crossed over to shut a skylight that I had opened. Lady Honour's voice and Willow's came clearly on the stilled air—

" Well, be sure you're there in time——"

" Oh, not a doubt I'll be there. Well, bless you, Cousin Honour. Beauty'll bite you bad over her chickens—take care, Honour——"

" Good night, my sweet——" and a laugh silenced short as the meek Morris engine started up.

Sadly as the Lord of Time Past and now of All Alone, Sir Richard came towards me feeling his way out of the rich dusky tropic. His face was as pitiful as that of a poor man lost among many trees, but it brightened into purpose almost before I had perceived this.

"There goes a right old bitch-fox," he said, as the car's engine died faintlier in the distance. "And *such* a charmer. You'd think Willow would have wit enough to see what a schemer she is—she'll get that child into trouble yet. But children are all the same, they know best—I did myself when I was young. Still, you know, Willow was so *fond* of me one time," his voice gained a sudden geniality at this short tender flight of his memory or imagination, and then again this softness perished from him. "Little she minds me now," he said with no sweet sorrow but bitterly as fathers do.

"I think you're wrong, Cousin Richard," I ventured.

But he waived my faint protest very properly aside. "Though you know her well, Oliver, better than most people do—she's like me, you know ; nobody can ever tell what she's at. But I know her better than she imagines—why wouldn't I ? and I know when she's fond of a person, and I know she's dam fond of you, Oliver. No. Listen to me, it's a fact. You have a great influence there, and if you choose to use it you could do a lot with Willow. I'm *not* happy about the child ; of course, with Honour, that's all right ; but Honour's friends are quite another thing—unless," and here he spoke a thought aloud, " they sicken her of going about with Honour."

Ah, frailty of old passions ! Only their unkindness endures as an abiding itch between those who have known them. Sir Richard would wound now with some of the fervour with which he had once loved, so long ago it might have been forgotten, and Lady Honour would taunt with shafts of venom well seasoned down the years. This was an old abiding pastime. But this why new and evil sport of bandying Willow and Willow's favour back and forth between them. Here was a jealousy past forgiveness. I did not like it at all. And his thought of my interference in the matter shocked me. None so quick as Sir Richard to see this and none so speedy or so graceful to turn the matter from consideration until, in a little while, I looked back on that revealment as though it were but a sickly imagining of my own, suckled to me until I had bloated it into an actual remembrance.

So I saw it the next day, when, together with Willow and Dick, I took the road for the Tincurry Agricultural Show, fulfilling my duty of sitting up in a car that it might go away with itself like blazes. We sat in the front seat, the three of us, and before we had gone very far on the road, stopped to drink a bottle of beer apiece, and fill the car with oil and petrol.

Not many garages combine a draper's shop and a public house with the motor business. We drank

our beer and waited, content now to wait; but
waiting many minutes before a small boy came
hurrying down the street, staggering as he came
beneath the weight of a large tin.

"We had to send up to the other garage for this,"
he said as he gave us our fill of oil. "We have an
oil-tank all right, only we lost the key."

We did not mind. Our hearts were warm and
careless within us. That beer, gold past belief,
had done our bodies good. The mountains on
either side of our road were blue, blue past belief,
as blue as the jersey of a woodcutter's youngest
son. Dick was wearing such a jersey, its high neck
tightened at the back by a safety pin which he
fondly imagined invisible, but the colour was beyond
ecstasy. Willow's hair was enamelled yellow and
her profile clearer and sharper than glass. They
talked of horses I had never known and races I had
never seen, of the servants of Pullinstown and their
faults, of motor-cars and drink; speaking with
serious consideration and unaffected grossness of
metaphor. . . "But Restoration comedy and hair
so yellow is not enough . . ." a poet says. I did not
agree. Not to-day, on this gay morning it was
enough. It was beyond reason to ask for more.

Presently our road took a turn towards the sea,
a sea of gross peacock blue that washed to the very
feet of the mountains in beauty so obvious as to be
near vulgarity. But again we turned inland and
lost sight of the sea, only its poignant, impermanent

breath on a sudden filled the car and as quickly died.

"We must try and buy some lobsters on the way home," Dick said. I think Dick does a greater share of the housekeeping than Willow. "Lobster mayonnaise would put the Sir in great humour."

"Yes, my father is very fond of lobster," Willow's voice was as primly filial as any one could wish to hear. But I am so accustomed to the changes that come on these two, making them sudden strangers to each other, that I am no longer shocked by them.

Silence reigned for a further three miles until we reached a little town and : "Here we are now," said Willow—with these words she invariably concludes any journey, however short—and she had tendered five shillings to the guardian of the car-park and driven through a narrow gate into the walled show-ground of Tincurry before Dick and I could begin to struggle our way towards our money.

"So you've got here at last. I was just thinking I'd have to rise up on the horse myself, y'know. Well, I was getting nervous, y'know——" Again I shook Mr. Billy Morgan by the hand, in a moment hardly spared from his excessive attention to Willow. "Willow," I heard him say as they walked away through the sunlight, "you are a little champion to come and ride him—I *do* mean it——"

Charming creature he was—lovely and bright in the sunlight—charming as a faun, handsome as a

railway poster. Tall and dark *and* handsome, and
his clothes, too, were delightful. No doubt Willow
was right—" He is such a lovely man," but she
had not said it kindly, I was glad to remember.

" Miss Redmond, you don't know my cousin,
do you ? " Dick introduced me to a girl as we
leaned against the rails of the ring, before Willow's
class came in, and I remembered her at once as
that sad third in the photograph which had so upset
Sir Richard. Still sad she was, and prettier far
than in her picture. She had a shy, quick voice
which in moments of excitement dropped to a
passionate whisper, and as she practically never
spoke unless excited she nearly always whispered.
A simple and girlish creature, by nature she was
scarcely fitted for the dire places of unhappy love.
But she loved as the uncomplex do, with a dreary,
undivided passion—yet who, indeed, shall judge
for another ? Are there not as many ways of loving
as there are different people in the world ? Now
she turned her sad regard from Mr. Morgan, whom
we could see across the ring exchanging words of last
import with Willow, and shook hands with me in a
very friendly way before she turned her back on me
to plunge into a very frenzy of whispering with
Dick.

" How did the gallop go ? " I heard, and :
" None too good. The horse he thought would
beat Jesus himself if he came down, didn't go any
too well." Her reply was delivered at speed and

without the smallest suggestion of irreverence.
"And the school?" "Well, it was such a thing
you never saw the equal of it—he set back into the
field and went at the fence and he *screaming*——"
the rest of the account was lost to me in the im-
portunate demands of a bawdy old creature whose
purple shawl and green skirt excited me furiously
by their ecstatic repetition of near mountains and
the nearer pellucid green of summer fields. My
shilling was received with a reverence which sunk
her bulk almost to the ground at my feet and drew
upon me the attentions of every beggar in the show-
ground. A fiddler came to make music before,
or more properly speaking, behind us. He played
a little plucking melody with his thumb before he
broke into a tune like curlews calling—as shrill
and wildly sad.

"I'll make the lady a prisint of a nice little
rack——" An insufferably sick old man thrust a
basket filled by Woolworth between myself and the
whispering girl. "Thims from Paris, mind you——
I haven't a trouser that'd cover me—see—me little
pants is tore——" But she repulsed him with an
easy tolerance which I envied exceedingly.

The judging of Willow's class had now begun.
"Hunter (gelding) or huntress, not less than five
years old, up to thirteen stone to fourteen stone";
and in a class of nine there were at least four really
useful competitors. The horse Willow was riding
would have caught a judge's eye in any show ring.

I rather wondered whether this expedient of Willow's riding would ever fulfil its purpose. Mr. Redmond's Brown gelding, Sandpiper, was unlikely to pass so quickly from the memory of a judge, even had he not cast that judge heavily to the ground. No doubt he was a very impressive, even a delightful horse, over sixteen hands, and yet giving the impression of a small horse ; he had great quality with plenty of size and substance, and as he walked past the rails where we leaned and looked, I thought I had seldom seen a horse with a longer stride. Yes, he should gallop. And as though speaking my thoughts I heard a voice ; a low, slow voice, behind me say : " Ah, walk, trot *and* gallop—— Oh God ! *What* a horse ! "

" Do you know my uncle ? " the girl asked, and continuing the introduction at lightning speed and some length : " Captain Pulleyns, Mr. Redmond ; Mr. Redmond, Captain Pulleyns."

Mr. Redmond enchanted me immediately. I have never met a man with more charming or more simple good manners. It is so easy to ignore young strangers or on the contrary to be over-kind to them, and he did neither. In appearance he betrayed none of his aristocratic if illegitimate breeding, for he was a man of mean stature and gross in the body. He looked as little like a successful horse dealer or trainer of horses as can well be imagined. I would be put to it, indeed, to have said what was his profession or walk in life had I known neither ; but at a guess might have hazarded bird-fancier (this because of his gentleness and his mild, untidy clothes) or auctioneer, for a certain look in his eye—undoubtedly cunning, incalculably swift, and entirely humourless.

As he borrowed my catalogue and leaned beside me watching the slow progression of the judgment, he spoke of many things, and between whiles commented with mild half-praise on the other horses in his class nor ever praised his own. He asked me whether I was interested in old furniture, and told me of some pretty pieces he had bought in odd ways and unexpected places. No one would imagine, he said, there could be any nice things left in farm houses, with all these jew-dealers poking about, but not three weeks ago he went down to a man's place, looking at a horse—an ugly little stump of a pony but a great lepper ; well, a sprung hock and a small foot and he'd lep the devil. He was about buying him for a very nervous lady—anyhow, as he was telling me, there was this delightful commode—two steps up to it— Sheraton. "What, child ?" This to his niece who had whispered a comment or a question in his left ear. "Ah, he's like all those Kosiosmo horses— he's a rotten ride on the road. Every stone that's before him he'll kick it from this to Connaught. But he's a great ride on the land——"

"He's a great lepper," she said ; she was discussing with Dick a grey horse with no middle piece and very indecisive action. "Ah, a brilliant hunter——" But Dick interrupted. "No, he's a horrible horse—a *bad* jumper, I'd say. I saw you riding him in that good hunt from Kilamon, and if he hit a bank a clout behind it was the most he did. He scarcely put a forepaw on anything, and if he did and he saw something he didn't like on the other side, he'd flute round off the top and back into the field with him."

"But he never fell," she protested. "He may have jumped the first three or four fences very ignorant ; but oh, what a good ride he gave him after that, he'd hop in on them the very same as a racehorse. Jesus," she whispered, "do you re- member that big dirty place leaving Coolbawn covert, straight and blind and trees on it and water rattling in under the bushes."

"Oh, a grave——" Dick shuddered. "Death on the other side."

"Well, he hopped in on the top of it and never a living twig stirred on the face of it, and he stood there and changed on it and lepped out into the middle of the field and *away* with him like chain lightning——"

I looked at the grey horse now with increasing respect, almost with awe, his praises singing still in my mind. Though he stood near to the bottom of the line that had been pulled in to unsaddle I discovered for myself certain things to like about him. But Mr. Redmond was sourly firm against him. "He's a small horse, too," he said. "I hate small horses of all classes. You pay seventy-five pounds for them, and you keep them for a year and feed them, and you sell them for seventy-five pounds."

Willow had been pulled in first ; she was showing the horse in hand now, which she did very nicely indeed. "And she's the best girl in Ireland to show a young horse or any horse in hand," Mr. Redmond commented contentedly. The girl whispered : "He does that well," as Willow jogged him back past the judges.

Across the ring where he stood, Lady Honour, wild with excitement, beside him, I have no doubt that her Billy Morgan was saying the same thing. One saw it in the very set of his shoulders, in his idle, contented sprawl against the rails. This poor girl beside me, I caught her eye on him more than once, very fond and unhappy. Unbearably divided she must have been ; if this horse won she must be pleased for her love's delight, and yet because of Willow's riding, no doubt the pleasure was not without its bitterness. And as the judging neared an end she grew more passionately silent, whispered no more to Dick and paid no heed to her uncle or to what he might say. When the horse had been ridden (and whether or not he was deceived in his identity, the judge whose verdict was so doubtful seemed to enjoy his ride to-day). I saw her face strained as though in prayer ; indeed

I know she prayed. And when in the end the judges conferred long together, and all emotion centred small in the bestowal of that red rosette on Sand-piper, I will swear tears were in her eyes ; and as she turned and said to Dick : " *Oh*, but Willow gave the horse a great ride," they overflowed in her enthusiasm and generous emotion.

But when, later in the day, they were beaten in the championship by a sixteen-stone horse, I did not dare to look in her direction and so was sur-prised to hear her say in a tone of matter-of-fact resignation, " Well, that's the luck of the thing. What one judge puts up, another judge'll nearly throw out," and away with her determinedly to whisper her sympathy to her love, Billy, and I could see that with him her passionate loyalty had a too sure worn value, easy as time past.

All through the bright hours of that day I saw her pain, and Willow so devastating and so entirely unmoved in her own lack of loving ; I saw that, too ; and Lady Honour, quick and greedy to observe, I saw that too ; and Mr. Morgan's very nearly graceful devotion, and Dick's entirely graceful insistence on accompanying his sister and this swain, did they go to drink at a car, or look at a yearling, or on a grave inspection of vegetables— all this I saw.

Oh, but she was sweet, Lady Honour, through the long bright day, involving me in ceaseless chatter and a very web of charm, deferring to my valued

opinion on all subjects ; the time to lunch and the
time to drink, and during a searching inspection
of a chestnut mare, which she had no intention of
buying it was : " Lay your hand on that leg,
Oliver—you'd know more about a tendon than I
would." How should I, indeed ? But I answered
masterfully and almost in idiom : " Well, I wouldn't
be one bit afraid of that leg."

" See now," said the young man who paraded
the mare for our inspection, " this is as nice a poor
bloody mare as ever I rode, and God knows he
had me in a critical ould holt one time. Well,
I made a marvellous escape ; 'twas going up on a
fence he should fall and to put me out over the
fence was what he done. When I looked up he
darkened the sky from me. Well, he come down to
me in the ditch afther, and he walked all up along
me and in the latter end all he done was to leave
the thrack of his foot on me coat. Well, only he
had such a nicety I was quinched."

" You were, Sylvester, you were quinched out,"
Lady Honour acceded amiably, and with that we
left him in high humour nor had we even bid him
for that kindly and careful creature of indeterminate
sex.

For an hour then or less we watched the jumping
competitions which grew as wearying as even bad
jumping can become if watched with any persistence. Who said : " Will we go and bathe
in the sea ? We will ! " It may have been Willow,

sitting on her stick with her back to the jumping contests in progress behind her ; or Biddy, worn past endurance by this spectacle which is always Willow ; or Billy Morgan towering ornamentally above us all, swift to bend towards Willow's lightest word and always kind to his faithful one—kind but inattentive. It was not Dick, he had just bought himself an orange from the ancient shrew who hawked a basket of fruit tirelessly about the show-ground. Now he peeled it skilfully and ate a section himself and gave a section to Willow in praiseworthy rotation. His mind was too idly full to give forth so active a suggestion. As for Lady Honour, she was a little tired now and sat on a mackintosh in a sweet silence that demanded all indulgence and protection. Her charming, sharp knees were drawn up and her pretty ankles crossed weary and frail before her. Mr. Redmond, alas, had left us, so it was never his idea. It was mine, I think—in fact I know it to have been mine. And for hours afterwards I was glad, although I went to bed that night with a wild feeling of sorrow in my heart, sorrow as acrid and as pale as those sea-sands where we had played.

For as in sullen Passions and evil tempers man's innocence so quickly dies, so by the sea, briefly it lives again. Oh, riotous inhibition of youth that causes man to clamour against the waves with song and shoutings, to run upon the sands as one who runs in a race, yet asking no worthier fellows in it than the old winds with which, head thrown backwards in unbalanced ecstasy, he ran in youngest days. Oh, gentle inhibition, causing man to lie in the sun, threading the supple sand through his fist ; finished his valorous doings in the harsh waters of the summer seas, a dim content his own. O, strangest of all these inhibitions that which causes man to sport roughly with his love (if he sports at all) by the seaside. The gentlest swain will here—urged by some savage nursery complex—lash his poor love with wide brown tails of seaweed ; or trip the girl and send her sprawling and squalling in the waves ; or run hand-in-hand with her to kiss her salty mouth without emotion.

So, with effortless and happy enthusiasm, may men play by the seaside. I have often observed them, but never with livelier interest than on this day when, having gathered in the harvest of shells which Lady Honour was solemnly sorting into their several kinds : " I send them to a children's hospital," she told me surprisingly. I lay beside her (the gentle inhibition strong in me), and observed those others, all so many years younger than myself, because of their charmingly savage absorption in themselves alone. They were quick of tongue, fleet of foot, lovely in body—and beauty is my delight—but there is no doubt they were savages. Now they ran and leaped in the sands. Willow was the fleetest runner. To please herself she ran and ran along the wet sea edge. Her

pale wet hair was solidly painted on her head ;
her pale reflected legs ran below her, where the
sand was wet enough to hold reflections, and (never
very far behind her) ran Mr. Billy Morgan ; and
(never far behind him) ran his forsaken sweet.
True, occasionally he lashed at her with wet seaweed—as lovers will—then she would run at him
screaming and fasten upon him for a moment's
severe buffeting, and shaken off, pursue again.
They ran like a painting on the walls of some never
found tomb or an unwritten phrase of music. But
know ye not, I could have said to Lady Honour,
had her mind been tuned with mine, that they
who run in a race run all but one winneth the prize ?
And know ye not equally that they who play by the
sea play all but one winneth the game ? So it was
this day, and I, godlike upon the beach, awarded
the prize to Dick.

Some solitariness of spirit had led him to a rock,
far out upon a spit of sand and there he had waited,
and the fatal tide had made it an island for him
surrounded by waters deep enough to suck the
purple weed back and forth, and turn the packed
mussel rows from indigo to wet sapphire. Now to
this stronghold his Willow came flying. Splashing
through the shallow water, she was lifted by him,
his flannel trousers rolled high on his thighs, through
the deeper channel near his sanctuary. Between
them they held the rock against those other two,
hurling great tufts of dripping weed with skilful

intention and sure aim until they routed the invaders. Even that strong, determined man, Mr. Billy Morgan was forced to retire to the beach to dry himself in the sun and his love's hair in a handkerchief (she enjoyed this, I daresay, poor girl), and presently they took a little walk inland. But Willow and Dick stayed on their rock together in a magnificent isolation of body and spirit— their four bare feet in a hot rock pool, they sat side by side, their backs turned to the sun and to us, the vulgar on the beach. They prized off shell-fish with a pen-knife and sought out crabs from their fastnesses, little green crabs, and raced them one against the other, handicapping the faster goers, they soon knew the form of each. Even when the sun had gone in and a salty chill hung low about us, and a cold small wind blew on the cold dark sea, they sat still on their rock and played with these lovely toys, the crabs, and paid no heed at all to the cries of Mr. Morgan or the shrill entreaties of the girl. I thought it quite likely that, like some of our forbears who would sit playing at cards or dice from day to day, they might sit on, racing their crabs and making their bets with each other until it grew too dark to see or until the crabs lost all power to go.

But at last they rose up, and coming back to the shore joined us in a very stately manner. Even Mr. Morgan forbore to chide.

"I'm afraid we'll have to go now," Willow said,

as one regretfully taking leave of an entrancing party, " we have to go and buy some lobsters for the Sir, you know ; and my car is not very speedy (although there's no doubt she is a grand car). So good-bye." She said, " Good-bye " all round with the utmost formality.

" I'll have the horse there for you to-morrow morning." Mr. Morgan wrung her hand at painful length, " and thank you ever so much, Willow, for riding him to-day."

" Oh, thank you very much. I enjoyed the ride——" And apart from us still, and dreaming between themselves, Willow and Dick silently pursued their way up the stony sea road that led back to the cars.

Indeed, I think they would have left me behind them had I not determinedly set myself down in the back seat of Willow's motor (it belonged strictly to the days of motors, not to the days of cars— this ancient machine). Here cold and contrary winds blew upon me to chill my person already bruised in transit ; for, though Willow's motor might not go as fast as she could wish, at least she drove it as fast as it could go, and, unhappily, neither the roads nor the springs were good.

At last we stopped, again by the edge of the sea, and here they bargained endlessly for lobsters, with a determined young seafaring man. It was late now. Lights shone wanly from the windows of little houses and, massed horridly in a dark box, the lobsters writhed their bound claws.

Willow and Dick struck matches and by this fitful light selected their purchases. The little flames flickered in small distortion on the wet blue shells, while the waves came beating, beating in from the sea—a Synge-like dirge of melancholy— and I stood shivering, shivering on the stone harbour jetty, and Willow and Dick tirelessly conducted their business.

"I *think* we robbed him, all right," Dick said comfortably as, the lobsters disposed now in the back of the car about my feet, we turned for home at last. I longed to sit in front with them, but they had forgotten me now and our faint love for each other, and I did not like to suggest it. So I sat on, lobsters stirring about my feet in dark distress, until one of them freed his potent nipper and seized me cruelly by the ankle. Then, indeed, my scream of anguish called back their tenderer feelings towards me and they stopped the car and placed me between them in the place of honour and warmth, and comforted me with kind words. Presently we stopped at a hotel and drank whisky by a hot fire and ate fried eggs and bacon—very good, before we continued on our way back through the mountains and so on to Pullinstown.

Here we found Sir Richard sitting in his study, rather pale and quiet in himself. He made no

motion of surprise at our late return nor did he speak
a word of inquiry or welcome.

"We were at Tincurry show, father," Dick
ventured at last. "We went on to the sea with
Honour and then round by Portlogue to get some
lobsters ; we didn't expect to be so late, you know."

"I see." Sir Richard looked up at the pair of us
over the top of his spectacles, carrying in his glance
a lack of interest only equalled by a sum of disapproval. "And where is Willow ? Mr. Billy
Morgan is driving her home, I suppose——" But
before we could answer with swift and appropriate
denial, Willow put her head round the door and
came in. Her tired, small face looked very harsh
in the lamplight.

"Hallo, Sir Richard," she said. "I'm sorry you
waited dinner for us—James told me. We brought
you back some good lobsters anyhow. James is
cooking an omelette for us," she said to Dick and
me.

"Why should James have to beat eggs for
omelettes at his time of life—at this time of night ? "
Sir Richard fired out. "What's the cook there for,
miss ? Eh, miss, what is that idle slut paid for ? "

"Mrs. Hogan had to boil the lobsters and play the
melodeon," Willow excused her handmaiden, " and
James really likes to do a stroke of cooking—you
know he does, father."

Sir Richard regarded his daughter in a silence
that accepted neither explanation nor defeat, but

he said nothing more and pursued no further the question of Mr. Billy Morgan. I found myself wishing very much that he would ; that he would fall on Willow with angry words which we might then, all three of us, refute—explaining and denying. But that I knew would not happen, for words could never undo that deep and knotted hurt which the very circumstances of life had dealt him.

I saw it suddenly in one truthful moment as we sat there together, Willow and Sir Richard in limitless antipathy to each other, Dick and I un-happy and watchful. I saw how Willow had stolen from Sir Richard his last romantic hold on life. With this cursed fashion she had taken of forever going to Templeshambo, and forever laughing and scheming quiet little plans with Honour she cut Sir Richard's romance away from him. She was Romance for them. She with her gold hair and her dangerous young ways—they loved and dreaded her, these ladies, and through her they might revenge themselves for old remembered hurts, beating Sir Richard with sweet words in their piteous spite.

" Willow is so *fond* of being with us——" " We love to have the child." " Oh, didn't Willow tell you that ? She told us a long time ago, but it was in confidence—of course I thought she'd have men-tioned it to you, Richard, or I wouldn't have said a word. I always was so *silly* . . ." Thus Lady Honour.

So the tale of race-meetings and horse-shows and

little scandals of the turf rose mightily with skilful
repetition until he knew they had taken Willow
quite away from him as she had cut them off from
him. For of what account now were his rare
Sunday afternoon visits to Templeshambo, in which
aforetime they had skirmished with old memory
and delighted in present company, compared to the
live flame of Willow's frequent presence? Ah, he
was bereft, alone in silly age, when even his power
to charm could betray him and his quick brain
served him more slowly every year. Loving now
where once he had been a king beloved; cute now
when once a brilliancy of deceit and acumen had
been his. And his Willow must devastate for him
this last conceit in life. His silence and his complaint
were bitter, as bitter as they were unworthy. Nor
could I see comfort for him anywhere until Dick,
rising from the chair where he had been reading
his post, handed his father a letter, saying : " That's
dam funny, Sir Richard. There's a bit of dirt
in that you'll enjoy," before he followed Willow and
me out of the room. And on Sir Richard's face
came suddenly a grave pleasure. He did not, as I
had done, see this as pretty behaviour, but as an
unmeditated small confidence. He was right, too,
and I wrong. The emotional vulgarity of my
surmise shocked me.

James was waiting for us in the dining-room. He
pushed in Willow's chair and reproved her as she
sat whistling a dreary little tune through her teeth.

" Miss Willow," he said, " strive now and behave like a lady should, and above all," he added, as he handed her her soup, " a whistling woman and a crowing hen are bad luck to a house."

Willow paid no attention, but she ceased whistling to drink her soup. Again she was sitting with her back to that pale ancestress in the green stomacher and pearls, to whom she bore so strong a likeness, and again the likeness touched me oddly. For behind all Willow's unkindness there is still something sweet and gently silly inherited perhaps with green eyes and hair so yellow.

" You'll want to call us early in the morning, James," Willow said towards the end of our meal. " We have to ride on to Piercetown and it's a good five miles. I suppose you told Pheelan, Dick? Of course you did. I meant to say I'd ride the pony on. I don't want to have one of Billy's boys messing about on Chatter—she'd fire them. Now that mare "—Willow stooped to the floor—" has a very deceitful way of bucking. She'll start *here* "—and she placed a forefinger on the carpet—" and *here's* where she'll finish up "—she drew her finger backwards, looking up at us as one who has made a really masterful exposition of a difficult subject.

" Oh, blessed Hour ! " James murmured his consternation, while Dick continued to stare at the carpet as though he might see there the solving of some further riddle.

" You're riding the show horse in the morning ? "

I asked, the reason for all these complications dawning on me at last. "What sort of a hunter is he?"

"Ah, no sort at all, but what does that matter? We'll only be airing ourselves round Piercetown woods. Looking beautiful, that's what we'll be doing. You might give my good field-boots a rub, James, if you have a minute—or tell one of those idle divils in the kitchen to do them for me."

"Me feet are tired," James replied, with sullen acerbity which took no account of Willow's last command. "I must go and put them in water."

"Do, James, do go and take a paddle out round the lake for yourself," Dick suggested cordially.

"It's in the sink he'll put them," Willow prophesied horridly, "when he's done lashing the silver round the pantry."

"May God forgive you, Miss Willow. I'd quinch out in the boots before I'd do a rude dirty act the like o' that."

"There was one time, Oliver," Willow turned to me, "James had the influenza on him and I went down to the pantry to give him a *Faivre* cachet, and there he was, dressed up in his coat and hat, sitting on the plate rack with his two feet in the sink, and a whole bottle of my bath salts a lover gave me and a big tin of mustard in the water, and a mug of hot buttermilk on one side of him and a big drink of the Sir's best whisky on the other."

"Ah, 'twas light in the head I was that time," James gave in agreeably. "I was killed with an inward pain and the girls in the house vexed me——"

"Have done, now! Have done—is this a proper time of night to be sitting up stuffing yourselves and keeping that old dying fool out of his bed?" Sir Richard, a candle in his hand and his purple skull-cap low on his brow, stood in the doorway. He looked at his children with tired, unloving eyes and sick of regarding their iniquity, turned from them in silence and walked slowly down the hall and up the stairs to bed.

We looked at one another darkly, our easy laughter quenched within us.

"'Twas whatever her ladyship told him when she come to him this evening vexed Sir Richard," James announced from behind the tray which he was at last carrying down to the pantry. "He was greatly knocked about in himself after she going."

"*Oh*, so Honour was here, was she indeed?" After prolonged thought Willow rose from her chair, saying: "Well, Dick, we must pin a note to the saddle-room door to say I'll ride the pony on in the morning. You wouldn't like to do it for me, would you, Oliver? You're the best writer of the lot of us——"

It was on my return from this errand that I passed under Willow's window and heard her laughter within the room, her laughter and Dick's low voice, and again suppressed shouts of laughter from them both—the insufferable, impious laughter of the young and unkind. I was swept by my pity for their victims, for myself stumbling up steps crude and unfamiliar in the darkness at their behests —for James whose lighted pantry window told that he served them still—for that poor whispering one whose love Willow had desolated. Of Sir Richard I would think no more and of Lady Honour only that she was likely to suffer further at their hands. And so, afar in spirit and apart from them in their pitiless youth I laid myself at last in my bed.

No quality of enthusiasm can take that dour sting from the awakening on a cub-hunting morning. The hour is unfit for man and man for the hour. James coughed and sniffed when he called me. The candles on my dressing-table burnt weakly in the heavy stealth of the day's delay. I looked out of my window into thick fog, low hung across the lake, and took myself shivering to the bathroom, when the day at last put on reality with the cheering sounds of busyness that came to me from the stables below.

A boiled egg, weak China tea and hoarse early morning voices are concomitants of cub-hunting. Serious and intent we gathered ourselves up and walked out of the dark, sleeping house into the morning that was not yet parted from the night. Dark waterfowl took to their heavy wings and flew low across the lake as we rode by. The lake water appeared as a solid black floor below the fog, untrue and surprising. Young horses moved blockily as cattle in the fogged half-light. All beauty was withdrawn. Beauty has hours.

We rode along silently, our thoughts shrugged together within us, hunching forbidding shoulders to any amity. Willow's pony was fresh and unmannerly. She beat her and called her rude names. Dick's horse—that chestnut horse, cultivated now from last year's brutality—was his delight. He rode him in thoughtful pleasure as one only rides what one knows to be a good horse. I had a brown four-year-old mare that I had ideas about buying from Sir Richard. Thus far she showed herself a reasonable and kindly creature, a bit green of her mouth perhaps. I would know more of that later, but a good ride I thought.

Presently in the changing light Beauty was born unto us. Unto us a day was given. If I tell of this hour it is lost to me, forever lost to me, its gift and its secret mine no more.

Willow cleared her throat and said: " You wouldn't see a fox go any earlier than this——" We were riding up a low road below a wood. The mist hung still as thick as milk about the mountains' feet and a milky bow was drawn across the sky behind the mist. On our left the wan black-gartered birch-trees flickered no noisy leaf in the still air. Cobwebs smoked about the heavy flame of the rowan berries, burning in sacrifice to some goddess of these groves. And then—unendurably picturesque—hounds, huntsman and servants were jogging before us down the road. The morning was shriven of all peculiar secrecy and the matters of the day began.

We embarked now upon serious cub-hunting, There was only a small field out and any one with a pretension to commonsense was sent on to watch some ride or corner where a fox might slip away. I found myself being piloted by Dick to a point of vantage above the steep glen of the wood. There he left me to consider my fate : to eat blackberries ; to be eaten by midges ; and to keep a rambling eye on the bracken-grown field that bordered the wood below me, while he cantered on to a more dangerous corner away at the top end of the glen. " Mind you, Oliver, if you holloa him away on an old fox he'll murder you. Now he won't leave a feather on your body . . ." and I was left to my lonely contemplation.

Willow was away on my right. She and Mr. Billy Morgan watched a ride, their horses head to tail, their vigil lightened by a hushed and earnest chatter. Now she had changed on to the show horse and I perceived that one of yesterday's judges was out, mounted by the master. No doubt Willow rode the horse very prettily, but my sympathy was all for Biddy Redmond, who knocked her green four-year-old about and whispered abuse at him. I wished that poor girl all success. She had ridden on with Dick and was in the next field but one to me, watching down a fern and bramble-filled tongue of glen. And as she passed me by on her way to her post I thought never had I seen such dark and lost unhappiness in any countenance. So deadly serious she was and seeing no reason in this matter but only an agony of unkindness. I thought I would talk to Willow myself about it. Then I thought No. Words make too much importance of trivial things. Nor could I ever face that blank incomprehension with which Willow or Dick suffer the consideration of the emotions.

Hounds were hunting in the wood—their voices nearly at my feet, then turning as their fox turned and failing farther from me. There was a scent in covert this morning. He must have turned very short, and they were at him again with no delay. Much has been said and much written of the beauty and the glory of hounds' voices, but ever again their music grips the heart towards a perilous ecstasy.

An old man came prowling out of the wood towards me. He had no shame for his romantical reactions. Tears stood in his eyes and he wiped his mouth on his hand.

"Dere is no music," he said, "like lishning to de bugle in de morning," and he stood beside me, gazing raptly down.

"Is there much young foxes in it?" said I, striving towards the idiom.

"Now a covey of young foxes, they do be abroad

yelling and roaring in it about the night time. There was two broods of thim rared in the moat above. The gintleman came to me a-Tuesday to put an ould stench bottle in the den. ' What use,' I said, ' what use in it ? Where the wild dog do make his bed, major, there he will lie. You will not change it, major.' . . ." His voice failed into silence. Again the hounds had turned and were hunting back down the opposite side of the glen towards us. A great place this to make young hounds, but, I thought, a horrible place to get away from in the winter months.

"'*Tis the lad himself*," the old man hissed, his face pearl-white with excitement, and indeed I saw, stealing in conventional style along the wood ditch a very conventional Old Customer. "Hush, man ! " said I, " it's the young brood they're hunting to-day. Don't say a word now," and our fox slipped back into the covert.

He threw out despairing hands. " Ye have no vinom," he almost wailed, " no vinom in ye for the chase, and you with your pride and your strong horse. Oh, pity ! pity ! "

" Now see," he said, " when I was in my prime I wrought in Devereux's o' Silver thirty year. Ah, those were the men to ride and the men to drink. And 'twas I incensed them and they young lads that time. I well recall," he said, " a day meself and the youngest little lad rode in to the fair of Cahin. Now such a day of rain I never see—the full of the skies was in it, there wasn't a stitch dry on the two of us and we crucified with the cold. Well, what did I do? *I gave him a little t'imble o' brandy.* 'D'ye know,' says he, 'I feel terrible well now. I never remember,' he says, 'to feel so well before. Wait till I tell ye what ye'll do,' he says, 'redden up the pipe and give me a couple o' draws at it for fear would the Uncle get the smell of the brandy off me.' He was in great dread o' the Uncle. Well, I did, I did. I reddened up the pipe and I took him up a little bye-lane and I gave him a couple o' draws at it. Ah, Master Hubert was a grand, unruly boy. . . ."

He left me with a feeling of faint distress. I could not bear him to think me such a very unsporting man, but saw no way to better myself in his opinion, being myself neither grand nor unruly.

I lit a cigarette and waited, listening now with shameless emotion to that nearing music and to the huntsman's voice echoing romantically off larch trees. Foxhunting overcomes me with excitement.

"An old fox," said I, riding down to the edge of the field as he rode up to the fringe of the wood, where his hounds were feathering, busily but uncertain now. "He came out into the field here and went back into the covert there——" As I spoke there came shrill and imperative from Biddy's corner a series of prolonged screams.

"Some woman in pain," he smiled. "It's Biddy Redmond, I think. Biddy'd never holloa me on to an old fox, anyway," and as a spectator subsequently observed : " He gothered himself and he blew a couple o' blasts out o' the bugle-horn to gother up the dogs and away with him."

Willow and Billy Morgan came along the ride below. They were talking in low and passionate undertones, their heads stooped together. Preparing myself to feel confused and angry, I heard : " She was jumping beautifully "—Willow's voice low as though in prayer—" She made a couple of lengths every fence she jumped—well, she *skipped* away from them——" So the green murk of the wood bred no more passion than this—well, how can one ever tell ? I turned my mind unto the chase again. And almost too late, as is ever the way, for the chase brooks no inconstancy of attention. As I pulled myself together those quick doubled notes on the horn came to us from the far corner where the huntsman had gone to Biddy's holloa, and the changed cry of hounds hunting in the open strove back to us on the heavy air.

" They're away," said I. " *Willow*, they're gone——"

" Ah, not at all "—Mr. Billy Mirgan put his cigarette case back in his pocket, however—" they'll only take a turn around the glen. B'God, Willow," said he, " they *are* gone."

Up a lane-way we galloped then, the three of us, swinging round hideous corners, opening two gates through a farmyard where geese ran at us furiously and a lean calf and a mangy white greyhound joined our numbers (we gave the calf a few savage clouts and galloped over the greyhound) and then I saw them a field on our right and hunting towards us. So we called a guilty halt, cringing in the deep lane-way. When it faltered and ended in a stony field, the hounds struggled through the blind growth of a high bank and had the line again over the field and away from the covert.

"God help us all now." Willow caught hold of her show horse and rattled him along. "This doesn't look very like a cub they're hunting."

A moment later I had a vision of Biddy's small face white with determination and justifiable terror as she shouted at her horse and launched him into the heart of such growth as six hard frosts would scarcely have subdued into a state to have made me think the fence a reasonable one. No doubt she meant having a desperate go this morning. Willow on the show horse slipped out through what was almost a gap—Willow has an eye for gaps only comparable to a fox's—and I followed her.

Hereafter ensued one of the grimmest and least enjoyable hours I have ever known in my limited experience of fox-hunting. The end of August is in no way a fit season of the year to ride over County Westcommon. A good blackbird might reasonably expect to see a hunt without disaster or mishap to his person, but for a man mounted upon a horse these banks grown over blind and solid with briars provide a much more difficult and dangerous problem. Besides they are so frightening.

I cannot now pretend to speak of what hounds did or did not do as they pursued their fox. I only know that scent was good enough to enable them to have their wicked way with him for miles and miles and hours and hours before it was in our power to get within a field of them.

And always Biddy was foremost in the contest; and always Willow was cleverest; and sometimes I was brave, and sometimes weak with cowardice. But I took turns with Dick in springing on and off my horse to pull gaps or open gates—oh, we were not too proud—while Biddy and that judge whose name I never knew rode the hunt together in a glorious and honourable fashion. Not a doubt but they won it completely.

" Well, my horse is a bad lepper and my bones are rotten little bones "—Willow waited for me as I climbed back on to my horse—" but *look* at Biddy. I ask you now, *look* at her ! " It was a high narrow bank and the top of it leaning towards her, but Biddy charged into it as though it was not there. The horse she was riding—a blood sort of brown brute with a mane and tail—such a horse as the heroine of such a hunt in Ireland should ride, never put a fore-foot on it at all ; he just hit it a kick behind and scratched somehow over the ditch on the landing side. Honour (I suppose) demanded that the unknown hero of the proceedings should ask his horse no less a question. The answer, however, was the wrong one. Valour deserved more fortune, I thought, as I skirted down a lane and took to the country again, and this time with a certain confidence in my lovely mare—for never think we had not jumped some hideous fences which an affectation of modesty forbids me to describe.

Some lucky turn put me now on better terms with the hounds, further behind their fox and hunting at a nice reasonable pace. And over a series of charming low stone walls I knew almost my first moments of enjoyment in the morning. The going was grand and my horse not quite tired enough to frighten me over these simple obstacles. I leapt them on Biddy's right hand and galloped beside her over the wide fields. Not a doubt in my mind now but I would buy this mare from Sir Richard. She was a great goer in her gallop, really got away with it, speedy too, I thought. Although her errors over banks had been many, they were forgivable and she sprang over these walls like a buck. Willow's show horse was getting under them and hooking himself over somehow—not a very flattering display of jumping, and I wondered what Mr. Morgan would have to say when he stiffened up on the knocks and bumps he must have dealt himself in the course of the hunt. Dick on his chestnut horse was smiling to himself and riding along with that absence of venom which my old companion of the morning had so deplored in me. Of the others, the master was always there, and the judge was joined to us again with his horse's head covered in mud and his own hat dented in several directions. Mr. Morgan took the matter quietly and sensibly and turned the lanes to good account. He was riding an entirely green four-year-old.

"Do you know where you are, Oliver?" Dick asked me the impossible question, put to all strangers in all countries when hounds have run a complete circle and are back in the covert where they found their fox, or else when the stranger is at the gate of the habitation from which he adventured forth in the morning.

So: "Pullinstown?" I hazarded cautiously, and Dick nodded surprised approval.

"A four-mile point from Piercetown," he grinned. "That was a grand, bold, determined cub Biddy viewed away."

Hounds had checked crossing a road and the master held them over it where they had it again up along the fence and hunted on towards the woods and through a wing of trees to mark their fox to ground in a sandy cavern high above the river's bank.

"Great stuff to dig in—sand." Dick smiled portentously as the fervour of the mark abated. "You'll soon know, Oliver. Come on now till we gather up the spades and terriers. The morning's work is only starting, boy. We won't be done digging here till teatime. It's a holy-God-terror of a spot, this is."

" As for you, Biddy—where is she ? " The master looked sternly about him. " Come here, miss. You're a very naughty girl. I thought you were the last person to do a thing like that—there's not one of you I can trust."

" Oh," Biddy was whispering, " it was a cub I hollaoed you on to. It was really. They changed, you know, they must have changed on to this lad in the bit of gorse they ran through two fields from the wood."

" *Not* very likely, I think "—he looked at her reprovingly. Anyhow you'll have to stay and dig now for your punishment. Where are those terriers, I wonder. Did anybody see the car in the road ? " He blew his horn again. I see him now—a stubby little man stooping in the sunlight to blow it, his mind intent on fox-catching alone, his thoughts for his hounds and his consideration all on the dig before him, its difficulties and probabilities.

It did not look an easy place either, this refuge and harbour for the thief of the world. There would be shelves in it and passages crossing all at different levels. The main opening, where the hounds shoved and scratched and growled in the sandy mouth was ledged below the woods where a bracken and bramble grown slope dropped its first steep flights down to a curling bend of river below. The sun was on the grey rocks that showed above the stream and shadows deep in the pools behind them, and the sun striped and bathed the bank in gold, roasting the blackberries and drowsing the blue-bottles that settled upon them. And behind again the woods were dark as old ivy and hollow as mockery. Tall green stones leaned together in them and elder trees gave forth their stale smells.

" Look ! " said Willow ; she was standing gazing in reflective consideration at her horse's legs, the sunlight hot upon her and the shadow green, " wouldn't a bottle of beer be great ? Well, now " —she turned herself about—" where is my pony, I wonder. If I had my pony, you know what I'd do, Oliver ? I'd send this yoke home with the boy before he's hopping lame altogether. I could tie my pony to a bush, you know, and ride her home at my leisure. I wouldn't like to walk home, it's a mile from here to the house. That's a long walk, Oliver."

" You can ride this animal down," said I. " I will ride your horse home now if the boy doesn't appear."

Then followed one of those difficult and inter-minable arguments which precede alike the de-parture and the return of horses from and to their stables. " If I ride your horse I can lead such another." " No, because the brute won't lead. He's funny like that." " Then I'll ride him." " But my saddle must go home." " Anyhow some one else can lead two horses quite well, why should you ? "

' No, but why shouldn't I ? " " Well, why should
you ? . . ."

Much such an argument proceeded now and Biddy
who had been up to this whispering excitedly to the
judge, her companion in peril and gallant endeavour,
joined us to say with surprising decision : " *Bill*y
can take both these horses back, Willow—yours
and mine—God, I was delighted with this horse.
How did that fellow carry you ? I was really
delighted with him."

" And this fellow'll make no bad hunter," Willow
conceded agreeably. " Mind you, this morning
was a wicked test of an ignorant horse, Biddy, and
though he gave me a few severe frights, I never
actually got him down. I didn't try very hard. I
was quite careful of myself. But that's a great
thing you're riding, Biddy."

" He is, Willow. Now I think he's a miraculous
young horse."

" And *I* think you're a miraculous young woman."
Full of enthusiasm and hearty admiration, the
stranger could not leave her side for a moment,
but must praise and dwell on his praises. I wondered
whether this poor Biddy would flower towards
them at all. Would their healthy balm heal her
shrill pains and callous the wound that Love had
dealt to her ?

" If you can send the horse home I'll drive you
back," he was saying now, and we entered again
upon giddy argument. Billy Morgan appeared,

followed by his groom on Willow's pony and matters
were sorted and horses dispersing when a sudden
presence was with us, a presence coming between
us and our morning amity as the shadow of a bird
comes between the sun and the grass.

It was Sir Richard who stood among us—Sir
Richard, lord of Pullinstown—a very prince upon
his acres and polite with the politeness of princes
within their own possessions. He bade Mr. Morgan
a polite good-morning ; spoke a friendly word with
Biddy ; and remembered acurately when and where
he and the brave stranger had met before. But I
saw anger and concern in his very gentleness and
in his silence towards Willow and myself : in his
lack of remark when the saddle was moved from
the show horse and put upon her pony : in the
quick, hooded looks he darted about him as if he
must know whether there were any other actors
concealed in this plot for his undoing. I think he
thought Honour might cry out at him, rudely
popping up from behind a near rock in the wood.
I, too, saw her there, dancing on little old sprightly
legs while Willow and Billy Morgan bade each
other a kind farewell—for he must ride home now
with the horses, he could not stay to dig.

The spades and terriers were here now and digging
had begun in earnest. Through long hours of that
gold day we dug in turns and lay by turns in the
sun. We sank long shafts taller than man and
broke down through sandy passages and still the

bravest of all terriers, the most renowned for valour and sagacity, stayed down with his fox, nor could we reach him though we could hear the faint echoes of his lonely courage.

Apart a little the hounds waited in vigilant expectancy about their huntsman, and he, leaning upon a tree, sometimes rated a misdoer, determinedly breaking back towards the earth, his voice strong and angry, but more often spoke in gentleness : " Vestal—Vestal, little bitch ! Vestal, poor little one——" or held low converse with his girl friends, Willow or Biddy. They entertained him, I could see, and it was their delight to do so, for he was a rare and charming man, bitter of tongue, malign and perceptive, worthy of entertainment.

Flung down upon blessed and sunlit grass in an interval of repose, I knew that delight of this moment was with me. And to know Delight, to put three rings about it forever before the anguish and the peril of its passing is to be as an immortal. Only when it is gone Delight is wholly ours. When it is with us the anguish and the peril are still to come, when its hour passes, they are translated into ghosts, holy ghosts and comforters, to walk by our sides. Now I knew the moment here : lying in the heat, the mountains on my right hand, the river on my left, I could stare down into its waters and deep into the folded mountains from where they came, and I could feel the shiver through the dark bird-visited woods behind me. I could hear Dick's voice and sometimes Willow's and the sound of the spades as I lay in quietness of mind and body.

I woke from this entranced reflection to see a very strange man come striding towards us through the wood. Tall he was and pale, a lean, long face and odd eyes—one blue, one brown—beautiful eyes. His limbs were long and loose and his clothes past the calculation of their age. He came walking fast out of the wood and straight into the middle of the pack where one old dog hound made a determined drive at him and ripped the pocket from his coat.

"What matter? What matter? Don't beat him, now," he said, raising his hand in deprecatory negligence as the hounds were rated into unquiet peace. "Look!" he said. "You's are digging a fox?"

"We are, Garry," the master allowed guardedly.

"Look!" he repeated. "You's have no dog like to my dog. Now I have a dog is the reigning dog of all."

"Have you him here?"

"No, but I have him with me cousin below," and he pointed towards a farmhouse two miles distant across the river.

"And the bridge three miles away!" The master's voice was significant. "I know these dogs that are such grand dogs when they are out of danger."

"See now"—the man was in desperate earnest—

" there's no fox nor badger but my dog would best them. Will I go get him ? "

" Do, Garry—good man," Willow encouraged him with polite indulgence. " Take the boat below."

" Oh, 'tis a gigglesome ould yoke. Look ! I'll be no length going."

" That one's as mad as bedlam," she said, " and he has three brothers as mad as himself. Look at him now—I ask you, look at him now ! "

Straight down the high rocky bank he had gone, and into the river where he met it, he waded and floundered to the opposite bank, the water sometimes up to his chin—" and I bet you tuppence he can't swim " ; Willow gazed after him fascinated, marking the straight line he took through the country towards that cousin's farm and his return, swift as a bird—he would have flown, it seemed, but that he was held down to earth by a large, reluctant dog attached to a short length of rope. Over the river the dog was towed, and I wonder he did not drown this single-hearted man in the deeper waters. But he did not drown. He came out of the water and straight on up the bank without waiting to shake the water from his hair, or stopping to see where a track led through the rocks and brambles. Never have I seen such bland intensity of purpose or so inhuman a display of bravery as followed.

There was a stir of increased excitement round the earth as he arrived there, for one of the shafts we had sunk cut down through a cross-passage and, very near now, we could hear the dog at his fox.

Garry leaped into the hole and plunged an arm and shoulder down the opening. " 'Tis rock above," he said, and struggled farther in. " I have the dog," he said.

" Take care," they said, " he'll whip the hand off you."

But a weary, grim little terrier with a wicked bite through his foot did no more than pant and growl as he was gripped by the skin of his back and thrust out and this other great creature forced in. I cannot say he went with any great keenness, and on his re-appearance a very few minutes later his master, in dreadful and silent shame and anger, seized and flung him, as far as strength and arm would throw, towards the river below.

" A pick," he bawled, " give here that pick ! " and we lesser men obeyed and gave it to him and saw him thrust down through the earth with the strength of madness : and saw him plunge his head and both arms into the opening he had en-larged : and saw him bring forth a terrible old boar badger, a foreleg and the skin of its back gripped in his bare hands : and saw its struggle and its escape within its dark retreat again : and saw, most wonderful, him plunge down after it a second time and draw it forth again to the bright and cruel hour. And as he stooped then gasping, his head a foot below the level of the field, terriers screaming and men shouting, eighteen couples of hounds broke from where they were held on the edge of the wood and poured over earth and man and badger. Nor even then did he loose his hold upon his prey till the hounds had him.

It was a strange and awful thing, wild in savagery, simple in its oblation of self to the moment. I see him, the light gone from his eyes, standing on the edge of the wood through which he had come to us, and his quiet words I well remember : " I must leave you now," he said in gentle courtliness, " I must go drown me poor dog. Here, *Lily !* Lily ! " and he went calling through the wood and disappeared at last in a grove of elder trees. I never saw him again, nor ever forgot him.

" Ah," said Willow, as I walked by her side back towards the house and towards food and drink and rest after this strong morning. " He's only out of the asylum three months in the year. He's very mad. I wonder will he drown his dog ? He will. No, but did you ever see the equal of it, Oliver ? "

" No, never," said I, and knew too that I would never look upon the like again. Nor on such a morning as that which was past from us.

Down a field road towards the house we were walking, and Willow delayed a little, I thought, she walked out across the field to look at a young horse and leaned upon a little bridge that crossed a stream that fed the lake and watched the swans oaring their lovely crafts of bodies on the waters and picking placidly at gold birch leaves that floated half in the shining air of afternoon and half on the bright and silver water of the lake. The swans swam through the reflections of the gold and red and blue willows planted by the lakeside and it was as though, invulnerable in beauty, they passed unhurt through fire and smoke.

" Not a doubt," said Willow, " but the autumn months are here." She lifted up her thin nose sniffing at the air, and a wind curled over the lake, its wintry reason brimming the little tide of excitement that rose upon her words. Near at hand, but not in sight, the smell of burning weeds was a bitter breath about the amethyst of Michaelmas daisies, before the banisters of those flowing steps, that which, dim as the miasma over a swamp, flowered are so lovely in Pullinstown's abandoned garden. The wings of the house stretched forth towards the outspread wings of the woods. There is nowhere so beautiful a house.

" Well." Willow laid her palms upon the stone parapet of the bridge and leaned out over the water, her weight upon her wrists as a child leans over water. " Well, that was a terrible morning, Oliver. What ? But the best of it all was Biddy getting him away on an old fox. Well, isn't she a divil ? "

" Why did she do it, Willow ? " said I. I knew. But I did not know what answer Willow would give me.

" All for a bit of fun, I suppose." Willow picked

moss from between the stones with a piece of stick.
" Or else she thought I might throw the show horse
down in a ditch in my excitement and annoy
Billy. I kept myself very quiet, didn't I, Oliver?
I'm not one bit jealous at this time of year—nor
at any other, in fact. Poor Biddy "—she laughed
inconsequently. " Love is a divil," she said. " You
wouldn't be rightly yourself, you know, Oliver, when
you'd be in love. So they tell me," she finished,
with an afterthought, and then we continued on our
way towards the house.

Dick met us in the hall where he had been waiting
for our arrival.

"Willow," he said—there was a foreboding
gravity in his approach near to us before he spoke—
" The Sir's *lepping*—lepping out of his body."

" Is he ? " Willow put her short leather-covered
stick down on the table with a defiant rattle. " Well,
let him lep. Let him get out of his troubles the same
way he got into them." There was a fine conclusiveness about this, although when I came to think
of it, it meant just less than nothing at all.

Dick took her by the elbow and walked her away
upstairs, and I have never seen Willow's face so set
and stormy as when she leaned over the banister
to tell me to go into the dining-room and start a
meal without waiting for them.

By myself in the dining-room a sudden forlorn
despair seized on my spirit. How should I, who
am made otherwise, measure the strength for good

or the strength for evil of these moods of passion that swept upon the Pulleyns of this house? How know their tenderness for one another, their cruelty to one another, their distrusts or their immeasurable confidences? I might not judge. I could not tell. I who had never lived as they lived, near to danger, untutored beyond the simplicities of life and therefore living the dramas that such as I observed. I have known Willow retire to her bed in the middle of the day because of bitter words which passed between her and Dick. "He's not fit to eat with," she had said, and meant it too. And their reconciliation was only effected by James who told each with secret subtlety of the other's fastings in unhappiness, so wooing them back to kindness once more.

Now he came in to minister to my wants and to hear my version of the morning's doings.

"'Tis a critical old place, God knows," he said, when I had at last accounted for my own doings, Dick's, Willow's, the hounds and their fox. "I well recall," he said, "a little fox I had one time, I rared a pet. He followed me out there one evening I was fishing for trout and he slipped off up to the burra; well, I was half the night in it afther— whistling and fistling and roaring and he's not come to me till near morning. Well, I was as fond of him I wouldn't bate him. Look, he was as cute ye'd love to see him. How did I get to rare him? On an ould foster I gothered, a collie bitch with one eye, an' I kep' him hung up in a bag from

a beam till he grew big and strong in himself·
Well, when ye'd call him be name, he'd strip
the teeth, lay back the ears an' wag a little
tail. God, he surely grew to be a noble fox
and only for Sir Richard he was living yet. He
had me annoyed and he had me enticed one time
to mate him to a terrier bitch and she got vexed
with him and choked him. Well, I was as sorry
afther him I had to cry afther him, 'twas pitiful——"
Again tragedy, I thought, and related as the merest
commonplace of life.

Dick came in and sat down opposite to me. His
expression was reserved and disconsolate, so I
continued to eat my pudding in silence querying
neither by look nor question into these hard matters.
James had more curiosity and less restraint.

"In the great name of God," said he, "what
should keep Miss Willow this length?"

"She's in the study," said Dick, "with Sir
Richard." And there was in his words so quiet
and sinister a ring that I felt almost sick. Nor were
my feelings relieved by the ominous silence in
which James received this information.

Looking back now I can hardly tell what it was
that I feared so much. It was a situation which
to those who might not guess at the inward cruelty
and beauty of this house and its people, must appear
as a most foolish dramatisation of very inconsequent
matters. A faint flirtation with an unsuitable swain—
what girl has gone unchidden for such an incident?

And what girl has not swooned in love and sulked
at parental chiding and gone her way for a space
and then forgotten ?

But this was otherwise ; for Willow did not love,
I thought, and Sir Richard, I guessed, knew this
too, and though he must battle with her on these
grounds, other ends were the true issue of the matter.
But Dick was so troubled. This added substance
to my fears. I saw dreadful visions in my mind
and dreamed sad dreams. . . . " If he knew I
could read and write half as well as I can, my dad
would have sent me off for a governess years
ago. . . ." Well, perhaps not a governess—the
simple bawdery of her manner would forbid that,
but there were other undertakings to which an
angry girl could fly, and in which she could change
—but change grotesquely and pitifully—from the
creature she now was. I saw Willow driving out
of the gates of Pullinstown in her absurd motor,
yielding to no entreaty to come back, grieved and
bitter and determined. Such a thing as this she
would do. There was marriage ; but Willow married
—the idea was absurd, almost painful. One did not
seriously consider it. And as I sat there staring past
Dick, suddenly he spoke aloud my forbidden
thought :

" If the Sir says too much to her, Oliver, do you
know what she'll do ? She'll gather herself up and
she'll marry Billy Morgan."

" *Dick*." The idea of it was still beyond me, pre-

posterous and grotesque. "She *can't* do it," I said,
"she can't possibly do it. Why, it would be absolute
madness, Dick. Hopeless. How can you think
anything so awful?"

"That's just why she'd do it," he said. "She'd
do anything that comes into her head when she's
angry. And that'll be the first thing she'll think of."

And I knew that in a sense he was right. This
terrible submission to the moment which this morning had given to one of passions very like her own,
the self-oblation to draw a badger with his bare
hands from its earth and hold on to it while eighteen
couples of dog-hounds raved around him, this very
same quality in Willow would encompass any
immediate disastrous action and enclose her forever
in desolation.

"Dick," I said, "Dick, what shall we do?"
The prospect of such calamity destroyed all my
calm. I left Dick tipping his chair backwards and
forwards, his head bent and his hands in his pockets
and I walked out of the house. I was stricken by
the awfulness of this, by the tragedy and the drama
and the golden lovely day. Pullinstown must not
be changed. Such bitter storms can envenom a
house, dividing it from us and putting a ring
sinister about its beauty. Thus as I walked for an
hour through the woods and the fields I feared and
I trembled for Pullinstown, for Sir Richard, shaken
in love and jealousy and old unhappiness, for Willow
whose haughty pride must cast her down so low, and

for myself and my great love of these cousins and of their house.

Faint on the air of five o'clock there came to me at last the unmistakable sounds of Sir Richard driving his great car down the avenue. I ran to the edge of the wood and I saw a little black figure step out of the car to open the avenue gate—James—saw him climb in again and heard the four merciless gear changes crashed home in their painful turns. And wondering much and trembling still a little, I turned my steps back towards the house.

Dick was sitting on a hot window sill, eating one by one the plums that some one had laid there to ripen. His Pidgie was lying in the crook of his arm, and now and then he kissed her and now and then spat a plum stone afar upon the gravel. I sat down beside him : " *Well ?* " I insisted, as he said nothing. I must and would know the end and the upshot of all this calamity that had so tried me.

" Ah, she has a great compromise settled up with the Sir now——" Dick for once was agreeable to my importunity, and with his words a mellow radiance flowed about me, from my heart to the house—dispelling all bitterness and woe.

" He's to buy the horse she rode to-day for her. He's not to sell him till the end of the hunting season. And what's more, he's to give her fifty quid into the heel of her fist and she doesn't care if she never saw Billy Morgan again."

For a moment I was indeed silenced. I felt quite

weak and shaken. "But where's he gone—now,"
I asked, "in the car?"

"He's off like the wheels of hell to Templeshambo to tell Honour and Beauty how he has them
bested again. It's little he knows they have a nice
back-hander to get out of the sale of that horse.
Willow and I have a bit to see too."

"But why fifty pounds, Dick?" My mind had
gone back to Sir Richard's compromise. "What a
strange sum. Why not a fiver or a million?"

"He hasn't a million to offer her," Dick answered,
"and that's not the one to give a man up for a
fiver. She has twice too much spirit."

THE END

VIRAGO MODERN CLASSICS

The first Virago Modern Classic, *Frost in May* by Antonia White, was published in 1978. It launched a list dedicated to the celebration of women writers and to the rediscovery and reprinting of their works. Its aim was, and is, to demonstrate the existence of a female tradition in fiction which is both enriching and enjoyable, and to broaden the sometimes narrow academic definition of a 'classic' which has often led to the neglect of a large number of interesting secondary works of fiction. In calling the series 'Modern Classics' we do not necessarily mean 'great' — although this is often the case. Published with new critical and biographical introductions, books are chosen for many reasons: sometimes for their importance in literary history; sometimes because they illuminate particular aspects of women's lives, both personal and public. They may be classics of comedy or storytelling; their interest can be historical, feminist, political or literary.

Initially the Virago Modern Classics concentrated on English novels and short stories published in the early decades of this century. As the series has grown it has broadened to include works of fiction from different centuries, different countries, cultures and literary traditions, many of which have been suggested by our readers.

Also by Molly Keane (M. J. Farrell)

TREASURE HUNT
New Introduction by Dirk Bogarde

For Consuelo, Hercules and Roderick, life has been a round of carousing, gambling and champagne in the Irish house, Ballyroden. With Sir Roderick's death, however, all grandeur must cease. Though boots are polished on dusty Chippendale and exquisite vases languish on floors, his legacy to the younger generation is a host of debts. To the outrage of their elders and servants, Phillip and Veronica decide to do the unspeakable and take in paying guests. A battle of wills commences, with Consuelo and Hercules doing their utmost to thwart the new regime. In the midst of it all is old and dotty Aunt Anna Rose, who *insists* that she has some rubies. If only she could remember where she hid them . . . Originally performed as a play, *Treasure Hunt* (1952) shows the inimitable Molly Keane at her comic best.

LOVING WITHOUT TEARS
New Introduction by Russell Harty

Angel, a woman of extreme charm and warm-hearted selfishness, awaits her son's return to the fold. She is the pivot of her children's lives – for haven't they always succumbed to her smiling manipulations? Now she has plans for each of them. Slaney, her beautiful daughter (who will make the perfect match with Angel's assistance); Julian, her young hero returned from the War (though still her baby after all); and even Tiddley, her niece (who lacks the sophistication of her own children, yet will surely be delighted to hover at Angel's beck and call). But sometimes a mother's plans run less smoothly than anticipated. When Julian arrives accompanied by his new fiancée, a stylish American widow, when Slaney seems adept at romancing without a mother's guidance, and even Tiddley shows signs of rebellion, Angel must sharpen her wits and struggle to maintain her tyranny.

FULL HOUSE
New Afterword by Caroline Blackwood

Poised between wild hills and the sea stands Silverue, a
graceful Irish mansion, ruled by the beautiful, selfish
matriarch, Lady Olivia Bird. To this house comes Eliza on
the eve of a delicate occasion: John, the eldest son, is due to
return, the 'tragedy' of his absence glossed over. In this
family of complicities, each member has their secret. Eliza the
confidante has hers too and John's reappearance will prove
the catalyst for their revelation. First published in 1935, this
is an exquisite novel with vivid descriptive passages and
concise placing of emotions. In unravelling and exposing the
precariousness of one family's security, Molly Keane has
created one of her finest and most intuitive works.

TAKING CHANCES
New Introduction by Clare Boylan

Since the death of their parents, Roguey, Maeve and Jer have
cared for one another and for Sorristown, their elegant home.
Here this companionable trio have fished and hunted,
unravelled secrets by bedroom fires and sipped gin cocktails –
a pattern of intimacy about to be broken by Maeve's
marriage to Rowley. A week before the wedding, her
bridesmaid Mary arrives. In contrast to acquiescent Maeve,
Mary is faintly pagan, elusive. Meeting her for the first time
Rowley describes Mary as "a factor for disturbance", little
realising the extent to which his prophecy will prove true for
each of them. First published in 1929, this novel perfectly
captures the leisured Anglo-Irish lives of that era, but most of
all it explores allegiances and love – and taking chances of a
desperate kind.

Also of Interest

TORTOISE BY CANDLELIGHT
Nina Bawden

'An exceptional picture of disorganised family life . . .
Imaginative, tender, with a welcome undercurrent of
toughness' – *Observer*

With the ferocity of a mother tiger defending her cubs,
fourteen-year-old Emmie Bean watches over her household:
her amiable drunken father, her gaunt, evangelical old
grandmother, her beautiful, wayward sister Alice and, most
precious of all, eight-year-old Oliver, who has the
countenance of an angel and the ethical sense of a cobra. But
with the arrival of new neighbours, the outside world intrudes
into the isolated privacy of family life and Emmie's kingdom
is no longer secure. Combining the guile of a young child with
the desperation of adolescence, Emmie fights to stave off the
changes – and the revelations – that growing up necessarily
brings. Powerful, heart-rending, but never sentimental,
Tortoise by Candlelight is a captivating excursion into the
landscape of youth.

Virago also publishes *A Little Love, A Little Learning* and *A
Woman of My Age*. *Family Money* is forthcoming in 1992.

THE MIGHTY AND THEIR FALL

Ivy Compton-Burnett
New Introduction by Hilary Spurling

'There is nobody in all this writing world even remotely like her' – *Guardian*

With his wife's death, Ninian Middleton turned to his eldest daughter, Lavinia, as a companion. When, some years later, he decides to marry again, a chasm opens in the life of the young girl whose time he has so jealously possessed. Convoluted attempts are made to prevent this marriage – and others – and the seams of intense family relationships are torn, with bitter consequences. Astringent, succinct and always subversive, Ivy Compton-Burnett wields her scalpel-like pen to vehemently dissect the passions and duplicities of the Middleton family.

Virago also publishes *Two Worlds and Their Ways. A Heritage and its History* is forthcoming in 1992.

A PARTICULAR PLACE
Mary Hocking

'Mary Hocking is an undisguised blessing'
– *Christopher Wordsworth, Guardian*

In this, her most memorable and triumphant novel to date, Mary Hocking is confirmed as the successor to Elizabeth Taylor and Barbara Pym.

The parishioners of a small West Country market town are uncertain what to make of their new Anglican vicar with his candlelit processions. And, though Michael Hoath embraces challenge, his enthusiasm is sapped by their dogged traditionalism. Moreover, Valentine's imperial temperament is more suited to the amateur dramatics she excels at than the role of vicar's wife. Their separate claims to insecurity are, for the most part, concealed and so both are surprised when Michael falls in love with a member of his congregation: a married woman, neither young nor beautiful. In tracing the effects of this unlikely attraction, Mary Hocking offers humour, sympathy and an overwhelming sense of the poignancy of human expectations.

Letters From Constance is forthcoming in 1992.